THE
WINSLOW
SISTERS

THE WINSLOW SISTERS

Michael Aronovitz

CEMETERY DANCE PUBLICATIONS

Baltimore

2023

The Winslow Sisters
Copyright © 2023 by Michael Aronovitz
Cover Artwork and Design © 2023 by Kealan Patrick Burke
Interior Design © 2023 by Desert Isle Design, LLC

Trade Paperback Edition

ISBN:

978-1-58767-948-3

Cemetery Dance Publications
132B Industry Lane, Unit #7
Forest Hill, MD 21050
www.cemeterydance.com

Police Log: Summary of Case 4922FB9:

Serial killer Michael Leonard Robinson murdered thirteen college coeds in early 2018, impaling them on poles and leaving them dangling there on various highway construction jobsites for the purpose of, "haunting the dawn rush hour." Police called him "The Scarecrow Killer," until he revealed in an otherwise cryptic note left for police on March 13th, 2018, that he thought of his "dolls" more as "sculptures."

On July 18th, 2018, Robinson targeted the Lower Merion Chief of Police, Bill Canfield, and involved the officer in a dark, psychological "game" that wound up taking the lives of Canfield's administrative assistant Erika Shoemaker, a junior officer at the station, Connor Mullin, the young man's mother Professor Rebecca Mullin, her estranged husband Joseph, and her daughter, (Connor's kid sister), Meagan. Additional related deaths on the same calendar day: Detective Ted Bronson and freshman coeds Melissa Baumgardner, Jennifer Buckley, and Bridget Ballentine.

It is believed that The Sculptor killer perished in a massive explosion at the Mount Airy Forge in North Philadelphia at four minutes to midnight, July 18th, 2018. Authorities recovered a foot in a rubber slush boot and one arm in the blast area. They could not find the rest of the body.

M.L. Robbins
Professor Brad Winslow
ENG COMP 101
27 October 2020

Proposal: Exploratory Analysis Paper

On October 19, 2020, it was reported that Jeffrey Toobin, CNN pundit and writer for *The New Yorker,* was caught masturbating on a group Zoom call by other magazine staff members. They had been simulating a political debate, and Toobin's role was to play "the courts," a stroke of irony as he wound up being the one judged. And while the more profound details have been left to imagination, it appears that he might have had two computers in the room, one left on by accident and the other providing the stimulant. Maybe he'd shared his screen and forgotten that even on Gallery View his shot remained visible in the top right-hand corner. Maybe he was hosting, and when he'd ushered them into their Breakout Rooms, he'd left a few back in the main screening area.

I find the reports to be deliciously intriguing and horribly unsatisfying.

I want to know all left unsaid.

I want to know exactly how this gorgeous catastrophe occurred: the time of day, the exact location of his wife, the room he was in, and whether he'd locked the door—the logistics, the lighting, the angles. Was he wearing a headset? Did he have on a dress shirt, a tie, and nothing else but his skivvies? Had his wife denied him morning sex, making him save up a gusher for vengeance?

And above all, who was his trigger? Was she a recent memory or an old stand-by from his Harvard days? Was she a "go-to" he kept in his Picture File, or had he surrendered to the gutter and tapped into Pornhub?

The fact is he got caught, and the miracle here is that the rest of us usually don't. We shamelessly categorize women and perform the dirty deed with Trumpian abandon and a hunter's precision after sorting and dividing the lovelies into two definitive columns: I Would Fuck Her or No I Would Not. The binary is as pure as it is absolute. There are no exceptions, yet men are quick to don masks of social etiquette, so form-fitted that the skin eventually seems fused with the rubber or factory plastic.

Do we ever really forget who we are? Of course not, we can't. The proof of the pudding is in the eating, forgive the cliché metaphor and its clumsy, rather childish parallel. First chance we get, we'll pull down the blinds, dim the overheads, and smoothly fold open the laptop. No one will see. Except us, occasionally getting that reflective haunt in the screen between web pages.

And in terms of the how, where, and when, we are shameless. The shower is convenient. On the toilet. In the den on a blustery Saturday when the wife has gone out to brunch with the girls from the book club, in front of the flatscreen at 2:00 in the morning, in the shadowed foyer leading to the basement, in the attic behind a dusty dressing table with the oval shell for a vanity mirror missing the glass. It is more than habit. We are odious spiders wired with a rather low cunning for finding the creases to crawl along, starving for a cheap junkie's climax, spewing our venom in our cars (highways are best), gas stations that would offer that lone restroom key on a chain tacked to a stick, and sometimes even at work after hours.

Newsflash.

There are even better secrets slithering underneath all the face coverings, more potent backstories, snakes in the larva, and you, Professor Winslow, are to be the explorer. You will provide me your person-to-person analyses and you will also be my deliverer. The alternative? Gore in the shadows, bone meal in the garden soil, body parts in the sewer tunnels. Before 2018 no one had ever bothered to notice me, and in response I delicately adorned your highway construction jobsites with slaughterous dolls. In 2019 I orchestrated a blood-puzzle of pornographic neighborhood violence worthy of worship, exposing the fault lines and fissures in local police bureaucracies, relationships, family, you're welcome. It was reported that I was killed in a massive explosion at the abandoned forge in North Philadelphia by the tire farm across from the train trestle at L and Erie Streets.

Newsflash: I lived. I was made blind. I am deformed. I am crippled, and you should feel kindled, inspired, awakened.

Here is the deal. Go to the police and I will skin your three daughters all to the bone one square inch at a time with an X-Acto blade and a pair of splinter forceps tweezers. It will be live-streamed. You will be duct-taped to a chair with your head in a vice and your eyelids sewn open.

Or...

You will be my Treasure Hunter, Snake Catcher, Lord of the Worms.

Michael Leonard Robinson is inviting you to a scheduled Zoom meeting.
Topic: Professor Winslow's New Naughty Activities
Time: Thursday Oct 29, 2020 7:00 AM Eastern Time
(US and Canada)
Join Zoom Meeting
https://us04web.zoom.us/j/74195378395?pwd=STh0VTg5MlcxRG
9keE0vUSswUWcz
Meeting ID: 741 9537 8395
Passcode: gVE9Qq

CHAPTER 1

Have You Checked the Children?

The girls.

Professor Winslow shoved up from his desk and banged his knees on the underside. He felt like an outsider looking in at his world in slow motion, and he made for the doorway, the hall, and the stairs. His heels pounded numbly. He told himself not to jump two at a time as he was wearing sweat socks, and taking a header or falling on his tailbone spelled "ambulance."

There were sounds, healthy sounds thank God, family clamor, in the kitchen as Esther worked the blender, revving it like a motorcycle…in the basement with the hollow *whap* of a tennis ball being hit off a tee and into the netting that he and Jody had hung in front of the wall-piping…and over in the sunroom where Pentatonix were singing *Bohemian Rhapsody* as Sage pattered to it across the hardwood floor in one of her strange, free-form dances.

"Honey," he called in to her. "Family meeting."

"After the Mama-Mia's, Poppy, okay?"

"K." He moved to the doorway to the basement and called down the stairs to his middle child.

"Jo-Jo, up here please."

"Workin' on it," she called back.

"Now."

"Five more. I'm lifting my chest and my shoulder keeps flying open, I can feel it!"

"Now."

Winslow stood there a moment, stroking his goatee, thinking, "So M. L. Robbins…Michael Leonard Robinson. Right." In the roll book he had that student listed as Mary Louise Robbins. He'd never seen her (or him) because, like most college freshmen, the camera was always turned off during the class Zoom meetings and she never participated. Well, now "she" had, hadn't she?

Winslow turned back and ducked under the archway. Esther, his youngest, was standing on one of the bar stools on the stove-side of the kitchen island, and just seeing her safe and within arm's reach was a relief. She was covered with baking flour and was stirring something in one of the silver mixing bowls. The tip of her tongue was poked out the side of her mouth, and for the umpteenth time Winslow achingly wished Georgia had lived to see this.

"Hi sweetie," he said. "What are you making?"

"Breakfast for dinner. Lots of eggs here." She stirred harder.

Winslow smiled. "What's the bag of flour for?"

"Fairy dust."

"What's that in the blender?"

"The shells."

"Why?"

"So we can feed them to the chickens."

"We don't have chickens."

She stopped mixing. "We have to *buy* them, silly." She smiled, scrunching her nose. She'd recently lost her two front baby teeth. "Hey, can I have a turtle?"

"Maybe."

"Can I have Slime?"

"Maybe."

"Can I use the eggshells to make a face mask?"

Winslow felt his forehead crease. "What for?"

"I saw it on a beauty blog."

"On whose computer?" he said. "You're seven years old."

"Seven and a half!" She pouted theatrically. Then the smile again, overly wide, as the kids her age always did at parties for pictures. "Make handprints with me on the cutting board, now, Poppy, *please?*"

Jody came in and brushed past with her DiMarini Voodoo bat set across her shoulder like a marching rifle. She was tall for an eighth grader, all knees and elbows. She had high girlish cheekbones that were almost severe, but she carried herself like a boy. A cocky one. They'd named her after the tomboy in Alcott's *Little Women,* and it was freakishly ironic how accurate that prediction was. Her color was high and her ponytail had come loose, giving her face-framing side-bangs.

"Friggin' eggs for dinner again, Peanut?" she said.

"Hey, no 'friggins,'" Esther said. She raised her chin. "And don't call me 'Peanut.' My nickname this week is 'Cupcake,' thank you."

Jody opened the door and looked in the fridge. "Poppy, where's the freakin' Gatorade?"

"We're out," he said. "And no 'freakins' either."

She turned. "But water's boring and milk makes my mouth taste bad."

"You've got it wrong," Sage said from the archway. "Your mouth can't taste bad because you don't have two of them."

Jody closed the fridge door. "Then it tastes like a dumpster," she said, and Esther snorted laughter through her nose. Sage smiled back without really committing to the expression. She had dyed her hair pink. She was experimenting with makeup and was wearing heavy smudged eyeliner and jumbo Fluffy Mink lashes so her *expressions would pop!*" Winslow knew she would need braces to fix that little gap between her two front teeth, but he doubted she would be too excited about it. Since her birthday was in September, she was one of the youngest of the sophomores at Lower Merion High School, and that was certainly the thing she wanted least to go around advertising.

Winslow cleared his throat. "Um, girls..."

He stopped. He wanted to tell them bluntly that he'd had a real scare because of that email and that he'd been dreadfully certain, if just for a moment, that one of them had been taken. He wanted to tell them how much he missed their mother, how inadequate he felt raising three daughters by himself, and that he felt a part of his heart had been stolen. Jody stopped fidgeting and leaned the bat against the fridge. Esther stopped mixing, and Sage put her hand on his shoulder.

"We miss her too," she said. Winslow closed his eyes hard, pursed his lips, and reached his arms out. He'd sworn he wouldn't break down in front of them, not again. They needed his strength. They all came into the embrace, family cuddle-puddle.

Sage's body spray was quaint and Jody smelled like a dude. Esther was in the middle of it all, hugging the hardest, and Winslow knew there were egg yolks and flour all over the back of his sweater now. Sometimes the best things were messy.

"Right," he said, letting go. "I got a strange note from one of my students today, and before I call it in I wanted to tell you to keep an eye out for weird texts." He looked at each of them meaningfully. "If a stranger contacts you, I have to know right away. Don't entertain even harmless conversations with those you don't know. And I want a look at all your social media platforms: Facebook, Instagram, Snapchat, the works."

"Total transparency," Sage murmured, turning back toward the sunroom.

"Don't play in traffic," Jody said. "I'm taking a shower."

Winslow rested his hand on the back of his hip. "Use the Dove Roll-On Pomegranate, please."

"Your Old Spice is better," she sing-songed back to him. Esther returned to her perch on the other side of the island-style prep table, and Winslow got out his cell phone. He moved toward the living room and dialed 911, working out in his mind how to put this. Most would probably see the email as elaborate monkeyshines, but Winslow wasn't so sure. The prose was odd, a bit uneven and coarse, yet it didn't have a college freshman's feel to it. There was a cruel joy and a certain...pompous bombast in the voice, as if the author was a damaged yet seasoned adult expecting the reader to find the dark writing poetic.

On the third ring, the dispatcher answered and said, "Lower Merion Police, what's your emergency?"

Winslow looked up at the ceiling. The voice was familiar somehow. It was the way the man pronounced his "s" sounds, not quite a lisp, but slurred with the tongue up against the soft palate. Winslow turned his glance to his feet and grinned sardonically. Somehow, some way, this was the same dispatcher who'd answered the false alarm he'd called in years back, in October of 2002, when the "Maryland Sniper" was picking off people in Home Depot parking lots and gas stations. The news had reported that multiple witnesses had seen a white van in the vicinity of various crime scenes, and when Winslow had come home from teaching a night class he'd seen a strange white van parked up the street. He had casually ambled over and noted that it had a Maryland license plate. He'd called the police, and the dispatcher, *this* dispatcher, had laughed him off the phone.

It turned out that white vans were simply popular work vehicles and were popping up all over the grid by default. The Maryland Snipers, a forty-one-year-old along with his seventeen-year-old sidekick, were actually using a blue 1990 Chevy Caprice. And yes, the dispatcher had laughed. Not as hard as had Georgia, however...

"Never mind," he said into his cell. "I hit the wrong auto-call button. Sorry to take your time."

He hung up and stared at the phone in his hand. He set his jaw. No more false alarms. If one had an issue with a co-worker, it wasn't procedure to go straight to the owner, now, was it? You went to the floor manager first. Or HR.

Esther was in the archway. "Poppy, help me with the extras."

Winslow nodded, put his cell in his pocket, and ambled back toward the kitchen. Tomorrow he would investigate this student with all the tools available to him through the college's proper channels, handle this appropriately. There was an anti-racist Zoom meeting in the morning, and he could ask in the chat if any other professor had had contact with this pupil. He would go to Student Discipline and contact Mike, even though he always tried to avoid talking to the Chair of the department at all costs; better to stand on his own two feet and all that. In the kitchen, Esther was working to climb back up on her cooking stool.

"We're out of the extras," Winslow said to her. "We finished the Ore-Ida's last night."

"Then use the leftover mashed potatoes! And fry up some Spam. Chop-chop, mister-man!"

She burst into giggles at her unintentional quasi-rhyme and Winslow bent to open the fridge. Tomorrow he'd go to a store, pick up some veggies, more green and fiber. It was a wonderful idea to indulge Esther this week and make her feel important, because she'd been having weird crying fits lately, but they couldn't do the "greasy spoon" every night. He had to do better. Tomorrow.

"Guess what I found," he said.

"What, Poppy?"

"It starts with 'Oscar Meyer.'"

"Then it looks like you'll be making bacon, Poppy-Pop. Yowzer! Makin' bacin!" She laughed so hard she almost fell off the chair.

That night it took Winslow a good while to fall asleep. After dinner he was both restless and exhausted, a typical feeling of late, and he gave in to the latter, which was not so much the norm. He'd gone up to his room. He stood in the silence and stared ahead listlessly. He got into his pajamas, shut off the light, and turned in early. And he wasn't thinking about "makin' bacin," or DeMarini Voodoo bats, or Pentatonix retooling a classic. He was thinking about the emptiness of this room. He was thinking about Georgia.

He rolled over to her empty side of the bed. He wasn't used to it yet, and it was better that way, at least for now. Getting comfortable meant moving on, and he wasn't ready. Better to suffer, to lie in the cold spot. When she'd died of a sudden heart attack last May, working the tail end of a triple double shift at Bryn Mawr Hospital, she'd been pronounced almost immediately. The administration had a plaque made for her. Winslow had been told that it was hung in the B unit where she'd crumpled to the floor amidst her bedridden Covid patients, most of them intubated and unaware.

Winslow started shaking with rage, toes curling in, fists tight, blood pounding up in his head. The death was so very senseless, so *Godless*. Every night, it took everything in his willpower not to throw off the covers, leap out of bed, and start thrashing at things in the dark. His breath rasped, he was drooling now, he wanted to rend, to rip clean, to bite down with all of the foot-pounds his jaw could manage and tear something to shreds.

He rolled over, ashamed. Animal instincts. Usually, they were far below the surface, and his girls deserved for him to keep this kind of shit buried. He opened his eyes wide, like that scumbag Rudy Giuliani, and he blinked melodramatically. Just the fact that he had to have this pep talk to himself lately in the first place almost brought the hot blood right back to his jawline. He made a concerted effort to steady his breathing, but it was getting harder and harder to concentrate when he was policing a psyche as if not his own, seething, churning, boiling.

He reminded himself of his duties as a father. That was the mission; that was the job. He repeated it to himself like an incantation.

He was on his side now, scalp still hot, throat rough like sandpaper, and then slowly but surely the nighttime carousel that turned in the mist brought him back around to thoughts of his girls, visuals that got him back to simply lying there in his own skin, and everything began to flow like peaceful waters under a soft moon as he drifted off…Sage was performing in the high school's dance ensemble, and Jody was making the boys' middle school baseball team for the second year in a row as the starting third baseman, and Esther… Esther was laughing, so full of life and so filled with joy.

"Poppy," she said, a harsh whisper. "Dad!"

Winslow's eyes flew open. It was dark. It was Esther standing next to him, shaking his arm with both hands.

"Wake up!"

"What?" he said. "Baby, what's wrong?"

"Shhh!"

He sat up. "What's the matter? Did you have a bad dream?"

"No."

"Did you fall out of bed?"

"No. I have to tell you something."

"What?"

"It's a secret."

She grabbed hold of his shoulder, and he could sense that she was up on her toes so she could reach his ear.

"There's somebody in my room," she said softly. "I can see his shadow and I can hear him breathing."

CHAPTER 2

Scared to Close My Eyes /
Scared to Open Them

Winslow reached over and turned on the bedside lamp. Esther had switched out of her Elf on the Shelf nightwear and had on the Fleece Footie jammies with the hood up. She'd pulled the drawstrings down so her face was a pale oval. She made to climb up onto the bed.

"You're too big for that," Winslow said. "Together we'll check every nook and cranny in your room, stem to stern, I promise."

She pulled back and pushed out the boo-boo lip.

"Promise," he repeated.

She stamped her foot and put her thumb in her mouth.

"You're too old for that too," Winslow said. She pulled it out, making a popping sound, and he took a brief moment to make sure his flannel pajamas were all buttoned properly. "Upsy-daisy," he then said to no one, and he tossed down the covers at the far side of the bed, grunting, making for the comfy-chair to get his robe. He slipped it on and pulled the belt tight.

"Sweetie," he said, "we could give the Snoopy nightlight another chance."

"My nickname is Cupcake."

"Cupcake then."

"No," she said. "It makes the shadows seem longer and it keeps me up hours and hours."

Winslow walked over and offered out his hand, which she reached up and took. Her hand was so very small...

"We could keep your door open," he said, walking her out to the hallway.

"No," she said, pointing across toward the laundry room. "At night the washer and dryer look like a person."

Winslow halted. "Then I'll take the dryer down. They don't need to be stacked."

"No!" she said. "Then they'd be trolls!" She took his hand in both of hers and bent her knees pulling.

"Come *on*, before the breathing shadow goes away and you won't believe me!"

Winslow looked down the hall. Jody had on her Galaxy Lamp Projector, and a pool of stars on rich purple backdrop washed out from under her door spreading nearly to the linen closet. Farther down, Sage had her door closed. Esther's was closed shut as well. Winslow looked down at her.

"Sweetie, did you close the door when you came out to wake me?"

"I don't remember."

"It's just kind of strange."

"Why?"

He paused. "I don't know, actually."

He stared at the door.

"Go ahead," Esther whispered, huddled so close she was almost behind him. "Open it."

He didn't want to. And this was ludicrous. It meant that in the back of his mind he believed that the prankster-student on the other side of that email was actually this *Sculptor* character, now back from the dead. Supposedly, this particular miscreant had been an expert with technology, creating "realities" through some new sort of projection technique that didn't require a digital theater, TV, or phone. He made pictures on the air—pictures that had physicality and dimension from all angles through superlative pixel distribution that addressed all five of the senses. Or something like that. Winslow was no cinema techie, but he did clearly recall reading that this monster spied on people, occupying multiple locations simultaneously, changing his voice, transforming himself through meticulous role-play and disguise. He read you and predicted you right down to your most intimate counter-strokes, he set booby-traps, made you self-mutilate, become a cannibal, filet your pet cat, kill your mother. Or was a lot of that rumor? There were whispers of a manifesto floating around that was possibly written by someone else and used by The Sculptor for hyperbole and misdirection.

Winslow had also seen on the news that the explosion at that forge in North Philly took out a whole city block. They'd recovered the killer's right hand and part of his left ear five hundred yards from the blast site. Or was it an arm and a foot in a slush boot? Didn't matter. Either way. The monster had been killed. There was nothing to fear here.

Winslow reached for the knob and slowly turned it.

He gently pushed and swept the door open. Hall light feathered in from behind on a slant, and everything looked the way it was supposed to, peaceful and wholesome, cleaner than usual actually, even deep in where the darkness still lingered. Esther wasn't so good with perimeters, as it seemed her clothes and toys often ended up cluttering the edges. Seemed she'd picked up. Winslow reached in for the wall switch, flicked it on, and the room was flooded with brightness.

The rainbow comforter with the pom-pom trim had been shoved half off the twin, but besides that it was typical Esther: bright, loud, and sassy. Her bedside dresser was crammed with books under the drawer and decorated on top with her Hello Kitty portable stereo unit and a ceramic water pitcher holding five plastic roses. The see-through fairy princess play-tent by the window was stuffed with throw pillows adorned with strings of alphabet beads and topped off by her old Grizzly Bear Teddi with an eye missing and both of the ears chewed down to nubs. Winslow hadn't been too good about rotating the wall art, which was still made up of old toddler posters, like T.O.T.S. and Zoomie Kids Watercolor Prints, but her bureau boasted seven—count them, seven—American Girl dolls, each with a variance of hair, outfits, facial features, and personalities. Winslow didn't see much difference between them, really. At two hundred dollars a pop, though, he'd made damned sure to go through the details thoroughly while ordering everything down to the smallest accessory.

"See?" he said. "No one here."

She squinted up at him. "Look under the bed, Poppy."

Of course.

He walked over and squatted down. If this was a Stephen King novel, his knees would have popped. He went to his palms and lowered his head, tilting it sideways. If this was *Trilogy of Terror—2020,* a little voodoo war doll would have burst out and jabbed him viciously with a razor-tipped throwing spear as the dolls looked on from above with those dead glass-ball stares.

"Nothing under here, Sweetie," he said. It was dark, vaguely dusty. There was the form of the folded-up futon and toward the front of the bed, a Flower Crowns Craft Kit she'd abandoned and forgotten.

"It's Cupcake," she said. "And you still have to check the scary place."

Winslow pushed up and briskly rubbed his palms together. Esther was pointing at the closet.

"He's in there," she said. "The breathing shadow-man is hiding in there."

Winslow's face darkened. The closet *was* a scary damned place after all, wasn't it? Well, the structure should never have been added to the rooms of children; it should have been a rule or something. He walked across to the door and yanked it right open, Band-Aid ripped off, one-two-three go!

He gasped.

He recoiled, took a step back. He couldn't breathe. It was sudden and it sure as hell wasn't fair.

It was the bow ties, all of them pinned to the long silk strips hanging next to the over-the-door canvas shoe holder. This had been Georgia's thing, the way she'd bonded with her precious six-year-old "girly-girl," the two of them collecting Preppy bow-ties: the Tomboy Chic style...the Straight Pink, the Kawaii and Tokyo Street, wearing them, playing dress-up. Though Jody had never bothered with the "fashion-play" as Georgia had named it, Sage had taken an interest in the Nu Goth Cravats, the Quirky, and the Grungy bowties, all during her dark phase last year in ninth grade. She and "Cupcake" were two girls on such opposite ends of the spectrum, a high school sophomore and a first grader posing together, *laughing* together, the Goth girl and the pint-sized diva proving that demons and reapers could still dance with unicorns.

Georgia was the Uniter-in-Chief. The sparkle in the darkness. She looked good in a skirt, looked good reading a book under a tree. She looked good washing dishes, for Christ's sake, and seeing the bowties triggered the memory of her fiercely, vividly.

He reached over and gently drew Esther in to his hip.

"See?" he said, making sure not to let his voice hitch with emotion. "Nothing here."

Not anymore...

His eyes filled up, and Esther pulled on his arm. "You can go to sleep now, Poppy."

He glanced down at her. "You sure?"

"Yessir, yessir, yessir, yessir!" She was yanking on his arm in rhythm as if it were a window cord in a trolley.

"Do you want me to leave the light on?"

"No."

"You want me to tuck you in?"

"Yes, silly."

He walked over to the bed and straightened the covers. She climbed in, and he bent and kissed her forehead.

"Night, Cupcake."

"Night, Poppy."

Winslow padded back across the carpeting, shut off the light, and closed the door behind him, leaving the room dark, like black ink. The only illumination was from the digital clock on Esther's bureau saying "11:17" in red squared-off numbers, and the light didn't carry much.

"Did I do OK?" she whispered.

"Splendidly," said the tender voice from the closet.

"But why did I have to play-act?"

"Because," the voice said, "I am not really in your room. Like magic, I am actually in my own room at my own place. I am also blind and partially deaf to background noise, so I would not have been able to see or hear your father if he decided to come and check in on you. He might have heard me talking and we would both have gotten in trouble."

"So now he won't come back?" she said, tone deadly serious.

"No, child, not tonight. Treasure hunters never dig into the same hole twice, especially if something in the pit has claws and sharp teeth. We can speak freely now, keeping our voices low, whispers only."

"You're nice," Esther said. "And your voice is pretty, like velvet. What do you look like?"

Pause.

"In time," he replied. "Soon, child, I promise. Now listen..."

CHAPTER 3

I Want to Play a Game

Winslow woke up with a start. He'd slept fitfully, bad dreams, Georgia. She'd been trying to tell him something, but her lips were sewn shut with a cross-hatch of 14-gauge baling wire. It was tied off at the corner of her mouth with a loop feed wrap-around, and Winslow had been working it with a pair of fishing pliers. He'd gotten it loose, but the wire was barbed, stubborn, sticking to her as he tried to work it back through. He'd then cut across in at the lip-line with a pair of rusted pruning shears. He slipped, he caught flesh. She sprayed the air red.

Winslow sat up and wrapped the blanket around himself protectively. Sage and Jody were watching him, both with their heads tilted in toward one another. Sage was twirling a tuft of pink hair and tugging on it. Jo-Jo was cracking her knuckles, one-handed, the left this time, using her thumb as the lever.

"You talk in your sleep," she said.

"But it sounds like another language," Sage added. "Something exotic, like Southern Bantu or Galician."

"Either way, it's time to wake up," Jody said. "You should set your phone."

"I usually don't need it," Winslow muttered, the effect of the dream slowly drifting from him. "And Sage, sweetheart, pulling on it won't make it grow faster."

"But she's caught in the middle," Jody said.

"In between statements," Sage added. "Like the orphan-girl in *Queen's Gambit.*"

Jody eyed her sideways. "You also pull on it because it hurts. It hurts the way you like it."

"Shut up."

"You shut up."

Sage rolled her eyes at her sister, then batted her lashes at Winslow.

"Can I get a tongue piercing, Poppy?"

"No. Ears only."

"But nose studs are cool, you have to admit," Jody said.

"Yes," Sage agreed. "Body Candy has cute rose-gold septum rings. Or I could get a philtrum lip stud like a Medusa labret or a barbell with a jewel."

Winslow smiled evenly. "Ears only."

"Can I get my eyebrows micro bladed, then?" Jody said. Sage's mouth fell open. She leaned her weight on her back heel and folded her arms. Winslow was just as surprised.

"Isn't that a tattoo process?"

"Yeah," Jody said.

"You're in eighth grade!"

"Yeah, and my eyebrows are too thick, yo. They don't match my cheeks. I need them shaved down and redrawn so they're sharp and arching."

Sage giggled. "Since when do you care how you look?"

"Since we have to wear freakin' masks all the time and it's boring. I want to give the boys something to stare at."

"No 'freakins,'" said Sage almost absently.

"And since when do you like boys?" Winslow said.

Jody shrugged. "Since always. I can't help it if I do everything they do better than they can. It's annoying. I want to punch them and pinch them and smack them and touch them."

Winslow put up his wag finger. "Let's be careful about touching in school."

"But I have skin hunger, bad."

"What?"

"I looked it up," Jody said. "And I like girls too, especially when they wear ribbons in their hair like prize ponies."

"What?"

She started cracking her knuckles again, other hand.

"They say it's best to come out early. Oh, and Poppy, I forgot to tell you. I'm a conservative. When I'm eighteen I'm gonna vote Republican."

"What?" he repeated.

Sage laughed. "You're a broken record, Poppy." She glanced at Jody sideways. "Don't conservatives disfavor the LGBTQ community?"

Jody looked at her sideways.

"That's why I can be a conservative, stooooopid. They lie all the time, make it make sense, and pat each other on the back. Oh, and Poppy, I almost forgot. I need you to sign the form."

Winslow pushed out from under the covers to get his robe, still trying to process the U-turn the conversation had just taken.

"What form?" he said.

"The one letting me play football today, varsity."

"Football!" He stood and made his way around the bed. "What, do they need a kicker?"

Sage laughed. "Middle linebacker, Poppy!"

"Yeah Poppy, you *chauvinist*," Jody added. "And I promise not to hurt Springfield's poor little running back coming through the B gap when I blitz. I mean, I won't hurt him too bad."

"Now wait," Winslow said. "You go playing tackle football with boys, we have a talk first."

"We did."

"Not so, and don't play around. I want to know their concussion protocol, locker room arrangements, their general liability. I also want to see the game and I have to check my tutoring schedule."

Jody put her hands behind her back and turned one toe in toward the other coquettishly. On her, it looked comically preposterous.

"Thank you, Poppy," she said. "I'll go get the form for you to sign."

She bounded out of the room. Sage patted him on the shoulder, shaking her head, turning to go.

"Sage, honey."

"Hmm?"

"Where's Esther? When I oversleep it's usually an event, party of four, you know the drill."

She looked at the floor for a moment, going pigeon-toed.

"You know, Poppy, a blood-red pedi with glitter would be dope."

"Are nail salons even open?"

"No, I guess not," she said.

"So where's Cupcake?"

"Latchkey."

"What?"

She sighed. "The church is a block away, Poppy. Literally. It was no big deal for Jody to walk her after making sure she ate all her oatmeal."

"But taking her over is my job," Winslow said. "And I like to say the last goodbye."

"Snooze, you lose," Sage said. She turned toward the hall.

"Hey," Winslow said after her, following. "That business about pretty ponies and skin hunger…"

Sage took a balletic pose and did a slow spin. "She's testing you," she said in falsetto, in rhythm.

"Clearly," he said. "Maybe." Sage glided away to the stairs and Winslow looked at his feet. How was he supposed to navigate the waters when his middle one told him outright that she was bisexual? It might have been the raw truth, or it very well might have been a way to garner attention.

He turned back toward the bedroom.

Even if Jody had been sticking a playful finger in his ribs, there were levels of truth embedded in jest. And what had been his reaction just now? Not much, in fact, he already could not remember exactly. The girls were too fast sometimes. Should he have been more supportive? More a guide at the beginning of her journey if there actually was one?

"We're going," Sage called up the stairs. "We have to catch our buses!"

"Bye," he called back. "Don't talk to strangers!"

"Got it," Jody said. The door slammed behind them.

Winslow started to make the bed. Did Jody even have her period yet? She hadn't as of last March, Georgia would have told him. And of course, these last months had been a blur, a family whirlwind, and he supposed he had assumed in the back of his mind that Sage would have helped Jody with that kind of thing if it came up. His shoulders sagged. There were never feminine care products on the shopping list, and it was a clear possibility that his eldest was currently buying them, possibly for both herself and her sister, with her own small allowance.

He tucked in the far side and bottom, pulling taut the quilt at the corner. Dammit, he should have known about this one way or the other. Esther was making eggs for dinner and hearing voices in her closet. Jody was experimenting with sexuality and walking Esther to Latchkey like a surrogate mother, just as Sage could very well be playing parent to Jody with the most raw and personal things. Winslow was slipping, losing this war.

His computer winked on.

Strange, he hadn't moved the mouse. The screen wavered at first, then came slowly to form. It was a Zoom meeting already in progress, evidently. Winslow's camera was off, and he was alone in the "room," his name printed in white lettering as he'd never bothered to represent himself with a profile pic.

He walked forward, head cocked a bit to the side. Last night he had not gone into his UDEL Zoom account in the first place, which would have required a user name and password triggering a robocall with an authorization code. He had not clicked "JOIN A MEETING," nor had he entered any Meeting ID. Still, he was in fact in a current meeting, alone in the Zoom Room in Gallery View. He reached for the keyboard, and the screen suddenly halved. He drew back his fingers, sucking air between his teeth. The other name that winked up was M. L. Robbins, followed by the "connecting with audio" alert and the snaking ellipses.

"Hello?" Winslow said, heart pounding.

Nothing.

"Mary Louise?" he tried. "We've, um, never spoken. You are always so quiet during the class times." He paused. "You know, you can't go threatening teachers, even if it's a harmless prank. There will be consequences for that proposal paper."

Nothing still.

Winslow cleared his throat. "It will be more than a failure, I am afraid."

Silence.

"I am going to have to contact administration. Have you nothing to say?"

Silence.

"Right," Winslow said. "Enough is enough." He reached for the keyboard a second time, and the computer blared back at him, loud, like one of those gymnasium basketball buzzers that made your teeth vibrate. Winslow froze where he was.

"Multiple choice," the computer said. It sounded robotic, insectile, as if the orator was using one of those cheap voice-changer apps.

"Beg pardon?" Winslow said.

"Multiple choice."

Silence.

Winslow grunted. He wanted to just click the "End Meeting" button and be done with this nonsense, but he didn't, he couldn't somehow. It wasn't that he was truly afraid of this in any way, shape, or form, not really, but the voice had played him in the same way that it was instinct to take something someone reached out and handed to you. Moreover, Winslow loved puzzles and he was a sucker for context, especially when it seemed he was one clue shy of some grand epiphany.

"OK," he said. "I admit I'm intrigued, maybe a little..."

"A lot," the voice said. "You cannot resist puzzles."

Winslow jerked his head back a bit and his nostrils flared. Was this some kind of mind-reading trick?

"Yes," he said. "And how on earth—"

"Your grading technique," the voice interrupted. "Student sentences are puzzles to you, and they inspire you to do extensive holistic grading on the papers, line for line, word for word. Obsessive, you are, as if your comments are some sort of high art."

Winslow put his tongue in his cheek.

"Mmm-hmm," he said. "So what is this about multiple choice? Are you asking for extra credit if you take a test for me? I don't do extra credit."

Silence.

"Multiple choice," the voice said.

"Yes," Winslow said, "what about it?"

"Multiple choice," the voice answered. "An assessment through which the student is prompted by a question or statement and is then afforded the opportunity to choose the correct answer from a selection of, most commonly, four possibilities."

"Yes, that is so."

"Two answers are often blatantly incorrect. One option is almost correct, and one is correct."

"Yes, so I've heard."

"Many get the correct answer on the first read, then talk themselves out of it, straight into choosing the second-best answer."

"Yes, I've heard that as well."

"And time is of the essence."

"Isn't it always?"

"Of course," the voice droned. "Multiple choice."

Suddenly, "M.L. Robbins" went to Speaker View, occupying the whole viewing area and putting Winslow in a small box in the top right-hand corner.

"I am going to share my screen," the voice said.

There was a wink, and the screen before Winslow went into quarters, each labeled with a number at bottom left: 1, 2, 3, and 4. He felt his fists tightening. 1, 2, and 3 looked like still shots, but only because the subjects were asleep; looking closer, he could see them breathing. These were recordings. From last night. From inside the house. Square 1 was Esther with the fleece hood still up, lying on her side with her knees pulled up. Square 2 was Jody hugging a pillow to her chest, and Square 3 was Sage, on her stomach with her hands tucked under.

Square 4 was blackened with a red X going through it. Winslow was so filled with rage and contempt he thought he was going to burst a blood vessel.

"You… were in my house?" he managed. "You filmed—"

"Multiple choice," the voice said. The pre-recorded Esther in square 1 and Jody in square 2 were in the same positions, but Sage, in 3, had rolled to her back.

"One must die, two will live," the voice droned. "Decide."

"Fuck off," Winslow said.

"Multiple choice," was the reply. "Choose the daughter to die:

"A—Square 1: Esther.

"B—Square 2: Jody.

"C—Square 3: Sage."

Pause.

"You have one and a half minutes, Professor Winslow."

"Fuck right off."

"If you do not comply, I will kill all three. Slowly and lovingly. If you decide to play, I will execute the daughter of your choice mercifully, quickly. Decide."

Winslow was trying not to shake.

"You have presented me but three options here," he tried. "In the introduction to this, you advertised four: A, B, C, and D. That's sloppy organization, poor focus. You can make up for it by giving me the fourth option."

"I don't do extra credit, Professor. Decide. Someone must die. You have one minute and five seconds now."

"My choice is not to play. You—you fucking dirtbag…you—"

"Decide. Someone must die."

"No."

"Decide. I am in the church, as is Esther right now. She is about to go in the bike room where I told her I would meet her. She will be my first of the lot. I will eat her eyes and choke her with her own liver. You have fifty seconds to decide."

Winslow's heart was pounding; he could feel it up in his ears.

"I don't believe you," he tried. "You're not in the church. Someone would see…"

"Splendid, how's this?" the voice said. "Esther has entered the bike room. Her sneakers are loose because she never untied them last night. Since Jody took her here to Latchkey, Esther defied you and simply worked in her feet before going out the door. Earlier this morning she had oatmeal, maple and brown sugar, and there's a small flake of it left on her cheek. She didn't use a napkin because you weren't awake to remind her. Also, she has a small mole on the underside of her chin, slightly left. Most wouldn't see that with a quick, passing glance. You have fifteen seconds to decide."

"Wait."

"Twelve seconds," the voice said. "Time is draining."

"Please…"

"Nine."

"No."

"Five."

"Stop."

"Three."

"Fuck!"

"One."

"Option D!" Winslow shouted. "D, God-dammit! You introduced the assessment with a four-choice option! Stick to your own God-damned foreshadowing!"

Silence.

"Yes," the voice said. "Of course. Option D: Box four only."

The red X in Box 4 dissolved and in a blink, the darkened square took over the entirety of the screen. Suddenly it was illuminated by a score of moving flashes as if someone was batting around a bulb on a wire. It flickered violently, and somewhere that felt a million miles away, Winslow thought of the climactic moment in *Psycho* in the fruit cellar, then modernized eighteen years later in the closet scene in John Carpenter's *Halloween.*

The light had stopped blinking, yet the bulb was still moving, the last swings of a pendulum, drawing the shadows in and out of the contours of a man's features and body-lines. He looked vaguely familiar, but Winslow couldn't place him. He was bound, hands behind his back, leather belly-belt pulled tight across his middle and fastened to the frame of the steel folding chair he was sitting on.

The man was smiling. Madly, it seemed, and for a moment Winslow thought of the happy-sad drama masks popularized by the ancient Athenians in their Dionysia festivals. This gentleman was doing the "Cheshire Cat" so hard you could see the top of his gums, and he had mask-lines drawn along the edges of his face from the corners of his lips, up the jaws, to the middle of the forehead.

The bulb was coming to rest, and now Winslow noticed the fishing hooks. They were punctured through the corners of the man's mouth and connected to what appeared to be fishing wire that pulled outward each side, slightly upward, forming the savage, theatrical grin.

The mask-lines were dripping. Tough to note the color as the shot was gritty, probably sixteen millimeter black and white film stock, but sure as all hell, that was blood. The mask-lines weren't drawn, but were actually cut into the periphery of the man's face, and suddenly Winslow understood.

"Don't do it," he said. "Don't you go yanking up on those hooks—"

"Too late, Professor Winslow. And remember, please, that his blood will forever be stained on your hands."

"Not fair," Winslow said through his teeth.

"Not quite," it replied, "that is true. But you are the one who stretched the boundaries of our game so cleverly. Besides, I will take care of the hands-on. You, conversely, might hurry over here to get Esther. There's something bloody and horrific going on in the kitchen. The police will be here. No place for a girl."

"I'll have a lot to tell them," Winslow said icily.

"You won't have time, Professor. You're on call, as they say. Later this morning there will be a new game. Later this morning, Winslow, you will kill a man. You will do it with your bare hands. He will see your face. Prior to this, you will study his profile, which I have provided in your school email. You will then kill him. Before noon."

Winslow said nothing.

"Choose your actions wisely," the thing droned. "You refuse or go to the police, and I kill the girls. Period. No multiple choice, no darkened checkboxes, no two out of three. This is more like true-false, either-or. And I'm rooting for you, Winslow."

"Are you... ?"

"Yes, of course. I'm an idealist, an optimist. I'm hoping that you can find yourself out there in the dark. I'm hoping, Professor, that you can be true."

Winslow shut down the computer and struggled himself into his clothes as quickly as he was able. The church was only a short block away. His Lexus was in the detached garage facing the back alley; faster to leave it.

Faster to run.

CHAPTER 4

What's in the Box?

There were already three police cruisers in the parking lot when Winslow got to the First Church of Christ at Haverford and Manoa Streets. There was no caution tape; however, no traffic cones, nothing roped off, and Winslow made for the side-basement entrance. He hurried down the steps and pulled open the door hard enough to make it clank dully against the wall of the stairwell, and he burst inside straight into the dark.

Where were the lights? He was sweating, breath heaving, and he'd forgotten his ever-loving mask. The door shut behind him, leaving him to fumble his way down the dark access corridor, soon opening to the large craft room, abandoned, and only slightly better lit with the egress windows letting in secondary light that was spidery and vague.

Winslow made for the door to the right, to the hall that led to the bike room, which sat next to the kitchen under the chapel, or so he'd been told. He hit the push bar hard, shoved through, and got light in his eyes, blinding. He raised both arms before his face.

"I'm Winslow, Brad Winslow," he said. "Esther's father!"

The lights lowered.

"I.D." a voice said, and Winslow dug into his pocket for his wallet. The after-image made the two officers in front of him look like silhouettes in one of those film noir detective movies from the 1940s.

"It's him," one of them said.

"Sir," the other said, "put this on, please." He handed Winslow a mask. "Come with me." Winslow followed. The officer pushed open the door to the bike room.

Winslow had never been in this space. It looked like a smaller version of the typical elementary school gymnasium/band room combo, with a polished wooden floor and a basketball hoop to the far right that could be cranked up to a horizontal position above a performance stage about thirty feet long and twenty feet back. To the left there was a scattered assortment of tricycles, most at the perimeter, a few kangaroo style sit-on-'em bouncy balls and a set of wrestling mats.

In the middle of the floor there was an industrial lawn and garden hose-reel case, around four feet high, top open with two lines of fishing wire fed out of it, drawn up taut to the ceiling between two LED lights and fed through what appeared to be an empty overhead pipe bracket at the far back edge of the room. Winslow squinted. The fishing lines next went through two small holes cut into the drywall about half a foot from each other.

"What's on the other side of that wall?" Winslow said. "Kitchen?"

One of the officers looked up from his notes. "Yes, the kitchen," he said.

"Where is my daughter?"

"In the chapel. She is being monitored there by Officer Fielding along with the three caregivers and the other kids waiting to be picked up. We called you, no answer."

"I was in the bathroom," Winslow lied. "I ran here as soon as I heard the message."

The cop gave a pert nod. "We would like to speak with her, Professor Winslow. Though it isn't required, we would like your presence and your consent."

"How is she involved in this?" Winslow said. "What's with the hose-reel case and the fishing line? What's going on in the kitchen?"

"Sir," the cop said, "all this is part of what is now an active investigation, and we just need your cooperation in reference to your daughter's possible involvement."

"Right," Winslow said. "And the less I know that you know, the more power you have to draw out responses open to interpretation and incrimination. I want to contact a lawyer."

"No need for that," a voice said. Winslow turned. The man was more than six feet tall, gray crewcut, big jaw, broad shoulders. He was wearing a white T-shirt, blue work pants, and a worn police windbreaker.

"Chief," one of the officers said.

"Canfield's fine," the man answered. "No need for titles."

"Are you in charge of this?" Winslow said.

"Not officially, no. Retired. Just. Wait here." He moved off toward the kitchen, his Timberlands making faint echoes. He pushed open the door at the back of the gym and slipped inside but only for about forty seconds. He came back out striding quicker across the hardwood than when he had left.

"Officers DeYoung and McCollough."

"Sir."

"You are excused. Go to the chapel. Wait there with the children and the caregivers. Don't let any of them out of your sight. Bathroom means you or one of the ladies accompanies, no exceptions. If any of the kids uses a stall, you're in there with them."

"Right."

After their exit, Winslow folded his arms up high on the chest. "What is this?" he said.

Canfield walked closer, but made sure to keep his six feet of social distance.

"There's a dead man in there," he said. "Late thirties, early forties, it would seem. Tall. Gaunt. Painter's overalls and boat sneakers. Do you know who it might be?"

Winslow nodded, thinking of the face he'd seen on his computer in box number four.

There was no choice... I was tricked...

"Probably the janitor," he said, amazed at his own steadiness. "Name of Harry Kendall, I believe. I met him once, but never knew him really. I heard about him, though, with all three of my girls coming up through the Latchkey program. He likes to help with the kids, doing read-alouds and monitoring dodgeball games. He also cooks them spaghetti." He looked at the floor. "That's Esther's favorite part of Latchkey, the Friday afternoon 'Harry Spaghetti.' He puts cheese in it, like macaroni and cheese but better, or so I've been told." He looked up. "You're telling me he's dead in that room?"

"I am."

Winslow pointed to the hose-reel setup.

"And this contraption has something to do with it? And Esther with the contraption?"

Canfield moved over to the industrial grade plastic casing and knelt beside it.

"I saw you noticed the fishing line," he said, "connected to the reel in here and suspended up through the bracket in the ceiling." He pushed up and pointed. "On the other side of the drywall, there in the kitchen, the fishing wire was fed through a spring-loaded wheel and pulley system, counterbalanced and tied to the lid of the freezer unit on one side of the stove and the hot-water push-spigot of the sink on the other. Before being brought back to tension, the lines on both sides were finally looped through the eyelets of the jumbo river bait fishing hooks impaled through Harold Kendall's mouth at the corners. There were runnels cut deep into his flesh starting at the two points of penetration, next carved up his jaws and across the brow, making the shape of a mask." He looked back at hose-reel setup in front of him. "When the crankshaft was turned out here, the hooks were pulled in there, and the 'mask' began peeling upward and off inch by inch."

"That's insane," Winslow said.

"Yes," Canfield said. "The trophy is currently hanging over the stove that Kendall made spaghetti on, at the front edge of the range hood like a morbid coat of arms. The raised lid of the freezer had initially let out frigid mist, just as the hot water from the sink was kicking up steam, like smoke machines, a stage effect. But the tableau is far from perfect in application and final execution. The mask is upside-down, first of all. And while that might have been the killer's equivalent of inverting a Catholic Cross or whatnot, the flesh of the relic was evidently fused too well at the left cheekbone and a spot on the forehead above the right eyebrow. The mask has rips, imperfections."

"And that killed Kendall?"

Canfield looked as if he was about to give a short laugh, but his eyes never smiled.

"No, Professor Winslow," he said. "The butcher knife rammed to the hilt through the middle of his breastbone killed him. Probably split his heart in two." His glance dropped again to the hose-reel case. "But I'm willing to bet that the steel came second, if you know what I mean."

Winslow nodded. "So what has Esther got to do with—"

"Winslow," Canfield said, "come with me, please."

The man started walking to the door, and Winslow was reminded again of the basic human instinct to follow orders given by another's body language. He stayed where he was. Chief Canfield stopped and gave a half-turn.

"I want to show you a video," he said. "Upstairs, in Sister Theresa's office."

"You have this on tape?" Winslow said.

"We have something on tape," Canfield said. "Best to have a look for yourself. Best to keep an open mind."

"An open mind? About torture and murder?"

Canfield hooked his thumbs in his belt loops.

"Professor, please understand that I know who did this. I was the one in charge when he opened his assault on this town two years ago, and I am imploring you to prepare yourself for this playing field. I need for you to keep an open mind about horrific possibilities." He paused. "I need for you to understand the way your daughter is caught up in the web of this fiend."

———

"PLAY IT AGAIN," Winslow said. Canfield bent to hit rewind, and the perverse images sped backward silently. Sister Theresa had already left the room. Somewhere, a phone was ringing.

"I have a temporal issue with this, you know," Winslow said.

Canfield stopped the tape. Esther had just entered the bike room, far left. "Temporal—"

"The time," Winslow said. "The damned timing."

"Time is on the tape, bottom corner."

"I mean *your* timing," Winslow said. "I'd left the house before the phone call from the officer downstairs because I was tipped off, I'm sorry to admit. In fact, I don't want to say more about it right now as it puts my three daughters in more possible danger." He squared his shoulders. "My point is that I want to know how you knew about this recording in the first place. You didn't arrive with the other officers. They were surprised to see you. It's too fast. The timing isn't right."

Chief Canfield straightened and came forward. A shadow moved across his face putting it halfway in darkness.

"Professor," he said, "I know you were tipped off, because I was as well. The killer got me on a Zoom call and told me to come right away to this upstairs office. He claimed he was going to crucify Sister Theresa, nail her to a cross leaving her entrails hanging from her naked belly like party-streamers. That was 6:40 A.M. I threw on some clothes and rushed over here, getting to this office at 7:05. I saw what you just saw on the tape, and I was studying it as you are starting to now."

"It's disgusting," Winslow said. "And I don't believe my own eyes."

"Professor—"

"Play it again."

"About the tip-offs, Professor, we have to do better. He wants us to hide things, suspect each other, keep telling half-truths."

"I can't go to the police."

"I'm not the police," Canfield said. "I retired last week."

"Play the tape again, please."

"Words matter with this guy, Professor. Technically, I am not a cop. I can't even carry a company firearm."

"Play. It. Again."

Chief Canfield hit the play button.

The screen jumped to life, and Esther skipped across the gymnasium floor doing her "flower-girl tossing rose petals" act. She hadn't taken her jacket off yet, and she approached the hose-reel case as if she'd expected it to be there.

"Hello," she said. Her voice sounded tinny on the recording, like a cheap replica. She was just tall enough to put her hands on the front edge of the case, go up on tiptoes, and look down over the lip.

"Hello, hello, hello," she called into it. A chill crept up Winslow's spine. He thought he had heard it during the first viewing, and this confirmed it. When Esther spoke into the device, it echoed as if she was calling down into a tunnel, or more the way she'd perceive it, a secret cave or a wishing well.

"Hello, child," a voice answered, rich and dynamic, as if the speaker was deep inside the hose-reel case. Esther jumped up and down, clapping her hands as though she'd just won money on *Family Feud*.

"Show me what you look like!" she cried. "You promised, you promised, you did!"

"Of course," the voice said. "First, Cupcake, just assure me that you are alone. Remember, I am blind, so you are my eyes. Clearly, this room is safe, but go check the hall."

Esther stopped celebrating and put her left palm under her right elbow, in the all too familiar "ready-position" she assumed when she was about to go sucking her thumb. But suddenly she stopped, seeming to will her arms to drop down to her sides. To Winslow, this was gut-wrenching. She hadn't broken the habit for him…

"I'm by myself," she said. "I told them I had to do…number two!"

She giggled.

There was no response.

She put her hands out as if to say, *What the heck?* and said, "Poop is *funny,* mister, like always!"

There was no response.

She stared, then pouted, shrugged, and put her head down and walked back camera-left, out of the shot. There was the faint, smooth sound of a latch sliding in and out at the opening of the mortise plate, a moment of silence, then the soft click of the door resetting. She came back into the shot and returned to her original positioning.

"There's no one in the hall, mister-man," she said. "So what do you look like? Show me. I'm asking really nicely, now, aren't I?"

"Yes, child."

"And if I'm nice, you'll treat me like a good girl like you said, won't you?"

"Yes," the voice said. "Back away three steps if you could."

She made a fist and drew it down slo-mo in front of her face as if to say, *"Yeees!"* then complied.

On her third step back, the hose-reel case started to change.

It began at its base and slowly fed its way up the panels in the form of tiny living crystals, not the bright orange fire-dance in what Winslow recalled as "The Genesis Effect" in *Star Trek II: The Wrath of Khan,* but a similar sort of super-animation depicting a virus-like spread, dots eating their way up and bursting from the top edge in the dazzling curve of a fountain-spray, soon hitting the floor and kicking up small wisps of red colored vapor.

"Cherry!" Esther cried. She stepped forward, closed her eyes, and stuck out her tongue as if catching snowflakes. Winslow made a concerted effort to unclench his jaw.

The spread was complete, the fireworks over. What had been a rather dismal-looking gardener's apparatus was now a gaudy red shimmering box with colorful side panels, each featuring a moving clown caricature. The camera's angle afforded a view of two of them: a hobo clown squirting himself in the face with a trick flower and a fireman clown with buttons on his body-suit that spun like propellers. At the bottom of the contraption were golden corner-caps shaped like lion's feet. And the lid on top was now closed, though Winslow could see the two lengths of fishing line still coming out the far side and leading up toward the pipe bracket.

"Esther," the voice teased, slightly muffled now, "I'm in here."

"Like a Jack-in-the-Box?"

"Yes, child. And you know what to do now, don't you?"

"Of course, silly!"

She reached for the crankshaft. The camera angle made it so the component wasn't visible, but when she began to turn it the music started, her head popping into view two times for each verse-line that was performed in those dead-bell, xylophone dongs:

> All around the mulberry bush
> The monkey chased the weasel.

There were a couple of other sounds too, and that was one of the reasons Winslow had wanted to roll this back for a rerun. First, it was Esther, singing along, and then, like everyone else on the planet, she didn't remember the third line: *The monkey stopped to pull up his sock,* which she replaced with *Da-da /da-da/ da-da-dee-da-da...*

"Stop the tape," Winslow said. "Listen to the song again, back at the beginning, back a few seconds up through the third line. Please."

Canfield rolled it back, and the two of them listened again.

"Stop," Winslow said.

Canfield hit pause. The back of Winslow's neck felt hot.

"Did you hear it?" he said.

"What exactly?"

"The harmony."

"Didn't notice, must have really blended. What harmony?"

Winslow smiled angrily.

"Yes, blended, of course," he said, "because this bastard employed the idea that everything we hear has a pitch, like a note. Train whistles, sirens, even percussive sounds like those of jackhammers fit somewhere on the musical scale, and he somehow worked it tonally that the bicycle bell or whatever he used to plink that God-awful melody was to be in perfect harmony with the real background noise. To hide it from Esther."

"Kendall's screams," Canfield said.

"Exactly. Hit play and let's watch this again to the end."

Canfield hit the button, and at the close of the verse when the box-top popped, it made Winslow jump even though he knew it was coming.

The loud snap was synonymous with a burst of glowing red pixel-confetti, and from within the box sprang a large tensioned coil, almost man-sized, covered with what appeared to be zebra-striped sock-puppet cloth. There was an arm on one side of it, black and rubbery with a Mickey Mouse glove for a hand, yet the other side sported only a stump. The oversized head was a smiling clown face, bright white with mime-lines, and its crown was topped off with dangling red and green joker tassels.

Winslow did not want to watch the next part again, but he forced himself to keep his eyes locked on the screen. The bobbing spring-coil was settling, and the thing pulled a Linda Blair, turning its head back ever so slowly. Back toward the camera.

Winslow shivered.

When he had taught Introduction to Film, the textbook had briefly discussed the Robert Zemeckis family Christmas film *The Polar Express,* starring (the voice of) Tom Hanks. Ironically, audiences found the characters to be creepy, even revolting, and it turned out that there was something at play called "The Uncanny Valley," a theoretical concept claiming that in our intrinsic search for anomalies, there was a point where the animation could get too close for comfort. Winslow remembered YouTubing a scene where the train became a roller coaster headed for a huge sheet of ice for a runway, and he'd marveled at the way the characters *did* skeeve him out, as if they were living corpses or something close to it.

The thing in the Jack-in-the-Box was worse somehow. The smile was too wide, the white-face too lifelike, as if the animation was shrink-wrapped over an actual skull. And the eyes were the worst, jet black and roiling as if there were maggots in the sockets under thin coats of tar.

The eyes flattened smooth before it turned back to Esther.

"Now, child," it said, and there was a blip, a blank spot on the tape. A second later, the camera was fixed on the hose-reel case in its original form, in the empty gym they'd just come from. Chief Canfield shut off the monitor.

"Well, that's it," Winslow said. "So what now? I don't know how this scenario ended. I don't know what this filth asked of my daughter, or what was the next directive or whatever you'd call it." He swallowed, felt his Adam's apple move. "Chief, question. Am I required to report all I know to the officers downstairs in the chapel?"

"I'd strongly consider it," Canfield said.

Winslow spread his feet. "I do not wish to. I've been threatened."

The retired police chief hesitated, slight but apparent. "Understood," he said.

"Should I grab my other daughters from school?"

"No."

"What then?"

Winslow's voice had risen and gained an edge he couldn't hide. He supposed that Canfield read it as a reaction to the imminent danger to his family, the scene in the kitchen, the technological marvels unveiled in the gym. But that wasn't it. Not even close, and Winslow hated himself for this.

Aside from the dead man in the kitchen, what bothered him most was the way Esther had responded to being ignored during the "check-the-hall" moment. This clown-faced deviant…this vulgar, intrusive piece of shit had given Winslow a helpful demonstration, and from it the professor had learned the best way to discipline his daughter. It was lose-lose, and he'd be a fool at this point not to take this advice. In fact, *not* utilizing it would be like trying to put toothpaste back in the tube, unsee what was just seen, go ahead pick your metaphor.

But it made the killer a partner in parenting. The smarter parent, the one more in tune.

Canfield squatted down to re-tie his bootlace.

"I'll tell you 'what now,' then," he said. "Invite me home for lunch and for supper."

Winslow smiled thinly. "Why?" he said. "Not to be rude, but it seems kind of…awkward and forward."

Chief Canfield pushed up and made for the door.

"Because rude has nothing to do with it. Because you and I have our feet stuck deeper in the muck than you think we do."

"How so?" Winslow said.

"We have roles to play." The chief was at the door to the hall, and he rested his fist on the knob. "He put us together for a reason, Professor, to even the odds." He stared down at his hand. "See, I'm one of the few who sparred with this savage and lived to tell about it. I know things, I know *him,* how he thinks, what he's capable of." He paused. "No offense, Professor, but to him I'm the one who is the more worthy adversary." He looked back, staring hard. "And I'm the one you're supposed to murder by lunchtime."

CHAPTER 5

Trust Is a Tough Thing to Come By These Days

Winslow did not invite Canfield for lunch, supper, or a glass of hard lemonade. What, was the man supposed to move in? Sleep in the guestroom? The whole thing was rotten, and Winslow didn't know what to do. He certainly didn't want this stranger just marching into his household, and if he went to the cops and spilled all as suggested, his daughters were dead. The killer had said so, and wording was important to him, right?

Enough.

He'd thanked Chief Canfield for his helpful insights and insisted that the best thing was to handle this within the family, keeping careful. To his amazement, Canfield didn't argue. Instead, the chief escorted him back to the officers downstairs and told them he had already questioned the professor, he who knew "no more than they did." The chief agreed to follow the officers back to the station to make an official report; next, he asked Winslow to take a walk outside with him for a moment while Esther remained safe in the chapel under armed guard. Winslow thought a stern lecture was coming. Instead, Canfield handed over a card that had his address and home phone number on it.

"Keep it handy, Professor," he said. "Not in the junk drawer, not under a magnet on the side of the fridge. Put it in your wallet, right behind the money. Please."

Winslow took the business card and glanced at it. Evidently, the ex–police chief had started a side business fixing lawn mowers, generators, and power tools in his garage. Winslow took out his billfold. The two of them had walked through the parking area and stopped at the far edge of it, across from the marquee board announcing Bible study times, worship services, and bingo on Zoom.

"He's like Covid, isn't he?" Winslow said. "He spreads into your life like infection."

"Yes, Professor."

"And he's everywhere. Watching us, listening."

"Not everywhere." Canfield zipped up his windbreaker. "From what we've heard and discussed, I think it's safe to assume that he's actually blind. I don't see a reason for him to lie about that. Giving away a truth about a weakness makes the game more thrilling for him, and I'd bet dollars to donuts he can't hear us outside. He's an expert with enclosed areas, somehow planting listening devices, making magic with his pixels or whatever they are, showing scary videos, writing haunting text messages."

And possibly using an accomplice to set up the fishing wire, pulleys, and bait hooks, Winslow thought.

"Then I can talk to my daughters outside," he said aloud. "Like a neutral zone."

Canfield made to turn back toward the lot, most probably for the black Ford F-150 parked next to the handicapped space.

"Yes, Professor," he said. "I'd guess that you can talk to them outside. You can make defensive guidelines, put a plan in place. Just know that this man's greatest skill isn't building wild and wondrous tech. It's his insights concerning your psychology. He knew I was going to offer you personal protection, and he also knew you'd refuse. He knew I would suggest, like I'm doing again right now, that your best remaining course of action would be to go back inside that church to give the highest-ranking shield the most comprehensive report you could manage—not leaving it to the watered-down version I just referred to them."

He gave a ghost of a smile. "But he also knew that you'd be just frightened enough of him to choose the third option."

"The third…"

"Yes, of course, dodging, delaying, hoping to outsmart him in the end by being subtle, clever, mature, and methodical."

Winslow shook his head. "He said he'd kill them if I reported the details, Chief. He said he would kill them slowly, and I believe him."

Canfield took his keys out of his pocket. "If he wanted them dead, Professor, they'd already be."

"So what do I do?"

"What you have to. Just remember, whatever you decide, he's already planned for it, like that checkers versus chess thing."

"So it's hopeless."

"No, it's grim, but not hopeless. Just try to see things the way the devil would see them. Take your girls, for instance. To him, they're not cupcakes, sweethearts, or pretty little kittens."

"What are they?"

"Collateral."

The chief stared an extra second to make Winslow look at him.

"You've got my card, my number and address," he said. "You know where I'll be."

"My thanks."

Canfield gave a short nod. "I'll be waiting on that call. Especially one coming near noon."

CHAPTER 6

Wanna Play?

Winslow rushed like a madman across town, one way then the other, to sign the girls out early from school. He'd scolded Esther in the car in front of her sisters for keeping a secret with a stranger, and he'd called it "betrayal," made her cry. Then he'd told them all enough about Michael Leonard Robinson and the death of "Spaghetti Harry" to frighten them into numb silence as Sage and Jody had immediately plunged deep into their cell phones, going on Google and looking up The Sculptor's past atrocities. It could have been worse. Winslow had kept hidden most of the details of the kitchen activity. And if that ended up on Google? Small potatoes, all things considered. Broad brush strokes were required, he was putting out fires.

At least they were all home now, all within arm's reach of each other. Sage was in her room listening with headphones to the K-pop group BTS, and Jody was in there with her, sprawled out on the beanbag chair, reading a book about Babe Ruth. She was eating sour-dough pretzels and drinking Dr. Peppers, belching every few minutes as if she were in a contest. It was a front; she was spooked. Though she and Sage got along, they didn't normally hang out together. They were all spooked; there was a cloud over their home. The idea that Robinson could be watching and listening was like having lice, grotesque and unclean, and Winslow was tearing apart Esther's closet. She was sitting on the floor out in the hallway, sulking.

There was no microphone in here. Old papers, board games, winter clothes, sure, plenty of bric-a-brac, but no microphone. He was on his knees with a flashlight. Nothing but dust in the corners, bare walls. The floor behind him was a cluttered mess. He'd accomplished nothing. All three of the girls had been filmed sleeping last night, the high, tilted viewing angles plain and clear, but there were no recording devices to be found. In case there had been small video units hidden in the lighting, Winslow had ripped down the ceiling fans in both Jody's and Sage's rooms, dragging them out into the hall. He'd turned the overhead light to its brightest setting. No cameras. Esther just had a bulb with a glass shade shaped like an umbrella covered with glistening frost. Winslow had put a crack in it. Ugly. No longer functional.

Winslow backed out and sat on the floor. This was over his head. Clearly, he had to go back to the police from the church. By now they had probably returned to the station, most probably the one up on Lancaster Avenue. Of course, he'd been threatened directly in case he decided to go down that road: *"You go to the police and I kill the girls. Period. No multiple choice, no darkened checkboxes."* He rubbed his palm along the side of his face. Maybe a professional search team would find things he couldn't in here. Maybe they'd put a car out front.

But for how long? And to what real effect? Michael Leonard Robinson had managed to amplify his voice from a closet with no apparent amplifying device. He'd found a way to film the girls with no cameras, peel a man's face off, and turn a hose-reel case into a super-sized child's toy, so, no, initiating a "professional" search of the place and then positioning a cruiser or two in the street didn't seem all that promising.

But wouldn't the officers see the tape upstairs in Sister Theresa's office? Wouldn't they come running here anyway, given that Esther's dialogue with the clown in the box suggested she'd had prior discussions?

He breathed hard through his nose. He'd have bet the house that the tape was erased. Robinson didn't seem the type to leave those kinds of loose ends. Winslow closed his eyes and turned his head to the side. So what about this "Chief Canfield," then? Concerning Esther, he'd covered for her (and him) by giving his brothers in blue the watered-down version for their report. Winslow laughed aloud. Watered down out of respect for Winslow's privacy? An attempt to shield Esther from questioning, to mitigate her exposure? Maybe the "chief" was nefariously involved in this, in cahoots with Robinson. Maybe he was pretending to *be* Robinson.

Or quite possibly, he had come to the same conclusions as Winslow, figuring that an official report and a squad car outside meant diddly-squat.

"What's so funny?" Esther said. She was in the doorway, pushing the heel of her hand in her eye as if she'd missed nap-time. Winslow sighed. Betrayal...by God, she was only seven.

"Nothing, sweetie," he said. "I mean Cupcake."

She came forward and dumped herself into his lap. He held her there on the floor. She mumbled something into the crook of his shoulder.

"What, Cupcake?"

She turned her face up toward his. "No nicknames, Poppy. Esther's fine."

He held her a bit tighter. Laughing clowns and killers aside, there was still only one Poppy around here.

"Come," he said, lifting her off gently, setting her down on her feet.

"Where?"

He pressed up and stood tall, looming over her.

"Sage's room," he said. "So that you can be with your sisters. I have to go onto Zoom and cancel today's English class. Then I'm going to catch up on some reading."

Esther scrunched up her nose."Like research?" she said. "On the bad man?"

"Something like that. Now go on, and knock first. You know Sage's rules."

Esther grabbed his forearm. "Will she give me a Starburst?"

"If she has them."

"A red one?"

"Of course."

Esther smiled. "Will she let me look at her Smithsonian glossy big rock-and-roll book?"

"You tell her I said so. Don't bend the pages."

"Yippee!"

She took off and ran down the hall. Winslow heard her knock.

Something was beeping. From his room.

Robinson, he thought. Right. The house was bugged. And it was just like this guy to wait until the conversation with Esther had closed. A peeping Tom with etiquette.

Winslow marched to his room, muttering sweet nothings under his breath. He'd been sloppy. He'd been conversing with the girls inside, when he'd already decided that all communications were best out of doors. The car was probably red-hot as well.

Winslow shut the bedroom door behind him. At least they hadn't said anything that would have given away some secret course of action, since they had no plan whatsoever. Winslow smiled up the side of his face. An ironic bonus.

The computer was up. The screen was populated with motion graphics that looked like threads of smoke as backdrop now for the headshot of a jester in whiteface with mime lines. The eyes were jet-black roiling tar, he was grinning.

"Professor..."

Winslow was rooted to the spot. The image on the screen was painful to look at for multitudes of reasons, but mostly it was the clarity, or rather, the "super-clarity." It was as if multiple cameras were filming the figure simultaneously, all zoomed at gradated levels, pinpoint to distant. It gave the image dimensions, more than three it seemed, *The Polar Express* on steroids. Beneath the makeup, Winslow could see divots and pores in the flesh as clear as the terrain of the moon through a telescope. Moreover, the comprehensive view gave the figure an amazing depth of field, as if the whole head was jutting out of the computer screen like the old Freddie Krueger movies where he pushed his face into the back side of a wall and stretched it in at you like an animal caught in a net, or a penis thrusting into a condom if you went with the psychoanalytic view of this fine piece of cinema. There was a scent here as well. Black licorice, pungent and dizzying.

"Professor," said Robinson, "you have been a bad boy. Did I not tell you to check your email and bone up on the life and career of the man you are to murder today? I know that you know it's Chief Canfield, and I know that he knows and revealed this to you, so let's not pretend things are going well."

"You son of a—"

"No time for name-calling, Professor. The chief has been a bad boy as well. He was supposed to wait at home for you, but he received an anonymous tip on a cold case thirty-two minutes ago, an unsolved mystery that has haunted him for half a year now. It takes precedence. I hope you're not jealous."

"Oh, go fuck—"

"Yourself, Professor. No easy emails on the chief now, no holistic biographies, no detailed employment record, not anymore. You'll get to know Chief Canfield by way of live bodycam. Dive into the mystery, Professor. Dive right on in."

"And if I don't?"

The smile on the evil thing gleamed.

"Oh, then it will be fun time, Professor. Girl time. Daughter-Poker. I can see it right now, I can taste it…real smock 'n' goggle stuff with car batteries, handcuffs, meat hooks, blood-spattered sink arrangements, boning and breaking knives, cleavers, hot brands, battle hatchets, barbed wire, walk-in freezers, and various high-revving power tools. Buh-bye."

The multi-dimensional head became small spheres that dropped to the floor and danced on it like marbles on granite before disappearing. Now, Winslow's computer was streaming what seemed a live view, slightly fish-eyed, fully in motion. It looked like a found footage snuff film.

"Professor?" he heard a voice say. It was Chief Canfield, and he was slightly out of breath. Winslow didn't want to answer. He didn't want to play. Still, he didn't see the advantage of shutting out Canfield as a source of information either. Whether he could trust that information was a different story.

"Yes, Chief," he said.

"OK, here's the lowdown. You remember the two local politicians that went missing last summer, right?"

Winslow looked up at the ceiling. This was new…

"Yes," he said. "If memory serves it was John, no, Jim Rutledge and Kathy McFee, both representing Montgomery County, one in the P.A. House of Representatives, one in the Senate, both from here, Lower Merion."

"Yes," Canfield said. "To be exact, Rutledge was District 149 and McFee was Senate District 17. Heated rivals: Rutledge the donkey, McFee the elephant, but McFee was always the outlier. Lower Merion is a Democratic stronghold. Been that way for years."

"And they both turned up missing."

"Correct. Same day, last June fifth," Canfield said. "Rutledge was supposed to be at a ribbon cutting, breaking ground for the new library, and McFee was meant to guest-host a charity function on Google Meet. Neither showed. And neither has been heard from since."

"Where are you?" Winslow said. "It looks urban."

The cam showed row houses at the perimeter and a commons with a quaint concrete walkway, a few sitting benches, and some hopeful-looking garden areas with black iron decorator fencing.

"I'm in South Philly," Canfield replied. "Cianfrani Park, 746 Fitzwater Street. I have been told that I will find the location of Jim Rutledge and Kathy McFee if I can figure out the riddle of the sculpture here. Robinson claimed you would help find the clues, that you're good with puzzles and such."

"And thar she blows," muttered Winslow, intrigued despite himself. The sculpture was bolted to the cement in front of the central floral display.

"So that's supposed to be art?" the chief said.

It was one of those absurdist pieces, looking more like junk than an aesthetic, purposefully childlike and visually cartoonish. It appeared to be made with a variety of flying saucer shapes for lack of a better word, as if a bunch of oversized drum cymbals were soldered and riveted together all along their rims, creating a series of two-sided hollow receptacles connected by tubing. Canfield stepped in closer.

The structure had been here for a while. At the points where the material was fastened together, the bronze had turned green in the recesses.

"Take a step back for perspective," Winslow said. Canfield complied. The structure looked like a man and woman with buckets on their heads riding a bicycle built for two. They were joined at the pelvis; however, sharing only one set of feet, those that were planted on the pedals at three and nine o'clock.

Wait a minute...

"Chief," Winslow said, "I think I see something tucked up under the rim of one of the buckets, the front one. Reach up and check, would you?"

Canfield approached and stretched upward. He went a bit higher unsteadily, must have gone up on his toes. *Yes,* Winslow thought. *Right there.* Canfield scraped at it, and from under the lip came a chain that had been seated in there, now dangling down four or five inches. Canfield pulled it and the bucket tipped up, revealing a face, a caricature painted in bright pastels on the bronze. It was that of a man grinning, and it looked vaguely familiar. From the news. Back in June. One of the missing politicians.

Canfield moved to the rear figure, found the chain, and tipped up its bucket, revealing the cartoonish face of a female, all teeth in a hideous apple-slice leer.

"Is that McFee?" Winslow said. "I recall Rutledge a bit, but I don't remember ever seeing the other one."

"That's her," Canfield said. "What does it mean?"

Winslow had a hunch. It hadn't quite come to fruition, but he knew he had something.

"Chief," he said, "a favor, please. Back off a step or two and aim down the bodycam."

"Down where?"

"At the base of the statue, the cement."

Canfield moved and adjusted the angle. Winslow edged closer to his computer screen.

"All right," he said. "It's shadowy, so confirm for me what I'm looking at, will you, Chief?"

"Sure," he said. "The concrete underneath the statue is old. You can see a big crack in it spiked out in perpendicular away from the base plate. And I would say this fissure was here before the statue got erected. Years maybe. There are weeds growing out of it."

Winslow nodded. "That's part of the artwork. Chief, approach the statue again, please."

Canfield moved back in to the edge of the steel base bolted into the ground.

"Closer," Winslow said. "Please." Canfield stepped in so his feet must have been almost underneath the belly of the thing. "Now," Winslow continued, "reach up under the groin area shared by the two figures. Is there something there? Something that feels different, like the ridge of a closed orifice, a small trapdoor?"

"Affirmative," Canfield said after a moment. "What is it?"

"Thematically, I'm pretty sure it's a rectum," said Winslow. "Open it, Chief. But get ready to jump back. You wouldn't want to wreck those nice boots of yours."

Canfield maneuvered and there was a scrape and a whooshing sound. He jumped out of the way and Winslow could see the edges of the retired police officer's hands up to the sides like goal posts. Quickly, Canfield positioned himself so Winslow could see the ground level in-frame and the steamy, bluish liquid that saturated the cement, spreading along the side of the base. Some of the liquid seemed to "sponge into" the concrete, and the overspill quickly evaporated.

The hue of the concrete was changing. Colors were coming up, as if the cement had been treated long in advance to be ready for the active agent to be poured over it.

The image came clear. At the base of the statue of two Looney-Tune caricatures riding a bicycle, sharing the same pelvis and feet, was an American flag. The crack in the cement seemed to split it in two.

"Do you get it?" Winslow said. "The message?"

"Not in the least," said Canfield. "And where are the politicians?"

"Right there at your feet," Winslow said, awed. "Our friend The Sculptor boiled them down or dissolved them. Then he played chemist adding God-knows-what to make the concoction to put in the shared steel belly here, same bowels. Don't you see? He's saying that it doesn't matter about Republicans, Democrats, Conservatives, or Liberals. He is showing you, quite literally, that it's all the same shit, poured out over a divided America. I didn't know our friend was so politically minded."

"He isn't," Canfield said. "But I have a feeling I know who is."

WINSLOW WAS STILL in his bedroom, sitting at the edge of the mattress, face in his hands. Of course, the killer was Harry Kendall, church custodian, creator of "Harry Spaghetti" and chemical mixtures that not only helped with the disposal of bodies, but reacted with concrete to paint political pictures. Of course, Kendall had secured the perfect location for this kind of dirty business, so oxymoronic it was cliché, horrors in the holiest of places, hiding in plain sight and all that. Moreover, as Chief Canfield had detailed over the phone, churches, being places of communal social interaction, had industrial work spaces, industrial storage of cleaning products and maintenance equipment, all ideal for industrial work, like synthesizing toxins, utilizing corrosives, and storing a hoard of dangerous acids. There was a small loading dock out back and a dumpster, and in the kitchen there was a professional drain grate in the floor, a small pressure washer, and solvents that they used to clean animal cages at the S.P.C.A. It was the hub for the perfect storm, conveniently closed to the public at night with knuckle-knuckle gears rotating, perfectly greased, until The Sculptor had thrown in a wrench. With a picture of Esther on the handle, *God,* why couldn't Winslow stop thinking in pedestrian metaphors? *Because metaphors are euphemisms. And the truth of it is, you liked solving the puzzle. Truth is, you put together two plus two quicker than the average Joe, or the above-average Joe, or even the 4.0 Joe. You had Rutledge and McFee boiled down and liquefied in your head long before even a pro like Chief Canfield had it figured. You're a natural. Yes, but a natural...what?*

Winslow messaged his temples with the pads of his fingers.

Canfield had told him that Kendall kept all the supplies for his bloody craft under the stage in the bike room. Perfect. The doors in front had a padlock on them. Kendall had the keys, of course, as did some of the nuns like Sister Theresa, but the stage was only three feet high. To get in you had to crawl. The youngest nun was sixty-three and the youngest Latchkey teacher fifty-seven. Pastor Kennedy was eighty-one. Arthritis, stiff backs, atrophied muscles, dust allergies. No one went under that stage except Kendall. Everyone was rather glad of it.

In the rear corner, stage left, were the tubs of muriatic acid and mixing drums. The chief had also mentioned a number of corrosive liquids with names Winslow couldn't recall at the moment. Rear left, there was a mini filing cabinet stuffed with pamphlets, mailers, memos, and bulletins, all propaganda, all conspiracy theories and paranoid hate literature. He had QAnon, Antifa, Oath Keepers, and Proud Boy shit. Represented also were 5G Towers, Anti-Vaxxers, Bill Gates's microchips, and various articles on the value of Socialism.

Lovely. Problem solved, at least here in Lower Merion.

You will be my Treasure Hunter, Snake Catcher, Lord of the Worms.

Really? thought Winslow. *A puzzle solver who can translate your clever vigilantism and assist in the dirty work through my unwitting daughters?*

Winslow rubbed his nose. He was already imagining the next step, possibly not so "unwitting," as it seemed he was being groomed to help The Sculptor kill killers now, John Wick's right arm, Dexter's puppet. But why? It seemed that Mr. Pixel-Robinson would have gotten along just fine with Sir Chemist-Kendall, heck they could have started their own YouTube channel.

"Competition," said Winslow aloud. "You're inducing me to help kill the competition."

He held his breath for a moment, half expecting there to be a reply from his computer or cell phone. There was none, and he suddenly ached to hold Georgia in his arms just one last time, run his finger along the ridge of her jaw, kiss her eyelids, rub her legs thoughtfully. Together, they could have solved this. She would have had an interesting alternate perspective, providing answers where Winslow had trouble filling in the blanks, and then they would have made love. But she wasn't here to warm him with answers. He was alone, protecting the girls.

He put his palms on his knees.

A corner of this didn't make sense, namely Chief Canfield. Why was he on the list to be murdered by midnight? If Robinson was wary of capture, he wouldn't have alerted the chief in the first place, and so, was Robinson making a point about the act of murder being subjective, depending on the uniform you wore and the cause in your head? How many had Chief Canfield brought down in the name of duty and justice?

Winslow shook his head. Robinson could have picked anyone in the world to be his assassin.

You're a natural.

"But for what?" Winslow murmured. "Teaching argumentative rhetorical structures to college freshmen? For figuring out puzzles?" He put his tongue between his teeth. The thing that would twist him into being Robinson's loyal "snake catcher," and the only thing in the world that could alter his instinctive behavior and principles, was three doors down the hall.

If he wanted them dead, Professor, they'd already be.

Yes, and they weren't just collateral either. That son-of-a-bitch induced Esther to crank the fucking handle, now, didn't he?

Winslow froze, cocked his ear. There were voices coming from down the hall, spatting and popping like grease in a skillet. He rose, thinking again of Georgia and how inadequate was his solo track record in setting a tone, holding down the fort, and playing referee when his angels were fighting.

CHAPTER 7

I'll Be Right Back

W inslow halted outside Sage's door, his hand hovering above the knob.

"No!" she cried. "I don't believe you. Show me your phone, I want to see the texts."

"Here you go, catch."

A pause.

"You changed the code."

"It's none of your business," Jody returned coldly. "Why do you care, anyway?"

"Because I know him, that's why. He's in my homeroom and my geometry class. He's dark and poetic, sensitive and a bit lost. He would never—"

"Really?" There was a rustling sound and then feet on the floor; Jody had pushed up from the beanbag chair. "Yesterday," she said, "when it was my turn in the batting cage, he stood outside the netting and whispered *'Cunt Licker'* at me."

"Jody!" Sage said.

"It's OK," Esther said. "I've heard all the bad words. What's a cunt?"

"Easy, Peanut," Jody said. "Your bigger sis needs to stop sticking up for this troll. He messed up my timing. We all know I don't do pitching machines very well—"

"Yes," Sage agreed. "When you can't see the pitcher spread, it forces you to do a load step or whatever."

"Then act like you know."

"Then act your age! You shouldn't be practicing with the high school team in the first place! You're only fourteen."

"Almost fifteen, and oh…I guess you still haven't thought of what to get me for my thirteenth, huh?"

"Not fair."

"Yeah!" Esther added.

"More than fair," Jody said. "It's been months."

"Since when do you care about presents?" Sage said.

"Yeah!" Esther said.

"Since you promised that I'd be the star of your first painting." Pause. "I got blocked."

"You can't get blocked. You're not a writer."

"And you're not a real girl!" Sage spat back. "You don't look like one, you don't think like one, and you're not going to go beating up on a boy just because you think you hear whispers in your head!"

Winslow turned the knob and pushed open the door. Sage had her fists by her sides. Jody was leaning in, a foot or so away from her. Esther was in the beanbag chair.

"Poppy!" she said, both arms up like a V.

"Two steps back, both of you," Winslow said. "Sage, what's his name?"

"Vincent."

"Vincent what?"

"Vincent Gatto."

"And you like this boy?"

Sage's eyes blazed and she looked right at Jody. Then her bottom lip trembled.

"He smiled at me. We talked about nineties music. He's nice."

"He's a pig," Jody snorted.

"Stop," Winslow said. "So he called you a name, Jo-Jo?"

"Lots of times. And he put dents in my best practice bat, banging it against the edge of a cement tire bumper in the parking lot behind the gym when I was doing the pepper drill inside. Lenny Schuster said so, he saw him do it. Then he rubbed dog shit in my glove, and I had to throw it in the trash."

Winslow folded his arms carefully.

"Language. And I've always had reservations about you playing with high school boys."

Jody's mouth dropped open. "So it's my fault? Seriously? The middle school doesn't have a good pitching machine and Coach Tornetta can't throw more than sixty. Neither can any of the players."

"Then we're going to have to alert someone to this. Maybe go and pay a visit to his house, meet his parents."

"No!" Sage cried.

"No way," Jody echoed.

Winslow stroked his moustache and glanced at her kind of sideways. "Can you take him?"

"Poppy!" Sage said.

"Easy-peezy," Jody said.

"Sweet!" Esther said.

Winslow looked at the floor. What was he thinking?

"Um, sorry Jo-Jo," he said softly, "I can't have you fighting a boy."

"What's to stop me?" Jody said, "You? There haven't been any rules in this house since Mom died, not really." She jerked her head to get a lock of hair off her forehead. "Fuck it," she said. "Later."

She leapt past, out of the room, and she was thudding down the stairs before Winslow could even begin to process this mutiny. "I've got your car keys now," she called. "Don't try and follow." The door slammed and she was gone. Winslow rushed over to the window. Of course, it was painted over in thick wavy rainbows from back when Sage went through her Frank Lloyd Wright phase. She was also terrified of heights, and having the window covered brought comfort to her. Winslow fumbled with the lock. He couldn't get a good grip, so he threw both hands into it. Got it, pinched a finger, he rammed it up, bent down, and stuck out his head. He'd parked out front, and he let out a long breath. She hadn't taken his car, thank God. He'd also not been quick enough to catch which way she'd run off.

He pulled back in and his glance trickled down to the bottom of the sill. He tried to imagine where she would go to fight—some place familiar, most probably. There was the Little League field across Haverford Avenue past the church on Manoa, but that seemed too obvious. Better would be the woods there, just past the outfield with its multiple clearings and nooks and crannies kids could hide in, playing hooky, smoking cigarettes, drinking, the works. There was the elementary school up Trent Road that would afford a 360 view from all four streets surrounding its expansive front lawn, playground, trailer area, and parking lot, but there was the Wynnewood Valley Park a few steps away down Remington. More woods, better for stealth.

"Are you going to go after her?" Sage said. "Make her stop?" Winslow turned. She was holding Jody's cell phone in her hand. "We can't track her," she said hollowly. "And you can shut that now too, if you could. Please."

He pushed the window closed and turned back.

"Do you know where she's going?"

"No," she said. "I could guess, but we'd be better off splitting up."

"No can do."

"Because of the bad man?" Esther said.

"Yes." said Winslow.

He felt old and helpless, ignorant and clueless. He reached into his pocket and got out his wallet, removing the card that sat behind the twenty-dollar bill. Next he got out his cell phone and tabbed in a number. And when the man on the other end picked up, Winslow said,

"I want to invite you over for supper."

CHAPTER 8

What Is Blood for If Not for Shedding?

Winslow started to explain the situation, but the chief cut him off.

"I already know about the fight, Professor. Hell, a third of the high school has emptied out to go watch. There are a couple of hundred gathered at South Ardmore Park, just below the 'B' field back by the restrooms. It got called into the station by the principal and a number of neighbors."

"Where are you?" Winslow said.

"Turning onto Haverford Avenue now."

"Meet you there."

"No," the chief said. "Stay with your other girls. This isn't the kind of sideshow you want them exposed to, especially the little one. You should also avoid crowds. They make you more susceptible. I've got this. There are two black and whites on their way also."

"How do you know?"

"I have it all on my scanner, Professor. I'm coming up on location presently. Damn..."

"What?"

"That might be more than two hundred."

The connection ceased. Winslow took the phone away from his ear and gazed at it stupidly. But wait...

"Stay here," Winslow said. Sage's running mascara looked crooked and tragic, and she put her arm around her sister. Winslow stalked out to the hall and made for the bedroom, hoping that the chief's cam-view would come up on the computer as it had for the park-sculpture incident. In the back of his mind, he reminded himself that all these viewpoints were only made possible by Robinson's technical and semantic manipulations, but the professor was too invested in his daughter's safety to go splitting hairs.

The computer was on, but there was no live footage showing. Winslow closed the door behind him. The only thing on the screen was a word in large caps:

EVOLVE

"What's that mean?" Winslow said.

"Evolve," the mechanistic voice droned back.

"Right," Winslow said. "You want me to evolve..."

"You are doing so already, Professor. You're just too close to see it. And I was talking about my own metamorphosis: larva to blowfly, ribbed egg to ghost shark, seedling to corpse flower."

"Good for you. Where is my daughter? Confirm for me that she's at the park. Now."

"Patience. We always rush to the human element and try to skip past the technology."

"What technology?"

"Projections, Professor, excuse the blunt alliteration. In 1999, for example, the world of film was opened to a new concept unheard of beforehand. I refer here to *The Matrix* and the Neo character's slow-motion dodge-dance through which we as viewers did a 360 around him in a faster slow motion. It was named 'Bullet Time,' filmed with one hundred and twenty cameras mounted in a roller coaster style arc, snapping single images in a computer driven, rapid fire sequence."

"Thrilling," Winslow said. "And I could one-up you and mention the latest jaw-dropping CGI, or I could go old school and discuss Shakespeare and the way we can easily measure his superiority when compared to his contemporaries. But I am not going to waste your time and mine, calling you a prodigy. Bring back that body cam and show me, Robinson. Show me my daughter. Show me right now."

"As you wish."

Winslow gasped. There had been no lead-in, no introduction, no plume of animated pixels forming the illusion of a solid taking on form and feature.

Jody.

It was as if she stood right before him, motionless like a wax figure, more depth than a picture or hologram, every crease in her Lincoln green Edgemont Tournament jersey vivid and pronounced like a raised relief map. Her sharp narrow face was a perfect replica, her dark lashes, the spatter of freckles around the bridge of her nose. But there was no breath in her chest, and her eyes were dead-empty.

"Go ahead," the voice from the computer said. "Touch her."

"No," Winslow said. "Make it go away. It's an aberration."

"Her hair feels like hair, Professor."

"No."

"You can take her hand."

"Never," he said. "Pack up your illusions and find someone else to torture."

"But Professor," said The Sculptor, "the match is about to begin. And I would never deny you the preliminaries. You, uh, might want to back up a few steps."

The professor retreated a half-pace, and the image of his daughter rose into the air, high enough so he could see a tiny pebble caught in the tread of her Nike Revolution 5's. There was a *pop* like a bang party-snap, and about ten feet abreast of her and a foot or so higher, there was another figure now floating on the air...red Converse All Stars, scuffed black jeans with a hole exposing his right knee, weathered blue hoodie.

"Enter Vincent Gatto," Winslow whispered to himself, knowing of course that this "low-angle shot" created an automatic hierarchy, forcing him and his daughter to look up to the creep, both figuratively and literally. The young man had dirty blond hair falling down across one eye, a small cut below his lower lip, and a cluster of blackheads in the cleft of his chin, partly hidden by a peach-fuzz goatee.

He drifted down to Jody's level and started to move, removing his sweatshirt, pulling it over his head. It drew his T-shirt up with it, and to the left of his belly-button there was a coiled diamondback rattlesnake tattoo with its tail dipping below the pants-line. The kid's stomach wasn't "washboard" by any means, but he was more solid than he appeared when covered in layers. Solid enough to stand his ground. Solid enough to do damage.

Professor Bradford Winslow had never felt so repulsed by a human being in his life, nor had he ever been so frightened for one of his own. The figure dropped the hoodie. He pulled his shirt back into place, and it said "Classic Rock Is for Fucktards" in bright yellow letters. He jerked his head to flip the hair from his face and his soulless blue eyes were laughing.

"Ladies and gentlemen," The Sculptor's voice said, still mechanistic, yet now enhanced as if coming through a microphone in an arena with an echo. "In the corner to my right, hailing from Wynnewood, Pennsylvania, coming in at ninety-eight and a half pounds, please welcome Jody-the-Hammer Winslow!"

Her "Avatar," or whatever one might call it, still did not move.

"And in the corner to my left, straight from Ardmore, Pennsylvania, at a hundred and thirty-one pounds, Vin-the Sin Gatto!"

The prick danced in place for a moment with his arms up like Rocky Balboa. Then he lowered his elbows and punched straight ahead at the air a few times. He stopped, pressed the middle knuckle of his right index finger up against the side of his nose, and blew out hard through the opposite nostril.

The mucus hit the professor on the cheek. It stung. He wiped at it, wide-eyed, disbelieving, rubbing it between his fingers like a miser gesturing about a payment.

A bell dinged. Both figures squared off and began to circle. Jody's face had life in it now, so real and distinct that Winslow almost wept. Gatto was a head taller. He was smiling, leaving his hands down barrel-rolling, jerking his shoulders a few times as if to lunge in, yet faking it, taunting, tonguing the cut under his lip. Winslow thought wildly that maybe the boy would go easy...showboating more than actually punching.

"Hey," he said. "C'mon, son..."

"Do not speak to the combatants," The Sculptor said. "And oh, he won't go easy on her, Professor, don't even think it. Vinny's 'besties', Ricky Tyler and Jaheim Carpenter, both know that this is going down. They have texted everyone on the baseball team and fifteen others in the friendship group, and they have spread it to the entire school as you already well know. If Gatto loses, he'll never hear the end of it. Oh, he's going to hit harder than he ever has, friend, so let's go through the potential scenarios. Jody's right arm is stronger and dominant, and she has the vague plan of roundhousing him into submission, maybe clocking him five times as if she's swinging a hammer."

The figures above Winslow went into slow motion, Jody coming forward, raising up her right fist.

"But Professor," The Sculptor said, "Vinny has two big brothers, one a Philadelphia fireman now, ex-boxer, bantamweight, and the eldest a car mechanic who owns his own towing service. At sixteen, that one did a year in a juvenile detention center for striking a teacher. They both taught Vinny to fight starting when he was seven, every year hitting him harder, making him block and hit back, and the old roundhouse isn't going to surprise him; in fact, he is not going to believe how simple this turned out to be."

"No," Winslow whispered. "No, Jo-Jo honey, too obvious, too open…"

Above him, she was coming in with her over-the-head hammer strike. Gatto countered easily with a forearm, brushing her fist to the side, and he punched her in the face three times, the vivid slow motion so achingly slow. Winslow was positioned behind her, so he didn't see the contact, just the effect. Her head jerked back each time like a puppet on a spring, and with each Winslow recoiled.

"Assessment," The Sculptor's voice said. The figures froze where they were. From over Jody's shoulder Vinny Gatto's eyes were blue frost. A grid winked on to their right, three-dimensional white graph-lines four feet or so by four feet, with the outline of a human face impressed into them. The left eye seemed to cave in, darkening, lines bending.

"Shattered socket," The Sculptor said.

The nose area on the graph then bowed inward.

"Fractured nasal bone, torn cartilage, damage to the maxilla bone, deviated septum."

Then the mouth, frontal view.

"Loss of both lower incisors and mandibular fracture in two places."

The graphic disappeared and the super-avatars sped up in reverse motion, stopping fast.

"Real time," The Sculptor said. "With sound."

It unfolded quickly.

Jody's head snapped back three times. The sounds were flat and percussive.

"Scenario two," said The Sculptor.

"No, I have seen quite enough," Winslow said.

"Lovely."

The figures started their slow circling again.

"Jody-the-Hammer Winslow," The Sculptor droned on, "is a big fan of collegiate wrestling. Her favorite team is the Ohio State—"

"Buckeyes," Winslow mouthed with him.

"If he comes in hands-high, she has been considering a double leg takedown, even though she has never attempted one on a live opponent. Let's see the results, now shall we?"

Above him, Jody crouched in slow motion, telegraphing, then dropped down to a knee. Gatto stepped in, set his left foot, and brought up the right one, all toe, like a punter. He got her flush on the bottom of the chin, rocking her head back farther than it looked possible it could go, and it brought her off her knees an inch or two.

"Assessment!"

They froze, Jody's head back between her shoulder blades too far, her eyes half-lidded, worse because Winslow saw them upside-down. Up next to the two fighters came the graphic, showing a representation of Jody's jawline from the side. For a moment Winslow didn't know what he was looking at. He had the face right, he could see clearly the teeth and the nose in the graphing, but there was some-thing in Jody's mouth. Something between her teeth.

"The apex of the tongue is entirely severed," The Sculptor said. "There are hairline fractures—"

Winslow's phone was ringing.

He struggled it out of his pocket, hit the button, and brought it to his ear. His heart was beating mightily.

"Winslow," Chief Canfield said.

"What?" he said. "Please, what's happened, Chief?"

"It's a MacGuffin," Canfield said. "A false lead. The two in the park are seniors, both male. Neither Jody nor Vincent Gatto are present here. If they're fighting, they're doing it elsewhere."

Winslow disconnected.

There was a *pop* and the super-avatars burst into confetti. Winslow palmed the top of his head to wipe off.

"Where are they, Robinson?" he said.

On the computer, the word "EVOLVE" took on a neon quality, the letters colored tubular blue with a pink moving border. The image burst into party streamers, and all that was left was a single word.

DOT

Winslow stared at it. What did a dot have anything to do with—Wait.

It was a puzzle. Simplistic.

Hell, it wasn't a dot. It was the short version of "Dorothy." *The Wizard of Oz,* and "There's no place like—"

"Home," Winslow said.

They were here. In the back yard, most probably, in the nook behind the toolshed under the cover of the snow goose cherry trees. He turned and opened the bedroom door, his eyes so wide they felt reddened and raw. His steps were long and clumsy down the stairs, Frankenstein with loose boots, stomping through the kitchen, pushing out the back, fresh keen air in the face, c'mon, *move!*

Winslow picked up the pace, going into a jog over the decorator pavers leading to the gate in the horizontal cedar fencing. To the right was the back side of the detached garage, and due left was the old shed that needed to be replaced or simply removed. It was a mini barn-styled eyesore, with dark gray weather-worn planks and an eroded crushed-stone foundation making the whole thing lean slightly right. Half the roof shingles were gone and the front wall due right had a slat missing like a yanked tooth. That made Winslow think of broken lower incisors, and he bunched his fists at his sides.

The shed was an embarrassment, its demolition put on the back burner because it wasn't visible from the alley or street. Winslow stalked alongside it.

From around the back corner, a figure appeared. He was putting his blue hoodie back on. His head popped through the neck hole. He had dirty blond hair, crystal-blue eyes, and a small cut under his lower lip. Both he and Winslow stopped fast before each other.

The boy smirked, and Winslow saw red.

Then he blacked out.

WINSLOW REMEMBERED THINGS, violent, piecemeal, flashes and starts, but it was jumbled, nonsensical dream theater. He was warm and sticky, hair matted down on the left side, a scrape of some kind in his ear. His lower back ached, and he knew he couldn't lift his right arm.

He was leaning over, bent at the waist, holding the boy up by the front of the T-shirt, two fistfuls. There was dark blood spattered up the professor's left forearm. The right was coated like deep red stained glass. Both the boy's arms were dangling down, his fingers touching the grass, and Winslow could not see his face, only the bottom of his chin because his head hung back like a trap door on a hinge.

Winslow lowered the boy to the ground. Someone was crying, talking gibberish.

"Quiet," Winslow said softly. "Sit."

From the corner of his eye, he saw Jody crumble down and sit Indian-style there at the back corner of the shed. She was gasping, hiccupping, working it up to another crescendo.

"Stop," Winslow said. "Deep breaths. And shut up."

He still hadn't looked directly at her. What lay before him on the ground was simply too galling, too fascinating.

It was a boy who once had a face. In a strange way it reminded Winslow of the infamous coffin photos of Emmett Till, the African American teen who was visiting family in Mississippi, 1955, and was beaten and shot for whistling at a white girl in a grocery store. The professor had always thought the appearance of the corpse was especially gruesome because of the cruel irony, the bloated, clownish facial expression that looked more like that of some comic old Brit than a fourteen-year-old who had just gone to the store for a pack of gum or a bottle of milk. Till's mouth was walrus-like, the nose a short pig's snout, the cheeks rotted cabbage, the eye-area nothing more than spoiled cheese left to bubble and burn on a grill.

Strange.

While Emmett Till personified savage bruising and swelling, Vincent Gatto was the poster-boy for omission, eviction, removal—a facial anatomy chart that offered the layers.

His nose was gone. Winslow could still taste it. All that was left were the exposed sinus cavities like those of some unearthly amphibian. His lips were raw, bloody hamburger. The left cheek was ripped clean, the teeth showing through in a pirate's leer. One eye was a smear of red gel, and the other was missing, the dark socket bursting with strands of ocular muscle and cranial nerves like wires in the wall where you ripped out a fixture.

"Poppy," Jody whispered. "Poppy, Daddy, please, I'm gonna throw up."

"No, you will not," the professor said softly. "Count back from one hundred, give your head a good shake, and stop swallowing air."

"But you SO didn't have to do this, Poppy!"

"Sit back down. And lower your voice."

"We weren't even fighting!"

"Sit."

"Okay, okay... but, but... but we weren't," she said. "I made it up, like an opposite, so no one would know we were hooking up. We kept it secret from everyone, especially Sage."

"Hooking up?"

"Kissing, Poppy! We were kissing! God!"

He looked at his daughter. Anyone who thought female tears were endearing didn't know what the fuck they were talking about. Her eyes were bloodshot and her pale cheeks had blotch-dots like clown paint. She had drool hanging off her lower lip and there was snot in her hair.

"Kissing," he said.

"Yes."

"How ironic." He looked at his hands and spoke to them gently.

"Darling, I am going to make two phone calls, and directly following this you are going to go straight into the house. You will go to the downstairs bathroom and wash your face. Soak a towel, the whole thing corner to corner, and then wring it out just enough so there is no drip. Rub it on your scalp briskly, then comb your hair down nice and straight."

"But—"

"No 'buts,' darling. After you have freshened up, and quickly mind you, I need for you to bring me some things. Down the basement in the white veneer cabinet next to the water boiler, you'll find the big canvas dropcloth with the paint splotches on it. Also, bring up the mop bucket, five Hefty bags, the Tub O' Scrub hand soap, and the jug of bleach that we keep under the splash basin. I additionally want the Rayovac search flashlight with the top handle, the roll of Gorilla tape that is in the pantry by the bag with the batteries, and five beach towels from the linen closet." He paused. "One more thing, Jo-Jo. At the back of the basement over the workbench you know I keep my hand tools on the pegboard. Bring me the hacksaw, please, the one with the frame that looks like a rectangle. There are also a couple of wood-ripping saws back there, and I want the longer one with the bigger teeth."

He slipped his hand into his pocket and winced. Tender knuckles. He hoped he hadn't broken them. He pulled out his phone and called Sage.

"Hello?" she said, "Poppy? What—"

"Sage, honey," he said, "there was no fight. Jody is fine, but I need you to lock your bedroom door and do not open it under any circumstances. If you have to go to the bathroom, take Esther with you and vice versa. Go straight through the laundry room and then return to yours directly. No detours, not even for a glass of juice. If the front doorbell rings, you ignore it. Clear?"

He didn't wait for a response. He disconnected and called Chief Canfield.

"Winslow?" the voice said. "I'm a block from your—"

"Don't come here right now, Chief. Keep away. Robinson's got the upper hand. You knock on my door; I lose a daughter. Period."

"Understood, but—"

"Keep clear, now."

"Understood."

Winslow hung up, then turned the phone off and stared at his feet.

"What are you waiting for?" he said.

Jody pushed up and ran back to the house, sobbing.

WINSLOW WAS GASPING for breath in here. He stopped what he was doing and straightened painfully. The cutting was a slow, laborious process. The search flashlight, perched on a milk crate in the shed's front right corner, cut a slant of a beam back in through the dark, illuminating a shelved stack of terracotta plant pottery and a pickle barrel filled with Georgia's gardening tools. The air was close and thick, the busted plank in the wall blocked up by a 50-pound bag of mulch Winslow had stuffed halfway through.

The body was bathed in soft secondary light, pitching long shadows to the rear left corner where there was a coil of chicken wire and all the rakes and shovels with their long handles sticking out of an old plastic trash bin.

Winslow had spread the dropcloth in here and had hefted the kid up over his shoulder out there, struggling for balance at first, waffling a bit back and forth, the corpse's head bumping him in the back, the swinging hands brushing his buttocks and upper thighs. It took all his will not to scream. When he stepped in across the landing his knees almost buckled, but he made it. Just. He bent forward too fast and the body slid off as if it was greased, the head thumping the floor like a melon that had just fallen from the shelf at the Giant.

Now the boy was stripped down to his underwear and was lying on his back—at least, what was left of him.

There had been a vague plan, to hack the body into manageable pieces and later transport them out of the shed one or two at a time in a duffel bag or suitcase. Winslow didn't know where he was going to bring these body parts; he hadn't thought that far ahead. All he knew was that dragging a dead body wrapped in a dropcloth to the car was an unacceptable option. The fencing and the cherry trees provided more than enough backyard cover, but once he dragged the body into the alley he was out in the great wide open. Someone would see, and he'd be even more exposed out front.

There had been other considerations as well, complications.

He had heard somewhere that bleach could destroy or at least muffle traces of DNA. Still, the exact way he would use the bleach was not clear. He would have to get rid of the blood evidence on the floor in here and out on the grass. But how exactly? Well, damn it all to hell, that was for later, just like the idea that he still needed to hose off before going back into the house. Gatto's blood had dried in places, making it so when he moved, the crusted edges pinched like old scabs. Other areas were moistened by Winslow's sweat, stinging in his eyes, dampening his shirt down the back.

And so how on earth *was* he supposed to clean off, anyway? He couldn't soak himself in bleach. Sure, he could use the industrial soap and the hose outside, yet the microscopic blood DNA would again be left out on the grass. For how long? Would a solid rain wash it clean? Winslow could get to the majority of his body here in the back yard with his clothes in a trash bag, going behind the ears and between the toes with meticulous care and such, but some would end up being tracked into the house, wouldn't it? Microscopic drops and flecks would be left on the carpets, the stairs, and the bathroom floor tiles. He thought he remembered seeing somewhere, a film maybe, that cops used a liquid product, maybe it was "Luminol" or something like that, which could make blood show up glowing like fluorescents under a blacklight. So again, how could he possibly purify the path with scientific surety and efficiency? He couldn't. It would be like trying to clean the trail of a slug with a toothpick. He had to cover the basics, get this all clean just enough so that no one would come back here looking, that's all.

First things first; however, he'd have to cut Gatto's body into reasonable portions. That was the goal. Things like cleaning the grass, showering, wiping the floor in here, and talking to Jody were all luxuries for later until he handled step one.

Jody, shit. Just thinking of her, visualizing what he had just put her through, was a knife shoved straight through Brad Winslow's heart. What kind of father was he? Why didn't he simply report exactly what happened? Canfield would believe him, that was for sure.

Winslow clenched his teeth and gripped the D handle of the wood saw harder. He had a responsibility to raise the girls right, and a confession would ruin everything. Found innocent or guilty, he'd be fired. College professors who adjuncted only did so with squeaky clean reputations. Would he work in a grocery store? Drive for Uber? And what if he went to jail? Who would look after his daughters? He had one living relative he talked to, Georgia's side, a half-sister who lived in a townhouse in Benton, Kentucky. She worked at a Walgreens and had an opioid addiction. Winslow had been an only child and his parents had been dead for years. His cousins, aunts, and uncles were strangers. Would his darlings become wards of the state?

Jody is ruined.

"Not yet," he said in a low voice. He had to be practical. Morals and ethics were one thing, but his daughters needed more than a mission statement. Symbolism and abstraction meant nothing when you were fighting for your family, your freedom, your way of life. He owed it to them to be strong. Of course, Jody would have to keep a secret and erase stuff from her mind, block stuff out, it happened all the time. In return, she would have a loving father, a comfortable home, and a strong family infrastructure. She would go to one of the big Division I schools that featured girls' softball, maybe Florida State or LSU. She'd play third with a full ride. She'd bat .650. She would have a boatload of friends and graduate Summa Cum Laude.

He cocked down his head and tried to wipe blood out of his eye with the back of his hand. Cruelly, he was reminded of the pain in his shoulder. That was one of the issues, as Winslow had to saw left-handed. There was an old joke that a man could masturbate with the non-dominant hand, and the touch of this new clumsy stranger would be a turn-on.

Winslow wasn't laughing.

He was trying his best to avoid putting himself through moralistic self-assessment as he just had and, at the same time, execute the dirty-work.

He'd started at the kid's left foot with the wood saw, entertaining the vague idea that the big teeth of the ripping blade would cut a nice furrow, taking him right through to the floor underneath with a few hearty strokes. If the bone was too awkward, he'd finish with the hacksaw. He'd gone down to one knee, grabbed the boy's foot with his right hand, and set the blade on the ankle with his left. He'd pushed hard.

It skidded up the calf, curling the skin back like tree bark. Winslow had cursed aloud, stood, and rummaged around until he found an old footlocker Sage had used last year for Girl Scout Camp. He dragged it over and propped up the boy's foot, thinking the better angle would yield more positive results.

After two good strokes, the blade stuck fast.

Winslow yanked it free. He was grinning, all teeth, and he bent in and set blade on bone up by the grip. To make a starting groove. He yanked backward, and it grated and bumped. He did it again, twice now, and then he switched saws. Slow progress. His left shoulder was already starting to ache, and the small-toothed metal-cutting blade got gummed up halfway through. Winslow had used the kid's T-shirt to wipe and pick it clean, and was forced to repeat the process twice before finally pushing through the bottom side.

Presently, he had removed both feet, both legs, and both arms. The ground cloth was soaked through, the beach towels bunched in five of the places the blood had most pooled, the body parts scattered between like lost toys. Amazingly, the arms had given Winslow more problems than the upper thighs, more specifically, the left, for which he had started too high on the shoulder and had been met with sinewy tendons that caught in the teeth of the ripping blade. The hacksaw had long become dulled and useless. Winslow had had to start afresh.

Now, the head.

Winslow looked around wide-eyed in the semi-darkness for something to prop it on, something pillow-sized as opposed to the footlocker, which would force him to set the torso into a sitting position. He grabbed the flashlight and followed the beam to the corner where they kept the holiday shit. There, on top of a plastic tub, he found the wrought iron Christmas tree stand. Perfect. It was a good height and had the convenient central orifice where the three set-bolts screwed in, the right size to cradle the back of the boy's skull.

He turned. The body parts were stiffening, the fingers and toes bending crooked like claws. In the middle of it all, Vincent Gatto looked like a broken mannequin, the trunk with its jagged vacancies, the stump of the left leg slightly longer than its twin. Winslow approached. Shadows passed over the boy's face, and the light slid through the right eye cavity, making it look for a moment as if he'd winked slyly. Winslow put the flashlight on the footlocker and set the tree base down on the floor next to the corpse. He bent, grabbed Gatto by the hair, lifted, and seated the head. He straightened and his palms went immediately to the back of his love handles. Girlish.

Tired. Miles to go before I sleep. Winslow turned and picked up the wood saw.

The blood streaked across the steel made it look like a shark's maw. Winslow took a knee.

He remembered from the early days, when he and Georgia were dating at Drexel University, the way he'd quiz her on slides she had to memorize for exams on musculoskeletal structures. He thought he recalled that the "softest" point in the neck was just below the Adam's apple, in through the hollow. He wanted to avoid the thyroid cartilage. He wanted to be in the middle of the cervical vertebrae where the tracheal discs were stacked. Was there spongy material between them? He thought so. Maybe he'd get lucky and pass through that part like a knife through butter. Maybe not. Didn't matter. He set the back end of the blade on Vinny Gatto's throat and pulled it back hard.

The skin opened, like a big widening grin. Blood filled the void and there was a sound like somebody sighing. Winslow switched knees and switched to his natural hand, moaning, talking to himself, shoving the blade through back and forth with his bad right shoulder screeching, grinding, grating, on fire. He got through the back side and the blade scraped metal to metal. The boy's head was entirely separated now, angled away, yet held in place by one long string of gristle. Exhausted, Winslow fell back on his rump hard enough to clack his teeth together.

He sat numbly, forearms on his knees, staring at nothing.

There would be an inquest. An investigation. Even if there had never been a school rumor about Jody and the boy…only fake texts between them…Chief Canfield knew. Sage and Esther knew. The boy's parents would look at his social media, as Winslow knew he would if he was in their shoes. All they needed to do was find one connection, one short conversation, and they'd camp out at police headquarters until Jody was brought in for questioning. She could keep a secret, but the SVU's finest were used to prying open young minds, juvenile delinquents with tougher scars and harder shell casings than Jody Beth Winslow.

Forensics would be here.

Blood-spatter experts, hardened professionals.

Winslow didn't even know where to bury the body parts. This was over his head, above his pay grade, pick your cliché, he was fucked.

Unless...

No. He pushed that thought away before it could even form into an idea, a possibility. But the cat was out of the bag now, and everyone knew what they said about pink elephants.

The idea solidified.

"Robinson," Winslow said aloud. "Help me."

———

"WHAT IS IT?" Winslow said.

"Fairy dust." The Sculptor wasn't using the voice-changer, and his soft, silky tone made the professor want to scratch out his own eyes. But, chop-chop, no time for fun.

"What do you mean, 'fairy dust'?" Before him was an industrial-sized bucket filled with pink powder. An ice scoop was buried in it to the hilt.

"Just what it sounds like," said The Sculptor. "Magic dust. Living pixie powder that is attracted to blood, addicted to it. Once you fan out a sprinkle, the dust will find the blood on its own."

"To do what?"

"Cover."

"Cover, huh? For how long?

"Long enough."

"Is it real?"

"Is anything? If it masks the splotches and spatters to the naked human eye, what difference does its origin make?"

Winslow took a deep breath through his nose. "What if it doesn't work?" he said.

"Have you any choice?"

"No."

"No."

Winslow reached over and put his fingers over the edge of the pail, gripping it hard. It felt real, anyway...

"So I scoop out the pixie pixel dust and spread it in here and out on the grass."

"After you have hosed off out there, yes."

"And I dust myself with it."

"Of course. Just to get you to the shower without leaving trace evidence."

"Then I douse the shower area with it."

"By George, I think he's got it!"

Winslow pushed to a knee and dipped his finger into the pail. Felt like laundry detergent; suddenly it seemed to creep up the back of his hand on its own. It spread almost to the wrist before it fizzled to a stop, making the blood residue vanish in its wake, showing Winslow's seemingly clear, supple skin.

"Can this stuff mask body parts?" he said.

The Sculptor sighed. Full and throaty. Winslow marveled again at this fiend's ability to manipulate sounds.

"Alas," The Sculptor said, "the fairy dust only likes liquids. Solids are a different beast altogether. And I would forget the little pail for now. That's like the icing, and we need to address the cake first."

It disappeared in a burst of pink flutter.

"So what about the solids?"

There was a low humming noise, similar to the one that had accompanied the appearance of the industrial pail. There was a *poof* of silver pixels, and then sitting by Winslow's knee was a machine, tabletop size.

"Sausage maker?" he said.

"Bone grinder, Professor. This is a state-of-the-art product designed and manufactured by yours truly. It has a metal auger drive and titanium, five-millimeter grinding plates. On eBay they say a device like this won't manage bones, but that is a simple falsehood. All the boy's skeleton will pass through it, every last splinter and chip. Then you transport out the powdered product in manageable increments. Go for a drive. Find an isolated patch of roadway thick with foliage and sprinkle the bone dust. Done deal, nice and neat. Your only limitation is that this particular mechanism is restricted to bone matter. Anything else will clot up the works like hot tar and get you positively nowhere."

The bone grinder disappeared in a poof of quick sliver.

"Hey!" Winslow said.

"Icing, remember? You don't need it yet, and we don't waste pixel productions as they sit in the corner waiting for use. My visual art is not a...permanent phenomenon. There is a shelf life, an expiration. That is why, in more favorable circumstances, I prefer to build machines of any kind with real materials."

"OK," Winslow said, "so then what about the rest of it—of him? How do I get to the bones?"

"Easy-peezy," said The Sculptor, and Winslow felt a pang of harsh guilt and shame: Jody's carefree words in what seemed like ages ago.

"What do you mean, 'easy'?" he said. "Explain."

"Well, there will be parts of the body that will be stubborn," The Sculptor said. "Tendons will have to be removed and snipped down to size with Georgia's gardening shears. Then, good news, you can run them right through the grinder."

"And the muscle?" Winslow said. "The skin? The...meat?"

"Ah!" said The Sculptor. "Right to it! Good. Let's stop playing games." He paused. "You, Professor Winslow, will handle that part of the process."

"How?"

"You will manage with the help of a tiny little pill that I am more than happy to provide."

There was another *poof,* smaller this time, this one in blue and red pixel glow-dots. Now there was a dinner plate there at Winslow's knee, and a pill resting on it. Large. A white capsule. A horse-pill.

"What does it do?" Winslow said.

"Similar to the pixie dust; Professor, it creates an illusion. I can't alter solids, but I can certainly alter you and your perception of things. Take it. Now."

Winslow dry-swallowed it. Easy-peezy. He waited a bit, counting to thirty.

"So what's different?" he said. "I don't see or feel..."

His voice trailed off melodramatically. His eye had fallen onto the dark form of Gatto's left foot, lying a yard away on the sodden drop-cloth. But suddenly it didn't look like a foot. It looked like a savory turkey leg, steaming hot and succulent. The smell was absolutely delightful, and Professor Brad Winslow started to scream.

CHAPTER 9

Oh, Mother of God, I'm Coming Apart

"But I don't *want* to wear a mask!" Esther cried. "It's gross. It's yours, so it's pointless, and it needs washing. It smells like bad breath! Let me go get mine in my room!"

"You lost it, remember?" Sage said wearily. "In the church before Poppy picked you up this morning."

"I found it!"

"Liar."

"*You* are! And I have a spare."

Sage reached for her own earlobe for no reason, massaging it.

"No, Es, you don't. Please. Pretty please with sugar and sprinkles. Poppy said that we need to stay put, and so we do like he says."

"But it's *so* stupid! I've been breathing the air in here for hours, weeks, years, centuries!"

Sage stared at her baby sister, who was in the beanbag chair, arms folded hard. Usually Esther's antics amused her, but she was just too tired to deal right now. She didn't like wearing a mask either, especially in the house, but this was a situation her English teacher, Ms. Giovanangelo, would have called *"exceptional."* Nobody really understood the pandemic, so you took all precautions. And Sage had come down with Covid-19, she was sure of it. The mask she'd given Esther was one of her spares that she hadn't worn in a week. She only hoped she didn't "have it" back then, or else her sister was right, it was pointless.

"Whether you think it makes sense or not," she said, "we do what we can. Those are the rules." Esther made to stamp her foot, but her laid-back positioning didn't allow it much vigor.

"Little kids don't get sick with it," she said. "The rules are... *churlish!*" She sat up and took on an air of superiority. "And Poppy says that when the rules don't make sense you can break them. It's heroic. Like Martin Luther King and Gandhi and Charlotte Perkins Gilhouse."

"Gilman."

"Whatever. What makes you think you have Corona-Beer anyway?"

Sage shrugged.

"I don't feel good," she said. Suddenly she thought she was going to cry. She wanted her mother. Her father. Someone to hold her and to be the grownup. She sank to the floor and sat cross-legged. "I feel bloated," she murmured. "I feel like puking, but there's nothing there. My thighs ache the way they do when I'm coming down with the flu and my breasts do too."

Esther giggled. "Your boobies?"

"Don't call them that. It's immature."

"Well, I'm a kid!"

"True." Sage frowned. The mask was itching her right under the nose. She'd never gotten used to these things, and suddenly she was sure that Esther was right, that her three masks needed a wash. Had other kids at school caught a whiff of them? Sage already had fear of heights and major test taking issues. Now she could add halitosis anxiety to the mix. Her eyes teared up and she made fists in her lap. *Vinny had never minded her breath...*

God, she wanted so much to...belong! She'd been known as an Emo middle school oddball, a fate she couldn't stop or help considering her weird habits. She almost laughed to herself and then almost cried. Mom used to joke with Poppy that as a toddler, Sager used to put anything and everything in her mouth. The household saying was that if Sage wouldn't eat it, throw it on the floor. Sage didn't remember this specifically, but she believed them. When she was thirteen, she'd found this old show called *Fear Factor* on YouTube and had become obsessed with eating strange things. In seventh grade math class, she'd swallowed two live Daddy Long Legs spiders that Adam Winetraub found in the cloak closet, and on a dare in eighth grade, when her classmates were more laughing at her than with her, she gulped down a dead frog that was there to dissect.

Esther clapped her hands three times rudely.

"Hello!" she said. "Anybody home? Go get Jo-Jo! I'm lonely and you're boring. Jo-Jo tells dirty jokes and funny stories."

"Poppy said—"

"I don't care! You're my sister and it's your job to make me laugh!"

Sage nodded her head and half shrugged again. It was true. It wasn't a rule, but it sort of always panned out that way, didn't it? There must have been a word for it. She swallowed hard. What *had* actually happened between Jody and Vinny? There was no fight, Poppy said so, and if there had been, he would have talked about it. So would Jody, but she was a silent enigma, locked in her room, quiet as a churchmouse. No deathcore heavy music like Genus Ordinis Dei, or RiseuP, or Whitechapel. No bouncing a tennis ball on the floor to kick up against the closet door the way she did when things were dull. The only way Sage knew that Jody was in the room next door at all was that the bed squeaked when she turned to her left side. Always had. But why was a girl so typically hype lying in bed before lunchtime?

A sudden fear washed over her. Maybe this was the doing of the freak-a-zoid Poppy had told them to beware of. In the car on the way home from school earlier, she had searched a bit on her phone, but this "Sculptor" character was almost too sick to be real. Worried that Esther would be sneaking over a glance, she'd shut off her phone, but she had continued her search here in her room when the waiting around had gone stale. She had read a bit more, then tabbed in "Sculptor's Scarecrows" and hit "Images." She wished she hadn't. The initial two pics were absolutely hideous, the first with a background of gray sky, featuring a bloody, disfigured girl impaled on a pole on top of a construction trailer, and the next with a different girl speared through and planted in a ring of rusted steel drums with flames leaping out of them. Sage had clicked off the page just in time. Esther had crept close and was about to look over her shoulder. She had begged to see, and Sage had refused. This spoiled the mood and led to the present argument like a disease, like Covid 19, *God*, did Sage feel like shit!

She pushed up to her feet and made for the door.

"Where are you going?" Esther said.

"Stay here."

"No! I'm going too!"

Sage turned. "No, you are not. You're staying put. If you move, I'll tell Poppy."

Esther's expression was so pained it was comic. "I'll tell on you first!"

"Good," Sage answered. "Tell him the rule didn't allow for me to check on my other sister, and I found it to be intolerable. You, put on the mask even if it stinks. Stay put. Don't even peek through this door, or I'll know it."

"Why can't I come along?" Esther whined. "She's my sister too!"

"Grown-up reasons," Sage said.

It was true. There was something going on here, something with Vinny Gatto or The Sculptor or both that had nothing to do with fighting, and it was pretty obvious that it would be above Esther's pay grade. Sage also knew she would have to whisper, for sure, maybe lead Jo-Jo into Poppy's room or the upstairs bath. That is...if she could "talk" her out of her room to begin with.

She moved out into the hall and closed her bedroom door behind her. It was chilly and there was a dim ringing in the silence that made it quieter somehow and ominous. Sage felt as if she was in the bizarro-zone between dreams. She approached and tapped her knuckle on the door.

"Jo-Jo," she said softly. "Jody the Hammer, Cave Woman, Super Girl..." She leaned her forehead against the door and doodled her finger in a nonsense shape on the knob. "I don't know any more of your nicknames. Maybe 'Clubber'? 'Jody-Bats'? 'Cannon'? 'Country Strong'?" Silence. "Do you want to talk? Sing campfire songs?" Silence. "Esther keeps begging for you." Silence. "I miss you for some reason," a whisper, silence still. Sage was suddenly reminded of the movie *Frozen*, when Anna sang through the door to Elsa about building a snowman. The age gap was about right, but Sage, as the elder, was on the wrong side of the door. Story of her life.

"I pay attention, you know," she said carefully. "The problem has always been that I care more about your feelings than I do about your stats, and so that's why I stopped watching your at-bats. It got too intense for me, especially the tourney all-star travel ball you started doing when you turned eleven, and I made it a point to go for a walk, to the bathroom or the snack stand. I had to. It felt as if I was dying inside when you stepped up to the plate. I know people have always said that you swing like a boy, but to me you always looked like a princess made of glass. When you made an out, it wounded me, not because I was disappointed, but more that I was terrified you might shatter."

Silence.

"Do you want to know my favorite moment?" she said. "Well, I'm gonna tell you anyway. Do you remember when you were twelve, on the Warriors? It was July, hot as Nevada, and you were always sad and pissed off, because you'd been seeing a strike out of the pitcher's hand and you were lunging, transferring your weight too early, hitting toppers back to the mound. It was your third tournament and they were thinking of benching you. First time ever." She sighed heartily. "I felt for you like I *was* you, but I couldn't talk to you about it because we were all sorts of passive-aggressive toward each other on the subject, all about my taking walks whenever you'd step out of the dugout. So I kept everything to myself. But like I said, I *was* paying attention." Her voice got even lower. "It was the Springford tournament, and you guys were already out of the running, remember? You were 0 for 12 so far at the plate. Then you played your consolation game against Audubon." Sage smiled under her mask. "I never mentioned this, but I hated that team more than sugarless oatmeal, with their fancy blue uniforms and red mesh vests, and the way they did those cocky little bunny hops before making their throws, and their parents and siblings, always on the left field side with their canopies and sparklers and face paint and air horns. And oh, their pitchers were the worst, with the way they acted after the warmups between innings when the batter was coming up, how they went in front of the rubber all pigeon-toed and cutesy, kicking at the dirt making the divots deeper."

She chuckled.

"Late in the game, I left Poppy in right field foul territory, but I didn't go to the snack stand or that dingy green cinderblock restroom with the water fountain that only bubbled up about a quarter of an inch. I walked around back and took the long way by the grill area where they were cooking brats, burgers, and dogs on the metal drums they'd cut in half, lying longwise and loaded with wood. I remember that smoky, buttery smell like it was yesterday. I made my way up the short hill, back in through the playground and over to the bleachers behind center field. I climbed up and sat next to an Audubon grandpa who wanted to get away from his son and daughter-in-law who'd drunk too many Michelob Ultras and were describing their most embarrassing family out-takes. I told him about your lunging problem, and he told me about his grandson's issue, still trying to tomahawk the high ones up at his eyes. Then he explained what 'Cal Ripken distance' was with the bigger infield and all, and he bragged about Audubon's closer-pitcher, the coach's kid named Max, supposedly able to throw an eighty-mile-an-hour fastball and a changeup at sixty-one that broke a foot and a half in toward a righty. And fifty feet from rubber to plate as compared to the Major League sixty? Impossible to hit. He also played for an AAU team from the Poconos called the Red Barons. Your game was in the last inning, five-to-three bad guys, your last ups, and you were leading off."

Sage giggled ruefully.

"Grandpa wasn't lying about that pitcher. You remember, Jo-Jo...he was six feet tall, skinny as a weed, windup all over the place like a junker car with the wheels flying off, and when he threw his warmup four-seamers, they thudded in the catcher's glove like gunshots. You were by the dugout in the on-deck area, leaning on your bat like it was a cane, watching. To be honest, you looked too young for the moment, too small, too unsure of yourself. First time

I ever saw that, and trust me, I wanted to die." Sage paused. "Then you walked to the box and dug in. I was slightly off-center, so I couldn't see in or outside as well as high-low, but everyone and their mother knew that the fastball he started you with was right down the middle, thigh high. And you lunged. Except it had never been a lunge, not really, you just never had a dance partner throwing hard enough to meet you dead-on at the front black stripe of the plate. Your swing was epic, and when I heard that thick *ping!* I knew that ball was not coming back."

Sage made a fist and bumped it gently on the door panel.

"High line drive over the fence," she said. "Almost hit the American flag, and pounded off the roof of a black Ford pickup with Yosemite Sam mudflaps in the parking lot. I remember, because I'd turned to see how far that dinger was actually going to go. When I turned back, you were rounding first for your victory lap. Your face was as red as the batting helmet, and you had your right fist up in the air. Your team flooded out of the dugout to greet you at home plate like you were an angel. Not a king. Not a queen. Not a princess made of glass, but a goddamned angel, make no mistake."

She pressed her palm against the door.

"You were a picture of joy," she said. "I wanted to paint it. Zach Epstein came up next and walked, stole second and third, and then Johnny Dean hit the double into the right field corner, you know the rest of course. Time was called and the man with the freckled bald head, the clipboard, and the whistle called the game on account of time, tournament rules, they had to get the next two teams on the field. You were left with a tie, five to five. I overheard Coach Bershad say it was like kissing your sister, but I thought what I had seen was heroic. And what's so bad about kissing your sister, right?" She paused. "Anyway, I saw the whole thing. I'm sorry I never told you, but I did now, because I think I've got Covid-19, and I'm frightened."

She whispered again.

"Won't you let me in? I'm wearing my mask and I promise to keep six safe feet of distance. Or you could talk to me through this door. Can you even do that?"

But all she was left with was silence. She tried the knob, wondering why she didn't do this in the first place. Locked. No response on the other side, and her stomach suddenly roiled.

Sage put her hand up over her mask, turned, and ran through the laundry room to the bathroom to puke.

—

AFTERWARD, SHE BRUSHED past the washer-and-dryer stack and made back for the hallway. She had managed to upchuck some bile and electric-tasting spit, and she flushed the toilet, then washed her face vigorously. As soon as she put her mask back on, small beads of sweat sprang up on her forehead, and she felt her stomach pitch again. She held steady. It wasn't heaven, but it would have to be good enough.

Someone was in her father's bedroom. Someone mumbling, soft and unintelligible, from behind the door down the hall which was half closed.

"Poppy?" she said. She approached slowly, passing the stairway to the right, moving even slower still. Finally she paused before the archway, listened for a moment for the sound she thought she heard but wasn't so sure anymore, and then pushed through and stopped. Her father's desk was its usual organized mess, with two piles of handouts stacked like cabin corner logs to the left, the German stein he'd bought at Disney World in the Epcot Center now holding his pens and pencils, a plastic tray with books that had Post-It notes sticking out the sides like porcupine quills, and the computer stage center.

The monitor was live, and on it was a split screen—two cameras, one that said Vincent Gatto on black backdrop, and the other a grainy shot of Sage in the doorway looking back at herself. She came forward slowly and studied her own advance, oddly displaced as if watching her twin in a cheap thriller.

"Vinny?" she said. The question of why he would be Zooming on her father's computer had crossed her mind, but it lost ground quickly. In the forefront was the delicious ache that had suddenly flowered between her legs and the desire for him to turn on his camera. He'd been her first, fourteen days ago after school in his older brother's sunburst yellow vintage Camaro, on the dirt road in the woods behind the goalposts at the Campbell Field on Reed Road. It had been raw and difficult, not to mention that her hip and the steering wheel never became best of friends. That said, it ended far better than it started, and he'd been super-gentle with her afterward. They'd both pledged love for each other. Neither was sure, they both well knew this about the other, and it hadn't mattered. It was the truth of a moment, a beautiful memory, a lovely gemstone exchanged that they could metaphorically wear under their shirts to keep close without ever letting anyone see.

"What's this issue between you and my sister?" she said, immediately hating herself for the accusation. Still, she pressed on, voice shaking a bit.

"Well?"

"Hello to you too," he said, and Sage breathed a sigh of relief. His tone reflected his usual countenance: confident and mildly amused, open without fear or guilt. And what a voice it was, deep and smooth-grained, like a radio DJ.

"Were you going to fight Jody today?" Sage said. *God*…said aloud, the words themselves sounded so *stupid!*

Vinny must have been grinning. "What do you think?"

Sage paused. "I don't know. Jody doesn't lie. She's one of those weirdos without a filter. I forget which movie it's from, but her favorite line is 'Why lie when the truth is so much more fun?'"

"It's all rumors," he said. "Toilet stall graffiti, you know how it goes. At indoor practice she was hogging the batting cage, making Jimmy Flynn keep feeding the pitching machine for her, not giving anyone else a turn."

"Who is Jimmy Flynn?"

"That kid with Down Syndrome in eleventh grade. He's like our mascot."

"Oh."

"Anyway," he continued, "I ask her if anyone else can get a turn, and she says her shoulder's flying open and she's stepping in the bucket."

Sage folded her arms. "Yes," she said. "I get that. She said the same thing last night, practicing down in the basement."

"Yeah," he said. "So I sort of insist that she move along, and she turns, yanks up the netting to crouch under, and walks out all pissy. Lenny Schuster said she was so mad that she started bashing her practice bat against a cement tire bumper in the parking lot. Freaky stuff."

"Where's her glove?" Sage said.

Vinny laughed. "A grounder took a low bounce and skidded between her ankles the way it always happens on gymnasium floors. She threw her glove in the trash. Said it was more useless than dogshit."

"And this fight I heard about?"

"Drama about nothing," he said. "She texted her friend Jenna Pressman, saying she wanted to kick my ass. Jenna texted Masha Knowles, who texted Rita McMartin, Brianna Richards, and Lori Finklestein, whose brother Brandon is in my homeroom and health class. He's still tripping over a spliff I got from him in the bathroom after fifth period, that I was going to pay for after he paid me for the Red Bull I fronted him out of my backpack the week before. He never paid up, so I called it even. He didn't, so when he got wind of the Jody thing he went to Twitter and Facebook and blew it all out of proportion. Then everyone heard that it was really Larry Fraley and Antony Combs who were fighting, and since everyone was so hype on fighting in general, the school emptied like it was a cut day or something."

Sage came closer so she was in a medium shot, waist up.

"So there's nothing between you and my sister?"

"No," he said. "Just that I liked using that practice bat she trashed. Shame."

Sage pulled over her father's cushy leather-bound manager chair, maneuvered into it, and put the points of her elbows on the arm rests. She webbed her hands in front of her chin.

"How did you get on my dad's computer?" she said.

"Right," Vinny said. "I got on *my* dad's computer, because like your dad, he likes desktops. Professor Winslow posts his permanent Zoom Room link in his teacher bio, so I popped in hoping to catch you at home. Better than using our phones, better visual to see you with."

Sage tilted her head. "You sure took a chance. What if my dad had been sitting here?"

"I would have asked him if Sage could come out and play."

"Ha."

"Yes, and I, uh, couldn't get you off of my mind."

"Same."

The air seemed to tingle.

"Why don't you turn on your camera?" Sage said.

"You don't want to know."

"How do you know what I want to know?"

"OK, then. I have a zit."

Sage giggled. "A zit?"

"Yes. Right on the end of my nose."

She made a soft fist and rested her cheek on her knuckles. "You're right," she said. "I didn't need to know that."

"I feel ugly today."

"You could never be ugly, warts, zits, and all."

"But still," he said, "what makes something good-looking versus bad anyway? What makes you so hot when other girls look plain, fake, or needy?"

Sage blushed hard. "You think I'm hot?" she said.

"Well, I don't think you're plain, fake, or needy."

Sage looked downward. "I think you're hot too," she said quietly.

"But why?" he said. "I have two eyes, a nose, two arms, and two legs like every other guy. What makes me any more special than Hank Rivers, or Gerry Feldman, or Russ Riven, or Nasr Mohammad?"

She leaned back in the chair and looked at the ceiling for a moment. "I honestly don't know, when you put it that way. To me, you're like a work of art. The others are not. They're just trade materials, background, concrete and ditches."

"So I'm work of art, huh?"

She smiled, leaned forward, and folded her hands on the desk. "Yes. Undoubtedly."

He cleared his throat.

"I, uh, thanks, I guess, but I kinda never got the 'art' thing. Or aesthetics in general. Seems like a bunch of propaganda, made up by people who want to make money off it."

"Well, dig you with the vocab."

"I'm serious," he said. "What makes something art versus garbage, anyway?"

Sage thought about this for a second. "I suppose it has to inspire people."

"Hmm," he said, "I guess. To each his or her own, though. People throw money at something, and you could call it art. Mass produce it, and you call it IKEA furniture."

"It's more than the money it generates," Sage said. "It's got to be."

"You're right," Vinny said. "Now that I think about it, art is more the mirror of the artist who has made something one of a kind. Then, at the same time, in kind of an opposite, there's got to be a few...ingredients people recognize. Staples. Benchmarks."

"As in?"

"Ah, fuck if I know. I think there has to be pain, but it has to have..." He was silent so long, Sage thought he'd screwed up his sound somehow. "What I mean is," he continued, "there has to be pain, but it has to have some sort of poetry to it. There has to be blood, sweat, and tears, maybe like a metaphor, but there's got to be an order to it. No, not 'order,' but a sense of—"

"Symmetry," Sage finished for him. "Even if the rules are odd, foreign, or blasphemous, the work of art has to obey those rules and laws that its own world creates."

"Exac-a-laca-lacalee," he said. "Like this."

"Like what?"

"Like this. Going throwback. My first doll."

Sage gasped. There was something behind her now, something in the camera shot that had not been there a second ago. A figure. A tall, bloody figure.

It was a naked woman impaled on a shaft set in a flagpole base. She was covered with a see-through sheeting pulled down over her and tied at the bottom like a patio umbrella, the inner side blurry with smears of her blood in a slashing, uneven masking effect. Still, her wide-open mouth was visible, pressed up against the plastic and shaped in a scream.

Big teeth, Sage thought crazily. Through the smudges and spatters lower down, she could also make out an elbow, a hip, and a dislocated foot pointing down like that of ballerina. Then, like a horror movie jump-cut, the corpse popped forward a few feet, literally skipping over time and space, close enough now behind her to touch.

Sage screamed, but most of the volume was in her head. She pushed up, sending the chair backward on its roller wheels, and spun around fast.

Nothing there. Just her dad's chair coming to a slow stop in the middle of the room, the seat rotating a half-turn and coming to rest facing away.

She turned back to the computer screen, and there on the monitor was the office chair, the backrest facing the camera.

"My dear sweet chrysanthemum," a strange voice said, sliding through the monitor speaker like moist, rotten fruit. "It's time," he said, "for a history lesson through which we will explore the past, then current events, and then the beyond. First, we celebrate what was. You just worshipped through fear, my first realized sculpture from a few years ago, Brittany Barnes, Shippensburg University, sophomore. The pain here was obvious, as represented by her blood, sweat, and tears, but the beauty, my darling, the poetry, was the thrill of terror that just raced down your spine. By default, then, the symmetry is your heightened awareness as compared to Brittany's lack thereof."

"What?" Sage managed. "What the fuck... why... where..."

"Ah, the evil W's, Sage. But we have no time for questions that won't propel us forward into blood and realization, bare truths and glory. Keep staring now at the monitor, Sage, please look at it closely. You have another visitor, the ghost of Christmas present as it were, or more like a reunion of sorts."

The chair behind her started turning to face front. Sage wanted to run, to do anything but stare at the computer, but she was rooted to the spot and transfixed. Her hands were up by her mouth. The chair completed its rotation.

Empty.

There was a sudden burst of green pixels, making it look for a moment as if the leather chair sat under a glittering weeping willow, the dots landing in a shower of sparks that emitted a fragrance, distinct and up close and personal. It was her mother's perfume, the good stuff, the Tom Ford Black Orchid she used to wear when they went to one of Poppy's school functions or a benefit sponsored by the hospital. Plum and amber, vanilla and balsam. Tears sprang into Sage's eyes. It was as if she could feel her mother's warmth, her breath, her embrace.

The chair wasn't empty anymore.

In it was a corpse, sitting daintily, wearing Georgia Winslow's black burial dress. Most of her hair had fallen out, making her witch-like and skeletal. The skin on her face had decomposed down to a patchwork, and beetles ran in and out of her eye sockets.

"Mother?" Sage said hoarsely.

It jerked at the sound, legs coming uncrossed, bony hands gripping the armrests.

The bugs scattered like oil drops skating off water.

Sage whirled around, and the chair was still facing away. Still presumably empty.

"My darling," The Sculptor said, making her jump for what felt like the umpteenth time. "I would expect your thanks for that lovely dramatic encounter, but your tragic fear was enough as reward. Let it be a reminder, then, that you must never lose sight of the art of a mother's death, the blood, sweat, and tears she put into you and your sisters, the pain of her absence, the poetry of your memories, and the symmetry..."

"The symmetry?" Sage said.

"Ah, yes, the symmetry, the replica."

"What replica?"

"Why, this one, of course."

She turned back slowly, hand still up at her mouth area in *Oh My GOD* mode. On the monitor was an ultrasound. Of a womb. Thanks to health class, she recognized the gestational sac with its double ring, and the dark spot in the middle winking closed for a moment, then opening like a camera iris. Sage's heart thudded hard in her chest.

"I'm—pregnant? You're saying that I'm pregnant?"

"Well, it's not Covid-19, dear."

"I'm pregnant." She said it like a statement. "I'm pregnant and somehow you're showing my ultrasound."

"No, dear," The Sculptor said. "You are only two weeks along, and this one is five and a half. The blood, sweat, and tears are poetic, since they are strange, equal byproducts of birth or abortion, the exquisite pain lying in the decision. The symmetry, my dear, is usually macro to micro, mother to child, point A to point B. Here, however, we don't just enjoy a vertical, linear representation. Here we go horizontal as well, multi-dimensional. Sister to sister."

Sage's mouth dropped open like a lap-puppet.

"Sister?" she said. *"My* sister? You're saying that Jody is pregnant as well?"

"Of course," said The Sculptor. "But no need to fret, as it's all in the family, like a fairy tale, a Netflix special. a movie, a dream. It's the perfect triangle, rare as a flame lily."

Sage finished it for him in a hoarse whisper.

"Because both unborn children are from the same father."

CHAPTER 10

It's Not the House That's Haunted

S age marched down the hallway. In her fist was the large statuette she'd taken from her father's desk. She did not remember looking for it, finding it in the clutter, and reaching for it, but she knew that it was special to her father in an odd, nostalgic sort of a way. It was a foot-high steel rendition of Gene Simmons of Kiss, posed like the Statue of Liberty, raising a torch he'd just used to breathe fire. Poppy talked about Kiss a lot, about seeing them live back in the day, about the way they were musically inferior (except for Ace Frehley), though state-of-the-art in their marketing strategies. Sage didn't give a flying fuck. The thing had an iron base, heavy as a five-pound dumbbell at least.

She was in front of Jody's door. She was not thinking logically, not quite, but more in terms of coarse practicalities. The door was nothing more than a symbol of etiquette. In reality, it was cheap and hollow, made of two thin pieces of wood with Styrofoam or something like it in the middle, had to be, as it was so light when you opened or closed it. She probably didn't even need the Kiss figurine to bust the lock clean. A good shoulder to it would probably do the trick, probably better, but Sage didn't necessarily want "better." She wanted to expedite this fiery rage with verve. She wanted to hit something, and a stabbing motion seemed it would be far more satisfying.

She reared back and pounded down hard. The figurine bashed a splintered dent as if the door was made of balsa wood, and the sound had been more than gratifying. She cocked back and smashed it again and again. The three divots looked like the grin of a buck-toothed clown.

"How 'bout two eyes and a nose then?" she said through her teeth. She brought the weapon down three more times, almost laughing for the fact that even in a state of violent passion she was drawing a picture. Always the artist. Always the oddball. Always the second one in.

This thought enraged her. She was second fiddle to both Jody and Esther, either/or depending on the semantics, and in this case, it had been Vinny choosing Jo-Jo. Same difference, as Jody wasn't the first Winslow Vinny had met, but he was sure as hell the first inside her, right? Sage got sloppy seconds. It was a stunning metaphor, but of course the prepositions were wrong or whatever, reversed and unparallel, making the linguistic device mixed up and stupid.

Sage was so *stupid!*

"Open up!" she cried. "Let's talk about love and sisterly stuff like loyalty, you slutty little monster!"

She was shaking. She stared at the door. The craters and spalls were ugly and some of the filler material had squeezed through. Looked like waffled cardboard.

The doorbell rang, and it ran a chill through her. It was the bad man, for sure, come to put an exclamation point on their recent Zoom call. He was The Sculptor, the mad creator of slaughterhouse dolls, a master of disguise, a man of dark magic.

She raced back to Poppy's room. The computer was off now, thank God for small favors, and his shades were still down. She stalked over to the one on the far right, giving it a pull. It snapped up, puffing dust into the sunlight. Sage squinted and leaned the right side of her temple on the glass, straining her eyes down and back-left. Looking down from the second story gave her a rush of vertigo, but she was determined. And it only required a peek.

There was no one there on the front step.

There was just the welcome mat that used to have "Home Sweet Home" on it, now dulled to the brown woven coconut fiber.

No one there.

Something caught Sage's eye. Movement.

Across the street, there was a man standing at the near edge of the tall evergreen shrubs that the Fergusons had put in along the sidewalk to block the view of their ramshackle carport. The man was tall, thick like a body builder. The hem of his dark blue windbreaker whipped in the breeze. He turned slowly. On his back were the white letters, "POLICE." He wheeled back around and put his out his arm straight ahead, palm up. Then he raised it, forearm at attention, letting it mechanically drop back to position, three times in a series, like an airport ground crewmember waving in a plane.

Come here...

Sage stayed where she was, staring back. Her jaw hurt. Her head hurt. Her stomach was still uneasy and she'd never been so unsure of herself. Poppy had called from wherever and said to stay put, to ignore the doorbell. A serial killer had just creeped her out person-to-person, and both she and her sister were carrying Vinny Gatto's offspring. Nothing seemed real. Hell, it might not have even been Poppy on the phone, and the cop across the street could actually be the killer.

Sage turned to look over her shoulder, eyes wide.

Maybe the freak-a-zoid was already in the house. Maybe she and Jody weren't pregnant after all, and The Sculptor was setting them up for a fight to the death so he'd have fresh meat for a flagpole and a new co-conspirator.

She turned and looked back outside. The man in the windbreaker had moved, but she was pretty sure she could see him standing behind that first evergreen.

Go to him now.

He was really a cop, he had to be, right? If she was wrong, she was wrong, but it was worse just waiting here, doing nothing. She turned on her heel and marched out of her father's bedroom.

"All right," she called out. "Enough is enough already."

Her voice died and she froze at the stairs. The bedroom doors down the hall were open, all three of them, Jody's battered one still creaking toward its resting place on the far inner wall.

"Jo-Jo?" Sage said. No answer. She whisked past and stopped cold in the archway leading to her own room. The beanbag chair was empty, still imprinted with the shape of her baby sister.

"Es?"

Nothing.

She stalked back for the stairway, stood for a moment there on the high landing, and next went thumping down, heels falling hard.

"Esther?" she called. "Cupcake? Jo-Jo?"

She got near the bottom, hopping over the last three steps to clunk down to the hardwood floor of the living room, and in the back of her mind she was thinking of high school girls in horror movies when they announced their presence in the killer's lair with a *"Hello?"* as if wearing a *"Please Kill Me"* sign.

She stood dead-still to think for a moment. Since she had already disobeyed Poppy's orders by leaving her room, all bets were off, she'd fucked this up royally. That is, if it was really him on the phone. If. And now her sisters were missing, the game had changed, and it was her duty to call the police. At least she would be speaking to someone authentic.

But wait a minute. Considering that The Sculptor could very well have been mimicking Poppy's voice perfectly...that he could make real-life images come out of the computer...that he made weeping willow trees that smelled like her dead mother...wouldn't hacking all the phones just be child's play? Wouldn't the sick creep just revel in it, faking as if he was a 911 operator as she poured out her heart and her plans?

There were two choices here. The first—search the house high and low for her sisters so they could all be together again. Option two was to run to the cop outside, pray he was for real, and tell him everything. Get some help. Some professional help.

Or professionally skewered like shish kabob.

Yes, OK, then fuck it, she could hide too! Possibly her sisters had heard some of the conversation with the fake Vinny Gatto from all the way down in Poppy's room, maybe not, difficult to call. Regardless, the bashing of the Jody's door was probably enough to send them running, and if Sage actually discovered one of them now, in the clothes dryer, down the basement under the stairs, in the attic behind the extra rolls of fiberglass insulation, she'd be doing her family a disservice. Her sisters would hate her for giving them away while they were smart enough to be hiding in the first place.

If they had been actually kidnapped; however, this would let the trail go horribly cold. It would play like abandonment, probably a crime, just her luck, right?

Sage bit her bottom lip. When it came right down to it, she just did not trust the man outside. And if her sisters had been taken, really *taken*, one of them at least would have screamed. Though the girls had rooms clustered together, Poppy had the privacy of, what?—twenty feet down the hall? Twenty-five? Sage wasn't good with that kind of math, but a violent struggle? One of her sisters crying out for dear life? *That* she would have heard even from down in the sun room.

Then again, maybe not.

It was complicated, and Sage didn't feel like analyzing anymore, splitting hairs. She had to do something, something now, something positive.

I'll hide, she thought, *just like Esther and Jo-Jo. It's the most logical option. Maybe I'll go out to the back yard, behind the tool shed by the fence. I'll leave the gate open. An escape hatch to the alley.*

She started to move back through toward the kitchen, and Jody stepped into the doorway from behind the wall. She was wearing her black Converse high-tops, black yoga pants, and her black throwback Slayer tee with the "Reign in Blood" logo. She had on her Nike Fury headband, and her eyes were crystal-red as if she'd been crying for hours. Still, for the sake of ironic contrast it seemed, she had also smeared on her tournament eye-black, circling both eyes to the rims of the sockets like carnival greasepaint. She was smiling. It was crooked. Her hands were behind her back and she went girlishly knock-kneed.

"Going somewhere?" she said.

"Out back," Sage said hollowly. All the rage had drained out of her, and her mind felt dulled, as her ears had been after the Blackpink concert two years ago. Jody's smile twitched.

"No, I don't think so," she said. "No one goes out back, not until I say you can."

"We have to talk," Sage said. "There are a couple of things you should know."

Jody shook her head. Closed her eyes. Opened them.

"No one goes out back," she repeated. "All secrets stay secrets. Back yard's off limits."

"It's my back yard too," Sage said.

"Not anymore," Jody said, "and my girly-knocker is bigger than yours."

She came forward out of the archway, and from behind her back she pulled out her DiMarini Voodoo bat. Sage had forgotten about the statuette in her hand the way you forget that your sunglasses are still propped on your head. Jody stepped closer and cocked the bat behind her. Sage dropped the Gene Simmons Kiss figure.

And she didn't just walk out the front door.

She ran.

CHAPTER 11

Wouldst Thou Like to Live Deliciously?

Esther was, in fact, hiding in Sage's closet.

Last night from *her* closet, the man with the royal silk voice had predicted that she would have the opportunity right around now to hide away, and that when this opportunity presented itself she was to be a good girl, crawl in, and "live small" for a while. Mr. Royal Silk Man wasn't the "Bad Man"—of this, Esther was sure. The Bad Man looked like a scarecrow. The Bad Man had been blown to pieces. The Bad Man didn't like girls!

Mr. Royal Silk Man liked girls, liked her, liked her the best, and everything he said that was going to happen actually did! Magic! Freaky spoons! Wacky dacky!

He had said there would be a surprise for her in the bike room, and the Jack-in-the-Box was amazing. He had said Poppy was going to pick up all the girls early from Latchkey and school, and that he'd be sulky and crappy and mean. He called him "Poopy-Poppy," and Esther had laughed so hard into her hands she thought she was going to wake the neighborhood. But last night Mr. Royal Silk Man also promised that Poppy would hold her, that he would stomp out of the house to a secret place, and that Sage would leave her room to go spit hot words at Jo-Jo like a cat having a hissy-fit. He even predicted the bashing noise, like a hammer crunching wood, and that was Esther's cue to get comfy. In Sage's closet. To wait for more directions, more clues, like a treasure hunt.

It was itchy in here. There was a big roll of burlap Sage had used for her plaster butterfly wall paintings, and because the other side of the closet was crammed with tubs of other art supplies, Esther had no choice but to sit on this prickly pillow. It smelled like canvas, like camping, and she hated camping.

There was that familiar buzz and whine, so light and delicate it was no louder than a baby bird finding its wings.

"Hi, Mr. Royal Man," Esther whispered.

"Yes, child," he said. "It's time."

"Time for what?"

"Time for truth."

Esther thought about it. "Sounds boring," she said.

"It won't be, child."

"Promise?"

"Of course. I want you to go see your father."

Esther smiled and nodded in the dark. "Oh, I'd like that Mister-Man! Where is he?"

"Why, out in the tool shed of course."

Esther pouted. "Why does it have to be there? I don't like that place. It's worse than this one. It smells like dead grass and nails."

"Yes," said The Sculptor. "But you've got to pay him a visit just the same, dear child. Together we have to figure out a way for you to get past Jo-Jo, but once we do that you're home free."

"Home free," she giggled. "You're funny."

"And you are anxious. I know, dear."

"Yes! To see Poppy!"

"To see Poppy, of course."

She crinkled her nose and squinted into the dark. "What's he doing out there anyway, Mr. Man?"

The Sculptor was silent for a moment, and then he said, "Eating."

CHAPTER 12

Death Should Be Repulsive
So We Don't Grow Too Fond of It

S age burst out the front door and jumped across the flagstone walkway. There was nothing in the flowerbed but dead leaves, and she ran through and bolted to the lawn, already breathless, listening for hard steps following. She had a brief, hopeful thought that maybe the mind could make the body do incredible things under stress, then slowed listlessly. Who was she kidding? She couldn't outrun her sister. And she had given up her weapon, the Kiss figurine. Not that it would have made that much of a difference. Jo-Jo was an assassin with a bat in her hands whatever the context.

Sage stopped at the sidewalk and felt her hand flutter up to her neck like a frightened sparrow. The man was no longer there, and she didn't think he was behind the hedge anymore. Tough to tell, though, the angle was different, and she made her way across the road half skipping, half trotting, amazed the she'd even had the sense to look both ways.

The hedge was thick. Sage didn't think it had ever been trimmed. There had been a bird nest in it once. She approached.

"Mister?" she said. She came to the edge and suddenly thought of the *Halloween* movie, the first one from the Stone Age, the seventies. Michael Meyers had briefly revealed himself next to a similar hedge, though that one was a perpendicular property divider instead of a sidewalk liner. Same difference. Similarly, he'd stepped back behind, and similarly, one of the babysitters had gone and popped around it for a look-see. Of course, it was a fake-me-out when no one was there.

Sage held her breath and stepped past the fringe.

There was no one here either. Just a lawn chair, an old gas grill with the lid up, a splintery picnic table, a dirty Igloo cooler, and a spade shovel next to a small hole seemingly dug for no reason. Sage turned, stepping back to the sidewalk, and there was movement at the corner of her eye, to the left, up the block. It was the police dude at the top of the gentle incline, in front of the house that had the black roof stains and the ivy growing up the chimney. Sage jogged toward him, and he ducked into the yard. By the time she made the crest, he was nearing the gate in the back that led to a stand of public woods that, straight ahead of him, gradually led to the Regional Rail stop for the Paoli/Thorndale Line.

Sage had explored those woods many a time. If he made a sharp left and backtracked, there was denser foliage leading to a right turn taking you down a mild ravine to a big stone culvert at the bottom that all the kids had thought to be haunted until realizing when a bit older that it was the perfect place to drink beer and smoke tree. To the right was an old horse path that went up a slow rise leading out of the forest to a large public garden, started years ago by a zestful middle school girl named Brianna Montgomery who was inspired by the book *Seedfolks*. Some of Sage's most treasured early memories were constructed there, but when Brianna went off to college the general interest of the neighborhood waned. Now there were just weeds, vines, and clutter.

The man turned right.

Sage moved forward.

Kids were trespassers by design, but she had always found this back yard to be spooky. The owner rented the space, that much she knew, but there were long droughts between tenants. Moreover, all the original kiddy stuff, or the remnants thereof, was left behind like forgotten dreams. The swing set had wild grass around the support posts, and the bumpy slide had moss on the steps. Sage edged past the tire swing, ducked under a low-hanging branch, and made her way through the back gate.

To the right there was a bend in the horse path, so she couldn't see the police guy. She took a few cautious steps along the wide trail, a few more, pace quickening, and something rustled in the brush to her left. Startled, she put both forearms across her belly.

The baby!

Her first thought: it was a squirrel, that was all, darting across the path a few yards in front of her.

The baby...

She didn't even know if she had been lied to about that. She breathed in deep, high in the shoulders, and started to move forward again. The baby...right. For real, she had to get a pregnancy test. Embarrassing! She'd have to find a Walgreens or CVS where she didn't know anyone. She especially couldn't let Poppy know. God, if people found out about this, she would die. When was she going to start showing? When was it too late to—

She stopped dead in her tracks for a second time: she'd had an epiphany. Her heart was racing and the back of her neck tingled. It was as if she had become two people in her head, the Sage that spoke her heart and the Sage that made decisions. Both were in agreement and both were amazed.

I was concerned just now for the baby's safety, because I want to keep it.

She put her hands on her hips and looked off to the side with a small, wry smile as if she'd become a third Sage who thought and acted like an outside spectator. Yes, she'd look stupid, for sure. But Isaac Newton probably looked dumb as all hell when the apple bonked him, right? She started walking again. It made no sense, none whatsoever, but it was a simple fact, like the world being round when it really looked flat. She wanted to mother this child.

The shadows were receding and the slivers of light winking through all the branches slowly gave way to the bald open glare of the sun. At the top of a short incline, the man in the police jacket stood waiting.

Sage shielded her eyes for a moment, then looked down at the ground. She pressed on, and another thought occurred to her. What would her child make of a half-sibling/half-cousin? Her face flushed. Wasn't going to happen. Conservative Republican wannabe or not, Jody was going to get an abortion. Sage wanted Vinny for herself. All of him.

The policeman had gone down the middle row, and on her approach Sage noticed that someone had cleared the trees on the far side, yielding a view of the Latchkey church steeple towering from over the rise like backdrop in a Gothic mural. She passed under the garden arch arbor, mostly skeletal except for the browned vines still clinging to the steel. Inside, the smell was vaguely unpleasant, like wet hay and swamp water. Sage stepped past an old chipped solar lantern. There was lattice fencing sporadically posted throughout the garden giving a labyrinthine impression, and the metal animal silhouettes on garden stakes, the decorative Amish wagon, the spiral spinners, camper's flags, and personalized magnetic signs all made the whole thing look like a cemetery filled with remembrances and grave tokens. There were even memorial garden stones and a couple of inscribed benches for the dead, partly obstructed by cattails and choke weed.

The police guy was waiting for her at a fork in the pathway, in between a display of old-fashioned milk jugs on a mule cart across from a wagon wheel, a war cannon, and a ring of flower pots surrounding a dry cement birdbath. His mask was off, but he had on mirrored sunglasses now, the aviator type, and he frightened her. He looked like a statue himself, a monument rising from the decay.

He put up his hand palm-out, as if to say, *Stop.* They were a bit more than six feet apart, and Sage took off her mask. She had to. She was so frightened she felt she couldn't breathe.

"Who are you?" she said, amazed that her voice hadn't quavered. "What is happening to my family?"

"I honestly don't know that, miss," he said, voice husky and militaristic. "Not all of it, at least. I do know that I am a part of it, and I am here at great risk. You need to listen and figure out what to do. You will most probably not have your father's help, nor any aid from your sisters. You are all alone in this and each of you will face different trials, torments, and ordeals. That's how he works. My name is Bill Canfield. I was the Chief of Police for Lower Merion Township until the end of last week, and I was the one a couple of years ago who went up against Michael Leonard Robinson, your *Sculptor*. I assisted in his defeat. I have also been compromised."

"What do you mean, compromised?"

"Mind control," he said. "And I haven't much time."

"What do you mean?"

"I mean," he said, "that I am in a sort of neutral zone out in the open air. He can't read or command me here, just as he can't read anyone out of doors including you and your sisters. But if I stay in a dead zone too long, he'll apply the punishment just in case, for insurance."

"Punishment?"

"Torture. With impunity."

"What kind of torture?"

"I'll explain in a moment," he said. "You'll need context."

"OK then, I'm in." Again, her apparent nonchalant bravery surprised her, and Canfield continued, voice low and even.

"After Robinson was supposedly killed in the blast at the forge, we found his rolling laboratory in an eighteen-wheeler. We tore it apart, reading his journalistic observations of victims, his plans, his blueprints. He was far more sophisticated than any of us could have imagined in terms of technology, and it was in one of those searches that I believe I became infected."

"With germs?" she said. "Like Covid-19?"

"Worse," he said. "Artificial intelligence. Nanobots."

"What are they?"

"You can Google it later, as my explanation will be overly simplistic in light of the time constraint. Still, I would ask that you take my word as-is for now. Nanobots are like small computers no bigger than splinters, and if swallowed, his are built to penetrate the esophagus, like live malevolent parasites, searching for and finding the nearest optic nerves, using the blood vessels as conduits."

"Optic?" she said. "Your eyes? They hunt for your eyes?"

"And nest in them, yes. They create an image for him, as he sees a version of what I see even though he is blind. And even when my lids are down, the bots have other functions, like high-tech crystals or semiconductors, perfectly seated, or rather, conveniently insulated, so The Sculptor can bounce illusions to his other victims. Again, my apologies for the remedial explanation, but please, miss, there's more. The nanobots inside me were dormant all this time, then activated a couple of days ago. I knew it immediately but could do nothing. He was still alive somewhere, somehow, and he gave immediate commands. I obeyed. There was no choice. If I diverted from course, he applied the consequence I first alluded to."

"Which was?"

"Headaches. Bad ones, delivered through the bots. There would be a few seconds of dull pressure like a last warning, and then..."

He put his hands behind his back, spread his feet, and tilted his chin.

"To the point," he said, "I had a dream last night. A vivid dream that I broke into the First Church of Christ at Haverford and Manoa Streets around the corner here. I dreamt that I struck a man unconscious. I went and got ladders out from under the stage area, and I rigged up a lethal hook and pulley system."

"Spaghetti Harry," Sage whispered.

"Affirmative. I 'woke' with my fingers stinging, the tips and edges around the nails. I have always had a nervous habit of chewing at the skin there, the cuticles et cetera, and the small slits and notches were sore and tingling. Then I remembered. It was part of the dream. I had used a cocktail of Harry's custodial chemicals to wash off the blood, then his industrial wipes to clean the bottles and cans. I wiped down the ladders, the hose reel, the eyescrew in the ceiling, the kitchen, the corpse. No gloves. Robinson, of course, wanted me to feel that the dream had been real, so I couldn't rationalize or deny it."

He paused as an airplane passed by overhead. He looked up toward it briefly, then off to the side and back, nodding slightly, flexing his jaw.

"Early this morning I got a message on my computer that Professor Brad Winslow would try to murder me before noon. I told your father as much, but obviously never experienced the confrontation, as it is 2:45 the afternoon now and there has been no more contact between us except by cell phone. Still, please understand, Miss, that The Sculptor does not make mistakes. I was told of this threat for a reason, most probably so my warning to your father would warm our acquaintance, making us allies. It was easy then for the fiend to induce us to join together in a short urban adventure while he toyed with other subjects in the timeline. Do you see what you're up against now? The Sculptor learns our psychology. There is an intensity to it as if it gives him sexual climax, pardon the reference, or something close to it in potency. Every move we have made he has considered, relished, and planned for."

Sage hugged herself. "Then there's no way out."

"There is always a trapdoor or porthole," he said. "Let's look at the conditions and variables. As said, I have discovered that this man cannot use me as a catalyst to broadcast his pixel-visions or to simulate sight for himself if I am out of doors—in other words, not surrounded by walls or barriers on all sides. When I cloud the transmission in this manner; however, he knows it and, as said, will begin applying the punishment if the picture doesn't resume in a reasonable amount of time. Again, as said, I am at high risk now as we speak."

"Were you in our house?" Sage said. "Did you plant cameras and bugs in our house?"

The man looked at the ground.

"No, Miss. At least I don't think so. There is no recollection of that, no dreams or visions. This fiend has many ways to engage his methods of surveillance, some we might never know or understand, at least with the knowledge we presently employ."

"But why us?" Sage said. "What could he possibly want with me, my Poppy, and my sisters?"

The chief looked at her expressionlessly.

"I don't know," he said. "But please understand that Robinson isn't so much about killing. He is more about fetish and voyeurism, participating in his own violent fantasies."

"So he can mind-fuck people."

"So he can wear them like body suits."

Sage gnawed at the inside of her cheek. "Then this conversation—"

"Might be a part of his master plan, yes," he said. "But I am hoping and praying it isn't. This morning I coaxed your father out to the church parking lot and, of course, was physically warned not to divulge information. The beast did it with the pain. Just enough to make me wary. In terms of our conversation here, I didn't announce or telegraph it. This is most probably a safe zone, but again, not for long."

"So what should I do?"

"The unexpected," he said. "Something that goes against the grain of your typical mindset, something uncharacteristic, even self-defeating. Outguessing The Sculptor is like outguessing yourself. Think of the thing you'd be least likely to do and do it. Don't think, just act. Minutes ago I took such a risk, stepping out of character and ringing your front doorbell. Your father had phoned earlier and warded me off, commanding me not to come to the house as there were new dangers, new threats. And it just so happens to go against my very nature to interfere in those situations. I don't believe in storming the kidnapper. I believe in paying the ransom. And so it is this small, inexplicable contradiction in action that brought us here, giving us a few minutes. It was a good gamble, a sort of micro-version of the way I tricked him in our first conflict two years ago. My move back then was to unplug a computer and eliminate myself from the flow of information. Do you see? I am a tactician, and to relinquish my power in that manner surprised our antagonist, if only briefly."

He suddenly made fists.

"What?" Sage said.

"He's on to me," Canfield said. "My head. The pounding, the searing..."

He bent over, hands on his knees. He straightened sharply and tore off the sunglasses, eyes huge and bloodshot.

"Execute the unexpected," he rasped. "Remember that, please. And don't let them bury me in a coffin underground. It would have the same effect as surrounding walls, making me his transmitter even after my death."

He reached behind for his waistband and brought around a revolver. It was thick, black, and short-barreled.

"No," Sage said, shaking her head. "Oh, no-no-no."

He put it to his head, right side, the temple. His breath was high, jaw tight.

"Please," Sage said, stepping toward him, and he stared back at her, eyes red like taillights. She put her arms out, palms up now like Oliver asking for more. *Wrong simile!* she thought. *I want less, so much less!* She wanted to grab him. Tackle him, maybe. Go for the gun at least.

Instead, she drew back her hands, making the praying shape in front of her lips.

"Please?" she said.

The gun roared. Sage screamed. Canfield's head jerked away from the muzzle, and the bullet came out the other side in a burst of red stringers. As he collapsed, his shooting hand seemed frozen where it was for a bare moment, bent at the wrist as if he was making a muscle as he crumpled into himself, a sack of bricks pinning his ankles beneath him. His upper body teetered for a moment, a rag-doll on a spring, and then he jerked backward, skull thumping the dirt like flat punctuation. His knees poked up irregularly.

Sage sank to the ground. She was tugging on her hair with both hands and made herself stop, unclenching slowly.

His eyes were open. Sage leaned to stare into them, her bottom lip trembling. They were so wide with fear, deep scarlet from pain, and so very dead, as if there were X's drawn through them.

His mouth came open making her start and draw back. A cicada whined by her ear, landed on Canfield's cheek, and flitted into the void, then back out, and then in again, down his tongue. He didn't move again.

She sat back on her haunches, palms on her thighs and she let out a deep breath, realizing that she had been holding it. Tears sprang into her eyes. The dead body was so sad, so disgraced. There were rules for this kind of emergency, procedures, but The Sculptor made you throw all those out the window, mistrusting your friends, disobeying your dad, despising your sisters, breaking the law and, at the same time, your morals.

She honestly did not know what to do.

Then. Oh my God, then she did.

CHAPTER 13

I'm Strong Enough to Kill You

Esther was terrified. It had been warm and snuggly here in the closet, and though the burlap was itchy, the Royal Silk Man's voice was smooth and delicious, like a lick of honey or a taste of frosting right off the whisk. He'd been so amazing! He had told Esther every move Jo-Jo was making downstairs as if it were a storybook, like *The Three Bears and Goldilocks* or *Little Red Riding Hood,* and he even compared himself to the wolf, only he was a good wolf showing the wandering girl the best way through the woods.

He had said that Jo-Jo made Sage run out of the house because Jo-Jo had been given orders from Poppy that no one was to interrupt him, not even Jo-Jo. Mr. Royal Silk had said that "Professor Winslow's middle one" was a good soldier. He claimed she had opened the kitchen door multiple times, popping out her head to check the back yard for "meddling strangers." She had gotten a piece of American cheese from the fridge and left the cellophane wrapper on the counter by the toaster. She had practiced swinging her bat in the kitchen.

A good soldier.

Guarding Poppy.

And Sage? He said that she was going to try and ruin everything, a real party-pooper, and that Esther had to get past Jo-Jo downstairs, almost like a game, a test, to show her closest elder sister that she was big enough to help protect Poppy too. Like outsmarting the smarty-pants. If she got caught, Jo-Jo would be mad as a hornet, but magically, if Esther *did* make it out to the shed, Jo-Jo would realize that her little sister was big enough now for the "meaty stuff," no longer the baby who never got to do *anything*. Jo-Jo would reward her, in fact. She would humbly take a knee before her and kiss her hand, rise tall above her and touch the collarbone on either side of her head with that aluminum bat, making her the youngest girl-knight in the land near and far.

It was a such an exciting game! Jo-Jo was the master Esther had to win over and Sage was the bad one, the dark one, the enemy.

And the Royal Silk Man had reminded her that Jo-Jo was no pushover as master of the house under Poppy, oh no she wasn't. Jo-Jo the soldier was playing for real, for keeps, and she already knew Esther was hiding up here, she just didn't know where.

"If she goes to the bathroom downstairs, you'll get your chance," he'd said. *"You'll have to be fast too, because Jo-Jo pees like a race horse."*

That one made Esther laugh so hard she'd thought she'd hurt herself. God, it was so much more difficult when you had to keep quiet! It took a minute for her to get herself back together: just when she seemed back under control, she'd picture her sister with her legs spread over a horse trough again, and a new eruption of giggles ensued.

"Wait a minute," said the Royal Silk Man. *"She's not going to the first-floor half-bath. She's coming back for the stairs. OK, Esther, now listen carefully. This is going to be tricky, and you're going to have to—"*

His voice suddenly winked out. It sounded like an old-fashioned radio making that cartoonish *blip* and *wee-o/wee-o* sound. There was a moment of static, then silence.

"Hello?" Esther whispered. Her hands made fists under her chin. "Mr. Man?"

Nothing.

"Mr. Royal Silk Man, I need you!"

Nothing.

"I'll be your best friend!"

Silence.

"Cross my heart and hope to—"

Esther put both hands over her mouth. She didn't want to hope to *die,* what a jinx! Besides, it was insanely stupid. Thinking this way, she'd never become a girl-knight. She also couldn't help but wonder if hiding here had made Jo-Jo mad as a hornet already. I mean... Esther liked Mr. Royal Silk, but now she could be in trouble, real trouble! And she hated hornets, yellowjackets, bumblebees, wasps! There had been a nest of bees under the overhang of the garage out back last summer. Esther had prodded it with the business end of a corn broom and the little nasties had swarmed out of their weirdo honey house in a savage crazy alarm dance. Esther had run away fast, but had been stung in four different places, under her right eye, inside the left ear, on the right forearm, and behind the left knee. She hadn't swollen up as if she was allergic or anything, but the pain had been throbbing and terrible!

The Royal Silk Man had hinted that it was okay to be mad at "Sage-the-Sissy," to hate her even, but again, Esther hadn't won the game with Jody yet, not by a long shot. Jody could be mean as an ogre, worse than a tough older brother. She had hit Esther three times in her life: on the flat of the bicep when she ate the Reese's cup Jo-Jo had hidden in the freezer under the crab claws...once in the center of the back between the shoulders when Esther had dropped down into the sewer the Silver Slugger signature ball Jo-Jo's ten-year-old Little League team's coach had awarded her for hitting .820 that season…and once in the stomach for stealing (and putting under her pillow) the Harry Styles picture in the oversized keychain from when he was on the cover of *Vogue* wearing a lacy Gucci gown.

All three punches still hurt as if it was yesterday—well, they almost did, like an ember in a campfire hungry for tinder. So unfair! She had only taken the Reese's cup because at dinner Jo-Jo had hogged the four-cheese Rice-a-Roni, leaving Esther all but a spoonful. As for the baseball, it had made her so mad and disgusted! Every player on the team had signed it, and to Esther this was yucky, gross, insane, and unheard of! Boys were smelly and didn't like girls. Boys were stupid, and the ball was like an evil eye, sitting on Jo-Jo's bureau staring at you, following you all around the room like a haunted house painting! And Harry Styles? Esther had never been more jealous in her entire life. Poppy had gotten it for Jo-Jo at the Springfield Mall in the store that had skateboards and the classic rock T-shirts he liked so much. And Jo-Jo wasn't even with them! They were shopping for book bags and lunch boxes for first grade! Esther had begged for her own impulse gift, fawning over a Minnie Mouse Zip-Up Stationery Kit in the Disney Store, a cute pair of rainbow strappy sandals at The Gap, and a twenty-inch Marshmallow Man *Ghostbusters* doll at Spencer's, but she'd come up utterly empty. Poppy hadn't even given in when she wouldn't stop pouting, and he purposefully skipped over the cherry slushi he'd promised her. What was a girl to do besides get revenge?

And pay the price. Getting hit. Sobbing. Curling up in a corner frightened, submissive, cautious, and untrusting, a baby, a little crybaby who was still too little, too young, and foolish to be included in *anything*. That alone made her want to weep and scream and scratch her own face! But there was no time for crying. She had to be a big girl now. The Royal Silk Man had abandoned her, and there was a sound out there on the stairs.

A loud spooky creak. Of course, it was the third step from the bottom, the one that always got you in trouble if you were trying to sneak upstairs or down for one reason or another. And this particular creak right now was five times as terrible because it was a continuing creak, not just a squawk, but a repeating phrase, mechanical and evil, like a villain in a top hat and coattails, winding a rusty crankshaft on the front of an old-fashioned hearse. Of course it was Jo-Jo, probably up on one foot, bouncing her weight on the soft spot, teasing and taunting.

She came off it out there and stomped her foot on the next stair, dramatically, mockingly, then up another and the next. Esther had the fingers of both hands in her mouth. There was a doubling, like an echo, thumping right after each of her sister's footfalls, and to Esther it sounded as if Jo-Jo was in fact turned the other way around, backing up the stairs, dragging a body by the ankles and letting its head bump clumsily against each new step in the rise.

Esther took out her fingers and rubbed them on her pants. Her spit tasted electric and spoiled. It wasn't a dead body. Jo-Jo was dragging behind her DeMarini Voodoo bat, letting it bunk against each carpeted step left behind her.

A soldier.

A yellowjacket-hornet-wasp with hammer-fists and a big aluminum stinger.

Footsteps came closer, hall, archway, room, right up to the other side of the door. Esther wanted to vomit. Her breath was harsh and stuttering, and she was sure Jo-Jo could hear it.

There was nothing but silence from the other side. Esther squirmed. Her sister knew full well she was in here. She knew that

Esther knew that she knew too. *I know that you know that I know that you know that I know...*

A harsh clap then. It shook the door, Esther felt it as much as she heard it, and she let out a short screech.

"Easy, Peanut," said Jody. Her face must have been less than an inch from the wood. "Have fun in the dark."

There was a thump that shook the door again, but not as much as the first. Then footsteps, quickly fading.

Esther pushed to her knees on the burlap and reached up for the thumb-turn. She gripped it, tried to twist it to no avail, and then tried both hands. The lock grated over, finally snapping to open, and Esther pressed her palms against the door trying to give it a shove. Nothing. Absolute blockade as if welded shut. She reared back and put a shoulder into it. Ouch! No give at all, and she sank against the door now with her back to it. Suddenly everything seemed close, as if there was no air, like a coffin inside that big hearse. She tried not to weep. She had to pee bad. And she came to the conclusion that Jody had jammed her baseball bat up under the knob, then stomped it down low at an angle to wedge it.

CHAPTER 14

I'm Your Number One Fan

S age felt as if she'd been walking for hours. Her brain hurt. Her feet felt as if they were made of lead, and she was trying not to think about it. The thing. The maneuver she'd pulled that kicked off all these grotesque contradictions.

She kept walking.

She passed the bowling alley and the Head Nut, the beer distributor and the D.M.I. Home Supply. Cars brushed past. She felt invisible. And she would stay invisible as long as she didn't walk into a building.

Don't think about it.

Tired as she was, it did amaze her that she could compartmentalize her mind like this. Her ears were still numb and ringing from the gunshot. She focused on the numbness so she didn't have to think about what happened just after. What she did. And the possible consequences. The numbness fogged everything, and in response she had discovered this wonderful trick...focusing on the numb foggy ringing in order to let her imaginary Vinny work his way through the haze.

She had never so desperately needed a boy. She needed to see him to discuss things, work out the kinks. She needed for him to hold her, rub her back, tell her that he was with her all the way with this thing.

And what if he's not?

Don't think about it! Numbing haze, Vinny stepping through it with no shirt on, wearing the silky gray shorts with the candy-apple red side-stripes, no socks, just high tops. Heavenly he was, simply heavenly.

She made a right up New Ardmore Avenue and bumped her toe on the lip of a turnbuckle in the sidewalk. It pitched her forward, and she had to take a couple of slappy-happy circus stomps to gain back her feet. Someone honked. She flipped up the bird, immediately regretting it. The last thing she needed right now was confrontation. Invisible was good. Attention of any kind was bad, very bad.

The car whooshed past, no catcalls, no drama.

Good deal, and Sage was thankful to have been thinking about it. Anything but...the thing...the act...the solution that wasn't a solution but possibly a seed of danger, a terrible calculation that was a black spot, then a blotch, then a monstrous stain overtaking the sun. A quick fix with consequences.

No! Numbness. Clouds and vapor. Vinny emerging from the haze just wearing his Fruit-of-the-Loom Micro-Mesh Breathables, mouthing, *"I'm waiting."*

Coming, she thought. *As fast as I can.*

He lived in one of those brick saltbox houses on the other side of the Elwell playground, past the tennis courts and the baseball field, on the other side of the street behind dead right center. He said he'd grown up on this field, learned to catch and hit and steal bases with his dad doing grounders practice and outfield fungo and home run derbies sometimes for fun in the rain and the mud. They were addicted. Vinny also met up with friends here, sometimes at night, like a hangout, their turf. He'd smoked weed for the first time behind the backstop, sitting on the dented brown JOBOX that contained the bases, lime bags, and community catcher's gear. Not his thing, the cannabis, no thanks, not again. The spliff had given him sludge mouth and made him feel too trippy to live. He claimed he liked drinking better, beer mostly, anything available, and when he was really feeling it there was Spiced Captain Morgan and Johnny Walker Blue Label. That said, the last time he'd knocked back the hard stuff, he had to be dragged home by Billy Berkshire and Will Snyder, both leaving him passed out in the driveway behind the vintage blue MG Midget up on blocks that his eldest brother Frank and his dad had been tinkering with. Evidently, Vinny had crawled around, opened up the back door, half climbed in, and ralphed all over the back seat upholstery.

His head had pounded the next day, as he'd recalled ruefully with a half-smile. And not just from the hangover. His dad had slapped him around pretty good, leaving room for Frankie to finish the task.

Sage winced. The idea of Vinny being abused in any way, shape, or form made her throat close. It was shameful, like defacing a religious artifact or precious national statue. She wished she had been there to cradle his head against her chest, to stroke his hair, maybe hum to him softly.

There was a slit in the outfield fence you had to scrimp through sideways, and past that was the strip between two properties divided by a waist-high stone wall that had a split-rail fence running along the top inner edge with bushes growing through it. The house on the right had its side windows blocked by two humongous hydrangeas.

Solid.

Invisible was good.

The sun was at an odd angle, and when Sage emerged to cross Elderberry Road her shadow stretched all the way to the corner mailbox, a stalker glued to her every step, and as it moved behind like something refracted in lake water, she was reminded that it was a part of her now, the darkness at her heels, in her heart, in her blood.

Move quickly.

Monsters, demons, and bad guys were a matter of perspective, maybe. Stop thinking about it. Sage hopped off the sidewalk and trotted toward Vinny's house, arms straight with the wrists bent and the knuckles cocked up, so freakin' girly!

Perspective.

She crept through to the back yard and positioned herself behind the tree that shaded the entire rear of the property, its branches stretching across part of the roof. There was a back patio, and from her vantage point Sage could see right into the kitchen through the sliding glass doors. That was where the family gathered even when it wasn't meal time. Sage knew. She'd been back here before, three times to be exact. Vinny wasn't aware of this, at least she didn't think he was. She looked down at her girly hands, her slender fingers. The black nail polish was worn and chipped halfway down. Sage had always secretly thought it looked better that way. Sexier somehow. And if Vinny did know she'd stalked him before, he certainly wouldn't think it was monstrous. She was pretty sure he'd consider it foreplay.

Vinny's mother was sitting at the table, on her cell phone, saying nothing, playing nervously with her necklace. She was a cold, beautiful woman, tall and hauntingly thin. She had on bronze eye shadow and winged eyeliner, exotic and feline. Her hair was jet-black with platinum blond streaks in it, done up in a casual princess ponytail coming over one shoulder.

Mr. Gatto entered the room brusquely. He was a foreman for one of those big construction companies that worked on bridges and highways. He had gray hair, bureaucratic eyes, and a rigid sort of posture one would expect from Marines or Navy Seals. He was wearing an industrial khaki button-down dress shirt, duck dungaree work pants, and engineer's boots. Under one arm was a white hardhat. In his other fist was a cell phone. Sage could hear it ringing through the window screen over by the stove, which itself was out of the sightline.

"Hang up," he said to his wife. "He left it home. Clearly."

She hit the button and re-crossed her legs.

"Then where is he?" she said. "It's not like him to leave his phone behind and it's not like him not to call. They canceled practice and Fetterman says no one has seen him since second period. Supposedly two older boys got in trouble for fighting and a bunch of the kids cut school to watch it. Regardless, it's 4:05. It's not like him and he knows that I worry."

Mr. Gatto hung his hardhat on a hook by the archway, turned back, and pulled out a chair across from his wife. He stepped around, squatted, and reached back between his legs to pull it in under him.

"I can't come off the job," he said patiently, "every time your routine takes a bit of a left turn."

"This is different."

"How so?"

"It just is. A mother knows."

He looked down at his fists loosely clenched on the table, as if considering, yet opting out of this particular argument.

"Maybe he's with Burnsie," he offered. "Or Mikey Flynn, Tzar Walker, or Bruce Phelps."

She straightened in her chair and gave a haughty look as if she'd just gotten scent of something mildly unpleasant.

"He's not with John Burns," she said, "because he knows I'm not talking to his mother, not after what she said about me at book club as if I wasn't sitting right there in the flesh. The Flynns took one of those impulse vacations to New Orleans, staying at the Hotel Monteleone, and Michael is with his cousins in Broomall. Tzar is grounded for sneaking out his window to meet up with that slut Erica Langley two nights ago at South Ardmore Park, and Bruce has been quarantined at his psychologist's suggestion because of Internet addiction."

"I'll bet it's that girl, then."

"What girl?"

"The weird one. You know, the artsy one with the pink hair and the dark eyebrows."

Sage blushed furiously. Mrs. Gatto leaned back archly.

"Sage Winslow?" she said. "She's nothing but a phase. Fast food." She stared at her husband for a moment, then shrugged, reaching for her cell phone again. "OK, what's her number?"

"How should I know?"

"It's probably in Vinny's phone."

"I don't know the code."

"It's his birthday."

"He changed it."

She put her own cell down carefully on the table. "Since when?"

Mr. Gatto pushed up to his feet. "Since he's growing up more every day, Mia. We don't own kids. We borrow 'em until they're big enough to start making decisions. Some start before they're eighteen, and if that's too tragic for you I'll get you a therapist."

She rolled her eyes and ran her tongue across her teeth. She set the heel of her palm on the table and clicked her long curvy fingernails on the smooth surface.

"This is not like him," she said, "and you damned well know it. I'm going to call information."

"No," he said, hands on the back of the chair. "You are not going to call some teenage girl we don't even know and get us involved in that way. It only spells trouble."

"Then I'll dial 911."

He straightened, hands raised palm-up, what the heck?

"On what pretext?" he said. "He's less than two hours late and it isn't even near dinnertime. And you're saying—what? That he's missing? Like a Megan alert kind of thing? Doesn't it have to be twenty-four hours? They have those timelines for a reason."

She reached back, flipped her hair to the other shoulder, and stroked it with both hands as if she was playing a harp.

"I tell you, something's wrong here, really wrong, and..."

She faded off as her husband was looking away, his "shoosh" finger pointed back at her.

"What?" she said.

He waved his hand at her, then disappeared from view. It must have been a counter- television on low volume, turned up now, and Sage heard the voice of a news reporter come drifting through the screen window.

". . . violence in an abandoned community garden just off Trent Road in Wynnewood. He was unofficially a part of the investigation of a crime scene close by, in the First Church of Christ at Haverford and Manoa Streets, though authorities will not divulge the specifics, nor whether the two cases could be related. William Timothy Canfield was the Chief of Police until a week ago yesterday, a decorated veteran, found on the ground with a fatal bullet wound to the head. We have been informed that he was wearing a 'small of the back' holster, but the firearm he was licensed to carry is currently missing. Again, this is disturbing, and we suggest you turn down the volume if there are small children nearby. We have not had to report anything quite like this since Michael Leonard Robinson, self-named 'The Sculptor,' terrorized Pennsylvania highways and finally Chief Canfield's precinct. Evidently, Robinson was finally killed two years ago in a massive explosion at the abandoned forge in North Philadelphia once rented by Mount Airy Steel. In terms of today's mysterious violence, we at Eyewitness News do not wish to imply things based on circumstantial evidence and conjecture, but it is our mission to reveal the verified facts that are here at our disposal. If there was another party present with Canfield at the time of death, he or she did not only confiscate the weapon. He or she took a trophy. He or she took both Canfield's eyes."

CHAPTER 15

We All Go a Bit Mad Sometimes

Esther was more than peeved and hurt. She was frantic. She'd peed herself. She'd screamed herself hoarse. She'd gone to her knees and banged on the door so many times that her fists felt as if they'd swelled to three times their size. She'd gone back to a sitting position, propped her hands on either side of herself, and tried kicking, both feet at once and then one after the other like a marching band strutting, and even though the wood felt different under her feet, slightly more "springy" than the wood at eye level, Esther could not budge the obstruction even an inch.

And it smelled in here, *God!* Odors usually didn't usually crawl down inside you like this, like multi-legged bugs, like snakes, so unfair! Usually a stink-bomb, a real *funk*-attack got you only at first, making you want to barf, but then you got used to it. Jody's number twos were a perfect example. Generally, it was best not to follow her into the bathroom in the morning, especially since Sage had protested using air freshener for "environmental reasons," whatever that meant. Following Jody after a poop was disgusting. But if you sat in the cloud of it for more than a minute, you forgot about it. Like magic, it went away like bad dreams.

This was new and different and fifty times *worse!*

The burst of hot urine Esther just couldn't hold any longer had not just seeped down her legs. Rather, it had gathered backward all over her rump, giving her road-rash-butt. It burned, and each time she moved it stung more, on top of the original fact that the smell of old wee was making her choke.

But if her stomach went "whoopsie" in here, she would die. Everyone knew that puke hurt your nostrils differently from anything else in the world, besides having Sprite or Dr. Pepper snorted back up your nose.

It was The Royal Silk Man's fault. He led her here.

It was Jody's fault for locking her in and walking away.

It was Poppy's fault for being occupied elsewhere.

And it was Sage's fault for being a traitor.

But wait.

The Royal Silk Man didn't abandon her. He'd been cut off with—what was the word?—*technical difficulties.* And Jody wasn't the enemy, but more, the superhero on a pedestal whom Esther had failed to impress. Poppy was the love of her life, the light in the dark, the king of the realm. And Sage? Well, she hadn't done anything to Esther, not really. She'd just pulled a no-show.

Like Mom.

The Royal Silk Man had been such fun, but was then yanked away like a mighty bullfighter's cape, or more, that magic trick where you ripped off the tablecloth and the dishes and glasses were left as they were, left alone.

The way Mom so recently left us all.

Jody had been Esther's hero.

The way Mom had been.

Poppy was "elsewhere."

The way Mom was right now.

Esther grimaced. She felt as if she was going around in circles with this, on a carousel filmed on a slant in a horror movie where the kiddie tunes were off-key, the sky was full of lightning, and the horses were bleeding. But when the carousel slowed and came to a stop, Esther was right back where she'd been just a minute ago, wasn't she? In a dark closet knowing full well this was all their fault, all of them! Like Mom, they were all *older,* the ones with the responsibility to pick apart the riddles, to understand the "people math." Mom was dead, dead, and deader, but Esther was the one locked up in a box, not the Royal Silk Man whispering to her like a witch with sicky-sweet breath...not Poppy, who'd suddenly become the slow kid in class who picked his nose, left his Legos a mess, and made it so they were denied snack after nap-time...not Jody, the bully, the meanie, the boy-girl, and not Sage, the know-it-all, poisonous garden snake.

If only Esther could get free of this closet. Make herself heard. Make herself...respected like Sage, revered like Poppy, held in awe like the Silk Man, and like Jody...feared.

Esther smiled slowly as an idea dawned inside her. Yes? No? Maybe? Of course. She pressed down, grunted, and managed to turn herself around toward the back of the closet, up to her knees on the roll of burlap. She felt around and found the bottom back shelf, the one below the second one that was bolted to the inside of the door overhead, making it so you couldn't stand up in here to save your darned life. She reached, resting her forearms on the edge of the low shelf, then strained up and in to grope around for the plastic tubs filled with Sage's art supplies.

The first one she pulled down and pried open had the paint brushes, watercolor papers, and sponges. She frowned, moved it aside, pushed around again, and stretched with all she had to get at the tub at the rear, the one that was the heaviest, the one with the goods.

She pulled it down, revolved back around with it, and sat with a hard bump. The treasure was in her lap. She pried the tub open and felt around. Smiled again, ear to ear.

No more haunted carousels, no more lightning, no more bleeding horses.

Just some respect. Some revenge.

And Sage's lovely stone carving tools.

CHAPTER 16

I Should Warn You, Princess.
The First Time Tends to Get a Little Messy

age had never been so frightened, so alone. There seemed nowhere to run, to hide, settle in, get her shit together.

Of course, she had taken Chief Canfield's pistol. It was a tiny thing, a Sig Sauer, and fit easily in the back pocket of her baggy hickory stripe overalls. How to use the gun, how to cock it, how to find the "safety" if there was one—well, that was experimentation she would have to dive into later. At this point she had to get rid of her footwear. Fucking pronto.

After the news anchor had finished his introductory speech, they'd switched to another guy "on location," who reported that police had found and "plastered' a clear footprint. It was a women's size seven, and they had surmised at least in a preliminary fashion that the individual with Canfield was most probably a teenage girl wearing some sort of slip-ons.

Sage paused at the sidewalk curb sewer and stepped on her heels to get out of her kicks. They were actually Tie-Dye Rainbow glitter sneaks, thank you, her favorites, and she had just dashed out of

Vinny's back yard as if her hair was on fire. She may as well have
been wearing a sandwich board sign saying "Suspected Teen Hippie
Killer Here!"

Sage nudged both sneakers over the edge, thinking crazily that
the clown from *IT* was going to politely hand them back out to her
saying that they would "float better" with her feet in them. Leaves
had washed and wedged into the right side of the orifice, and Sage
used her toe to push a couple of clumps in over the edge after the
footwear. It was like using a few feathers to hide a soccer ball on a
gymnasium floor, but it was the best she had at her disposal.

Her hand fluttered up to her throat and she looked all around.
The sun beat down on her forehead, yielding a bug-under-a-microscope
feeling, and she knew she had to get out of here, now. She made for
the strip back between the two houses at the edge of the baseball field,
noticing absently that the grass felt a lot better on her bare feet than the
pavement. This was bad. It was highly probable that she was going to
have to run at some point, not in a trot, not a lady-like jog, but a fucking sprint—balls to the wall. And now her feet were going to bleed.

Blood, yes.

Crimson copper, she could still taste it. Compartmentalize,
right, sure, go fuck yourself, girl!

Do NOT fucking puke!

Of course, she had swallowed both of Canfield's eyes. Back at
the withered garden, before stealing his firearm, because the shock
of witnessing a suicide, blind terror, and sick desperation made you
do crazy things and take crazy chances.

It hadn't been easy. Not even considering the psychological shock
or the physical gag reflex she had to overcome twice, yanking out
someone's eyeballs was a damned chore. First, digging in your fingers
behind the slippery things was tricky. There were nerves and tough
stringy fibers acting as obstructions. Sage would have used a trowel or

garden shears if she'd taken the time to look for them, but this was a hold-your-nose-and-jump kind of deal. Worse, once you got a finger under, it made the eyeball move as if the corpse was making faces at you, going cross-eyed and sarcastically calling you a klutz, looking up in frustration (*what am I going to do with you?*) and peering downward in what looked like a cartoonish mimic of Sage and her vertigo. Consequently, the best footprint wasn't the one they claimed to have found in the dirt. There was one on each of Canfield's cheeks, where Sage had set the sole of her sneaker both times for leverage.

Each eye had come out with a suction *pop* and wet snaps of muscle. Sage made the grave mistake of looking closely at her "prize" the first time, almost losing her resolve, the wet trails of veins, arteries, and optic nerves making it look like a blood-soaked one-eyed baby jellyfish from Mars, dead-alive somehow, watching her baldly. She closed her eyes for a moment, going back to her middle school mindset, that's right, just a live Daddy Long Legs, a frog from a jar, and she used both hands to shove it in her mouth, swallowing it whole.

Unfortunately, she'd mostly grown out of her *Fear Factor* phase, and she almost ralphed.

She squatted, one hand pressed hard over her mouth, the other scraping the ground for dirt. Why she thought this would help was still beyond her, it was an instant's intuition, but she took a mouthful of soil and swallowed, not the whole handful, just enough to grit up her throat for traction.

She coughed like a cancer patient. Spit. Coughed some more, but didn't vomit. Somehow the dirt was so flat and specific, it made the taste of the eyes have less after-effect, muted aftertaste. There was no water to wash out her mouth, but she used eyeball number two as its own lubricant once she snapped it out of its socket.

More dirt. She wondered how she had the stomach for this, and she sure as shit didn't know. She guessed she got it from Poppy. Not that he knew anything about wolfing down someone's body parts, but anything she did well she associated with him. Always.

She'd stumbled back into the woods like a drunken sailor, to the ravine, down to the creek. She squatted at the edge. She cupped her hands, leaned over them, and pressed them into her face like a caveman. She drank, gargled, spit, again, and repeated three times. She didn't ralph. She washed her hands and forearms. She didn't ralph. She washed off her face. No ralphing here. No twenty-twenty hindsight, no guilt, no regrets.

Plainly, she'd done this all on pure instinct, a whim.

Talk about a gamble, hell, Sage was no scientist. She didn't hang with tech geeks and computer nerds, she didn't get their vibe, didn't speak their language. But she'd swallowed Canfield's eyes just the same, because he'd said that the nanobots nestled behind his irises made him a transmitter. Because he'd said that burying him was the same as putting him in a room, making it so the bots could be activated again. Because he'd claimed the bots could work their way through the esophagus, and Sage had figured that if they could do that, maybe they could work their way through an intestine, through a stomach wall, to the *closest available* eyes only just developing right next door inside of her womb.

Could she "trick" them this way? Totally undetermined, probably not actually. Then again, she'd taken the risk because it made a sort of artsy, dramatic, and poetic sense, at least if you liked your poetry dark. They were automated parasites, able to penetrate tissue to nest in the human eye. Once in their home, however, Sage figured they wouldn't be so quick to reverse course, not as rapidly as their first journey through the throat, and again, once past that check point achieved in a quick swallow, she was hoping, begging, praying that they would next find the home ports most convenient.

Did a two-week-old fetus even have anything resembling eyes yet? Probably not.

Would the bots remain in her womb, waiting for the new nests to take form and grow all around them?

Probably not.

Would the fact that the baby's eyes were shielded and encased in Sage's body as opposed to being an eyelid away from the open air keep The Sculptor in the dark, so to speak? Was the extra layer even relevant?

Probably not. She'd find out when she entered a room.

Crazy. Poetic, hell. This was insane. There was also the question of taking the pregnancy to term. Could she actually give birth this child in the end?

Probably not. Please welcome to the world The Sculptor's new super-transmitter. And that was the paradox, the awful contradiction. She'd so wanted to keep this baby, but keeping it now meant being its slave, or just as bad, The Sculptor's next victim. Most probably, anyway. On the other hand, aborting it could work, but then again, that removed "the layer," didn't it? Same thing as Canfield in a casket. Would a cremation kill these things? A total unknown. If not, they would be right there in the open, ready to transmit from the urn, or better yet, to "infect" the cremator, as if they were alive. I mean, how exactly had Chief Canfield been "infected" in the first place? By touching a container of nanobots he found in The Sculptor's Mack truck? By going hand-to-mouth to chew at his cuticles? There were so many variables here, so many unknowns. Besides, she'd been hoping before all this that Vinny would want to keep the baby as she initially had.

But Sage just didn't know exactly how she felt anymore. Too many layers, lol.

She felt like a toddler trying to do calculus.

Still, she was pretty sure it was fifteen weeks before the state banned abortions; she'd have to Google it when she could get back home to her phone.

Fifteen weeks. Almost four months to figure this out. That is, if she could enter enclosed spaces in the here and now without becoming a tool of the maniac pulling the levers and throwing the switches. She needed Vinny. She needed her father. Her family. She couldn't go through this alone.

She worked through the slit in the outfield fence and scurried across right field, the basepaths, the on-deck area on the visitor's side. There was a short stand of foliage behind the steel bleachers, and she pushed in, physically taxed, mentally exhausted, falling to her butt and sitting on the thin dirt path that led to the Havertown Apartment complex, just above its parking area.

Mostly, she needed her father. She needed to tell him everything: her feelings for Vinny, the baby, the buried eyes hiding behind just one extra layer, the whole enchilada. She and Jody needed a pow-wow as well. Truth. Younger sister was going to yield to bigger sister and get herself an abortion as quickly as possible. Sage's beautiful child was not going to have any half-brothers/half-cousins tagging along, weighing everyone down like the village idiot in a bad comedy.

Truth. It hurt sometimes, but rationalization was for fucking pussies. Sage grinned in a way that wasn't really a smile. She absolutely abhorred that expression, but it was the only way to address this particular situation with gusto, with punch, with...truth.

Sage was no pussy. She was no snowflake, no hippie-girl, not after today.

It was time to act like a grownup.

It was time to go home.

CHAPTER 17

Here's Johnny

Esther took Sage's two-and-a-half-pound stone carving hammer, two-handed it over her head, and smashed it into the door. There was a resounding thud, but no give. It sent vibro-shocks up her arms too, didn't tickle. She frowned so deeply it felt as if she was faking it, mocking someone else she thought was a baby, and it made her so mad she wanted to spit and cry and scream and have what her sisters called one of her "hissy-fissies." Why-oh-why were the closet doors TREE TRUNKS? Why was she locked up in here with no ice cream, no dollies, no light, and NO TOILET!

She raised the hammer again and brought it down.

She'd been ready for the shockwave this time, but there was no progress, no budge. Esther reached up to where she thought her two strokes had fallen, where her fists had naturally landed earlier, and she felt a small divot. Where was the other one? She'd hit the door twice.

Her hand moved lower, and while she didn't find the other hammer-mark, the surface under her fingers changed and slanted inward, feeling sort of "ribby" for an inch, and then it went flat like before when she went kicking and the wood felt "springy" beneath her feet. True! Yes! The first divot and the one she couldn't find had been banged into that cruel, unforgiving part of the door that had hurt the heels of her hands!

Esther put the hammer in her lap and reached up to where she'd just been, feeling all around like a blind woman groping on someone's fat face. Yes! The divot was in a long part, like a cross thingy, or crossbar or cross-section. She got mad again, as she didn't have Poppy here to help her with the hard words, but she screwed up her mouth and made herself think. The cross-sections of this kind of door were the unfriendly parts. The indented flat square sections below were weaker and were called…PANELS!

Esther smiled for her small victory, but the expression quickly vanished. She'd been thinking in CAPITAL LETTERS, and Sage had told her that it was RUDE to do that in a text or the old-fashioned emails that Poppy sent to his students, and Esther didn't CARE and she fumbled for the hammer and grabbed it by the handle.

The panel wasn't quite in the striking range for bringing the heavy tool over her head, too low, but she moved to the left as far as she could and gave it a try with her right-hand sort of "sidearm," as Jo-Jo would say.

It was no home run, hardy-har, but it wasn't a strikeout. Even though Esther didn't have nearly the power from this position, the panel was definitely friendlier, no shocks or vibrations as it *boinged* the hammer away as if made of rubber. She scrunched down, lying sideways, all on one hip, face parallel with the panel as far as she could tell in the dark, and she tried doing it again with both hands this time, from over her head sort of—

Boing!

The door panel did its trampoline-rebounding effect again, and the flat back of the mallet popped Esther in the forehead.

"Oh!" she cried, dropping the hammer, jerking to a sitting position, hands to the face. "Sugar pops!" she screamed into her palms. "Shitake mushrooms! Gosh darn, son of an ever-loving corn-shucking biscuit!"

WOW, did it hurt! It made her head ring like the Liberty Bell, and that old thing had a CRACK in it! Then Esther smiled ruefully.

At least it's an excuse to use Sage's makeup!

That made Esther pause, and she tried to snag the idea floating right there in the dark just out of reach it seemed. Sage equaled makeup, and makeup came in a kit. You used different brushes for different...what did Sage call them? Applications, yes! And if the makeup kit had different tools for different jobs, brushes, eyebrow pencils, powder puffs, then so did the tool case here in the closet! Esther reached far right where she'd left the tub of art supplies. She fumbled around, fingers tracing themselves over a variety of short steel chisels, and finally she found one with a pointy end instead of a flat one.

Now the key was to be able to use the hammer and chisel in the dark. Suddenly, Esther pictured *just* missing by a fraction and hitting the bone in her thumb or scraping hard and rough down her knuckles.

Scaredy-cat!

She backed again to the left, got to her knees, and felt around to find the middle of the low panel. She put the tip of the sharp chisel-point against the wood, leaned in, and tapped ever so lightly the tiny flat end cap. There was give in the wood, just a tad, she felt it.

She pulled the hammer back a bit more, maybe three inches, and she tapped it across. There was a satisfying sound to it and she swore she'd felt the chisel-point embed itself a bit more. She was in the wood now, and she slowly, so slowly, drew back about a foot. It seemed like forever that she remained suspended there, aiming in her head, thinking it, being it, and she brought the hammer across to a hearty clap, bullseye! More give! Progress! Patiently, Esther repeated the twelve-inch hammer-slammer once, twice, and again, hitting her thumb only once and not all that badly.

On stroke number five, the chisel-point punched through the door, and when Esther pulled it out, a sliver of light beamed in across the darkness of the closet. Now Esther could see what she was doing, at least better than a second ago, and she repositioned the point a few inches from the hole she'd made and gave it a whack on the end cap.

Score! Soon there were two slivers of light, then three and then four, all making a rough square the size of a peanut butter sandwich. She pulled out the chisel-point and sat Indian-style all the way to the left, going two-handed on the hammer, using her shoulders and hips, and bashed at the panel between the four points of light, hearing it splinter, and the hammerhead banged all the way through the wood. Light poured in around it like sweet lemonade, and Esther worked the hammer free and then went on a rampage, banging, breaking, thudding, and smacking, and the panel became a jagged hole. She thought she'd heard an echo, but it was no echo, as there were hard heavy footsteps coming up the stairs. Hall. Closer. Inside the room, and Esther felt the wrathful presence on the other side of the door like static electricity.

There was a dull *thwack!* and the baseball bat made a hard *bonk-bonk* noise as if it was sent cartwheeling across the carpeted floor, giving a thick *ping* and a *bang!* when it met Sage's writing desk by the window. The closet door whipped open, colder air flooded in, and it was too bright. Esther squinted upwards with her hands around her eyes the way you looked out a window close up when there was glare on it.

She'd been expecting Jody, of course.

Surprise, it was Poppy. He was a dark giant towering above her in silhouette.

"Do not look at me," he said softly. Esther glanced down immediately. This was serious. He only used that tone when she was to be punished. Severely.

"You have been making quite a ruckus," he continued. "The neighbors might hear you and that will not do. I said, do not *look* at me!"

Esther shrieked, looked down at her hands, and started to moan.

"Shut up," Poppy said.

Esther almost gave the auto-reply, "No shut-ups!" but that was Poppy's saying, and when adults broke their own rules, especially the rules that made you more polite and ladylike, you did what they said. To the letter.

"Where is Sage?" he said.

Esther shrugged. "I dunno," she murmured. You'll have to ask Jody."

"She locked you in this closet?"

"I was in here already."

"Why?"

Esther shrugged again, and made the face with the boo-boo lip. "You'll be mad."

"I'm already mad. Why were you in Sage's closet?"

Esther opened and shut her mouth three times. The words just didn't want to come out.

"I—" she croaked. "It wasn't my fault...the Royal Silk Man said to. He predicted everything. He talked to me in my closet and here. He made me do it!"

"What else did he tell you?"

His voice was still totally soft, even quieter than before, but the edges were more razor-like. Esther kept her eyes down and let everything gush out all at once.

"He said I had to hate Sage and I had to trick Jody and go visit you in the shed because you were eating and it would make me a big girl. But then his voice stopped like a wack-a-doo radio or turning off the TV and then Jody locked me in here and I peed myself."

"He wanted for you to see me in the shed, huh?" he said, tone different now, almost as if he was talking to himself. "See me in the shed to shock you, terrify you, damage you, make you shattered and broken and loyal."

"Huh?"

"Don't look at me. How did you get that bruise on your head? The bump."

"I hit myself with the hammer."

"Don't lie. It was Jody. She will pay."

"No!" Esther cried. "No! She'll punch me and when she does it in my stomach it hurts me for days!"

"Keep your glance down. Keep it there. She will pay."

"Please, Poppy!"

"Quiet. And listen. Things have changed. Your 'Royal Silk Man' was talking to me too, and then he got cut off. If you hear from him again, you will tell Jody immediately and have her come to see me in the shed. You are not to leave this house. You are not to go anywhere near that shed, understand? You will walk across the hallway into the shower, clean up, re-dress in something comfortable, and stay—in—your—room. Clear?"

Esther was scared to ask, but she couldn't help herself.

"Is Mr. Royal Silk a good guy or a bad guy, Poppy?"

Her father didn't respond for a long moment.

"Both," he said carefully. "For now, however, he is our friend and the police are the enemy. That is why I came up here. I could hear you banging that mallet all the way in the back yard. I thought I heard you yelling and pounding with your fists beforehand, but I couldn't be sure and I was busy. The business I am tending to in the shed must not be interrupted again. If someone comes to the front door downstairs, you ignore it. Pretend you are asleep and didn't hear it. Have I made myself clear?"

"Yes, Poppy."

"Don't lie to me ever again."

"Yes, Poppy."

"The minute you hear from Sage, tell Jody, and she will let me know in the shed."

"Yes, Poppy."

"And again, if the Royal Man gets back his...wavelength, you tell Jody that too so she can tell me."

"Okay, Poppy, yes."

"Take a shower. Change your clothes."

He moved out of the doorway, flooding the closet with light. Again, it hurt her eyes, but she'd gotten a quick glance of her father just before he'd turned to make his way to the hall and the stairs.

His eyes were sunken and lifeless.

And there were layers and layers of blood in his beard.

CHAPTER 18

Welcome to Prime Time, Bitch

S age took a shortcut that became a longcut, bringing her right back into the heat of it.

Of course, the quicker path would have been straight back down New Ardmore Avenue, left on Haverford all the way to Penn Wynne Elementary, then a quick "right-left-right" as they said in the Army. Still, Sage wanted to keep off the main roads, so in a rough diagonal she cut back across County Line Ave and moved through the small "nook and cranny" neighborhoods common to Lower Merion Township between its main arteries. At one point she crossed the lawn of a Baptist church she had never seen before, and then she hurried through a small cemetery spattered with dark, weathered headstones. When she climbed over the stone wall at the far end and crossed through a couple of properties without fences, she wound up at the back edge of South Ardmore Park, with its four baseball fields, basketball courts, and walking paths between decorator trees.

She didn't recognize it at first, because she usually entered off Argyle Road on the other side. This was the back corner with the dirt infield and mesh batting cages of Field B. It was the place where Jody was supposed to fight earlier today, and there was a police car parked on the grass in right field foul territory, most probably where the crowd had recently gathered to see Larry Fraley and Antony Combs have their "pushy-pushy."

Sage hid behind a tree and allowed herself to lean ever so slightly so she could just see a sliver from around the wide trunk. The cruiser was about ninety feet north of third base, facing away mostly, yet angled so she could see the shadowy form in the passenger seat: broad lines, big shoulders, and the militaristic shape of his police cap. He was talking. Sage could hear him. And this was amazing because it was the shadowy glare on the closed window that made him look like a sketched illustration in an old-fashioned detective novel. Was the driver's side window open? Wouldn't matter. His voice was right near Sage's ear like a lover whispering sweet nothings. It was too personal, too up-close, and Sage instinctively crossed her forearms in front of her womb. Then it hit her.

The baby. Though no more than a couple of cells at this point, her precious child was actively bonding with two parasitic nanobots and becoming a transmitter. Could The Sculptor hear this conversation as well? Was he tapped in? Did he know she was here, hiding from the cops behind a tree, or was she still in the safe zone?

Of course she was. This was the first communication between Sage and her baby, her super-child. It was private, between them, it had to be!

Suddenly Sage stopped gushing to herself and brought the knuckles of her hand up to her lips. The cop was starting to talk about relevant shit. Personal shit. Personal to Sage.

"There's no way," he said, "that the chief would just go and off himself, and we owe it to him to go get this guy. Or 'gal.' Want your Starbucks?"

Sage saw that the one in her sightline in the passenger seat had moved forward slightly while talking, as if reaching for something.

"No, thank you kindly," said the other voice, thinner, less intense, and more measured. "You have it." That one was clearly the driver, as the gesture of the former seemed to be aimed for the top of the dash where the extra cup probably was. "Thanks," he said, settling back in perfect rhythm with the words, and immediately the dramatist in Sage gave them nicknames. The coffee drinker on the passenger side was "Officer Hamlet," looking for revenge for his father figure, and the driver was "Norman Bates," trying to keep his voice smooth while checking in Marion Crane.

"You're jumping to conclusions without real evidence," Norman continued.

"You didn't know the chief very well," Hamlet answered. "I did. I was there when he took on Robinson, figured him out, and ended him."

"Inaccurate," Norman said. "No one knows who caused the explosion at the forge, but it was either Robinson himself, Erika Shoemaker, or the tenth-grade psychopath Meagan Mullin. All were killed. I read the reports. I didn't have to know the chief like a pal at the watering hole."

Hamlet turned to look out the window, his face an unintelligible smear of glare, flesh, and shadow.

"You just offered a mouthful," he said. "And the answer's right here under our noses."

"Are you claiming one of them survived the blast?"

Hamlet turned back toward him.

"Not necessarily," he said. "I think something's going on with another teen girl in the mix, possibly a psychopath as Meagan Mullin had been. One who leaves footprints and goes taking trophies."

"Now hold on there, boss," said Norman. "I know the size seven prints are telling and incriminating, but use your common sense. Tell me, what on earth would a teenage girl want with Chief Canfield's eyes?"

"It's all in the writing."

"What writing?"

"The manifesto."

Norman laughed. "I may be new to the station and all that noise, but I'm familiar with Michael Leonard Robinson and his clever scenarios. I read the manifesto back at Eureka Springs."

"Oklahoma, was it?"

"Arkansas, Fifth Precinct. And I read the thing multiple times, we all did. The case became a conversation piece, like a game of *Clue* where you proposed alternate endings, speculated in the gray areas, and next tried to figure out how he pulled off each piece of theater. Caused some prickly debates, to be honest, but the thing we all agreed on for sure was that the manifesto was an exceptional load of horseshit, written by Meagan Mullin's mother, Professor Becky Mullin, as was reported, under the pretext that she was penning a fictional journal entry in the voice of a real-life uncaptured criminal. Robinson manipulated her into authoring this abomination that became its own legend. It has been reprinted as a short story, published in a ton of periodicals as a true confession, and regurgitated over and again by those actually adding falsehoods and subtracting facts for the simple thrill of twisting the narrative."

"I know that."

"Then you see that Robinson still taunts us all from the grave. That manifesto was crafted purposefully to sound so much like truth that it would become one, or a bunch of truths more accurately. Nowadays, the average citizen can't decide who the killer actually was. Get a hundred people in a room and ask them who murdered those girls impaled on poles on highway construction sites, and your odd twenty will swear it was Professor Becky Mullin making an actual confession *meant* to be taken as a fake. Twenty will swear it was her lunatic teenage daughter Meagan who also killed a police detective. Twenty will blame Meagan's brother Connor, as he was found dead in the eighteen-wheeler used as 'The Sculptor's' rolling lab, and twenty will blame Canfield or his dead receptionist Erika Shoemaker. Then the leftover twenty settle on Robinson or some other story thread trending on Facebook."

"I concede all that," Hamlet said, "but you're missing the point."

"What point?"

"The fact that you read a different version of the manifesto than I did. If that wasn't the case, you'd see the glaring implication like a rat on a wedding cake."

Norman laughed thinly. "If so, different precincts in different states have different depictions of what's supposed to be pristine case-evidence. It means Robinson managed to manipulate the data behind the blue line."

"Agreed," Hamlet said. "And trust me, this is cut and dried. As basic as a lady's sneaker size seven."

"A small woman."

"Or teenage girl."

"Paying some kind of random homage to her dead hero?"

"Negative," Hamlet said. "Like I said…a rat on a wedding cake, anything but random. In the version I read, the killer ate the eyes of the victims."

"Oh," said Norman. "Fancy that."

There was a silence in the police car, and Sage herself was struck numb. She couldn't remember ever reading or hearing the manifesto in full all at once, but the scattered pieces she *had* gotten wind of never said anything about eating eyeballs. She felt as if she'd been hit by a truck. Hamlet gave voice to this new fear immediately.

"You see it, right?" he said. "A country in the middle of a swirl of doubt and misinformation, and the youth caught up in the cyclone, looking for answers, for something to hold onto. To be noticed. That sneaker print came from a teen girl looking to make a mark, and she picked up right where Robinson left off. She found The Sculptor's arch-nemesis, got rid of him, and put herself through ritualistic initiation by eating his eyes. Self-inflicted baptism. We have a copycat here, and unless some dude found a way to fit into a girl's size seven, we just have to pull a Cinderella and find the darling who fits the glass slipper."

"And pump her stomach if we find her soon enough."

"Damn straight."

"But our perp didn't remove the head and sew it back on."

"Of course not. She didn't impale him on a flagpole either."

There was a momentary silence.

"But you really think some teen," Norman said, "some *kid* actually ate the chief's eyes? The manifesto is fake, so we have no way of knowing if Robinson did the actual dirty work." He paused. "I just can't picture some teenage girl making herself do it. The mechanics. The actual…swallowing."

There was a burst of static and a voice sounding tinny and official said,

"Five Charlie Niner."

"Copy," said Norman. "How are you, Melinda?"

"Just came on shift. How 'bout you?"

"Even-Steven. State your business."

"Check. We have a call concerning a missing boy, Vincent Gatto, age sixteen. His mother, Mia Gatto, thinks there is reason to suspect that a classmate named…Sage Winslow might know his whereabouts. She lives with two sisters and a widowed father at 389 Trent Road in Wynnewood. She has hair an inch or two less than shoulder length dyed-pink, you can't miss her."

"10-34 Emergency!" Norman barked back at her. "Under the requirements of order 197-46432, we are required to have secured South Ardmore Park and cleared it of stragglers. There are twenty-seven minutes left on that work order, and we request an immediate replacement, over."

"Noted," said dispatch. "I can have another unit there in approximately eleven minutes. Hold until then."

"Out."

And Sage was already running. Away from the cruiser. Home. Desperately.

For the name "Winslow," no duh, had been on one of the precinct's early morning work-orders, over at Latchkey a block from their house where Spaghetti Harry had been discovered dead in the kitchen. Damn, for all she knew, Hamlet and Norman Bates could have been the ones who questioned her father and sister!

Sage had to beat them to the house.

To stop Poppy, Esther, and Jo-Jo.

From answering the door.

From welcoming in the police and unknowingly forfeiting samples of Sage Winslow's footwear.

CHAPTER 19

Oh, No Tears Please.
It's a Waste of Good Suffering

E
sther had finally stopped crying in the shower. When drying off, her face tingled and her eyes felt raw. Now her damp
hair was hanging in loose strands in front of her face, and
she was back to digging inside Sage's closet.

Oh, she would have rather been doing something else, for sure.
She wanted to see what Poppy was doing.

She wasn't allowed.

She wanted to hide from Jody.

She wasn't allowed.

She wanted to scream, to bang things, to scratch her own face.

But she wasn't allowed to do *anything!*

And that last one fascinated her, the hunger for gouging herself.
It literally felt as if her head was going to burst with thoughts, and
she craved the relief of letting some of that go. She wanted to yell at
somebody, but no one was near. She wanted to *squeeze* something in
her fingers, but she didn't have a stress doll. There were no pieces of
bubble wrap to pop, no Styrofoam to push crescent moons into, and

she could almost *feel* how satisfying it would be to dig her nails hard into the soft meat of her cheeks.

She had heard about teen girls cutting themselves, and she'd always thought that was so *stupid!* Not anymore. Not since getting down Sage's sewing kit just now and finding the sleek silver needle that would cut even more effectively than her own fingernails, well, sort of at least.

She had stared at the small implement, so thin and beautiful and deadly. It was like a miniature sword in some old-school French swashbuckler like *The Three Musketeers,* the Disney version, thank you, and it wasn't the sword she would wear outside on her belt as the fourth Musketeer. It was the secret one she would bury somewhere in her clothing, the dangerous treasure so small and thin it was more like a stabbing dagger. It was her secret weapon. Her last resort if things went downhill, and it would be hidden in her sock, tucked under an elbow patch, or even sewn inside the hem of her cape.

She had not brought the needle to her face. She had not even experimented with the flesh of tougher fiber, like the back of a heel or the calloused skin at the corner point of her big toenail.

Instead, she'd rummaged through Sage's artsy-fartsy stuff looking for thread. She found a spool of gray, one of white, and one that was black.

Back to the "rummage sale," ha!

She dragged over the desk chair, set it at the edge of the closet, climbed up, and got on her tippy-toes. Back behind a bookbag with a broken strap she found an old throw pillow shaped like an elephant that Sage had discarded years ago. Esther tossed it back in the middle of the floor in the general vicinity of the pincushion shaped like a tomato with the needle in it and the small spools of thread. She stepped down carefully, leaned in, and raked through some of the plastic tubs on the second shelf. Finally she found a drawer with buttons, safety pins, doo-dads, and ribbons. She scooped out a big handful, padded back to the middle of the floor, and squatted by the sewing stuff, making a nice little pile with the accessories in the vague shape of an anthill.

Back to it.

She needed one more ingredient. Something stickie-wickie, like leather or rawhide.

Esther smiled and she felt that she looked evil doing it. Leather or rawhide...Puhhhlease. Jo-Jo absolutely lived in rawhide, smothering herself in it like a pig in mud, with baseballs and infielder's mitts and outfielder's mitts and first base and catcher's mitts.

And, of course, batting gloves.

Esther knew Jody was a bit of a slob and also a hoarder. She still kept tee ball and Little League jerseys from way back in the wicker basket in front of her bed. And tons of batting gloves, some so old, wrinkled, weathered, and small, even Esther would have trouble fitting in her fingers.

But she didn't need to fit them. She just needed to get her hands on a sharp pair of scissors. To carve open the elephant throw pillow for the stuffing, and to cut up a couple of pairs of batting gloves, saving the palm parts.

For the paw pads, of course.

And for the inside of course, to make friction.

So that Esther could have satisfaction.

So that Esther could make herself a new stress doll.

CHAPTER 20

I Know You're There
Because I Can Smell Your Brains

S age came through the front yard, going tree to tree until she was parallel to the sun room on the side of the house. The window screen second-in from the rear had a broken lock. Sage was pretty sure she was the only one who knew about it. She'd used it to sneak out multiple times, a couple of them to see Vinny Gatto, and even though it technically left the family at risk, she'd always felt that the feeling of security was mostly a fallacy anyway. A penknife or a sharp scissor, even in the hand of a child, could cut through a screen faster than a seasoned criminal pulling on each to see if one would slide open.

Did Esther know about it?

No. She disliked the sun room. She said it smelled "rusty."

And Jo-Jo?

Doubtful. Her domain was the basement and her bedroom. She only came out to the sun room to get the bicycle pump or a mini umbrella or a pair of old snow-shoveling gloves in the odds-and-ends box Poppy kept in the corner under the clipper ship painting.

Sage walked across the grass, stopped, took a deep breath, and ran her finger along the screen, second to the back. It had the remnants of a spiderweb in it, mid-top left, and it made Sage consider the ironic sort of hypocrisies kids lived by, many preferring the woods to the rec room, the dingy cellar to the den, and the garage to the studio, almost as if teens wanted the shit no one else did, a hand-me-down existence in the metaphorical sewers and junkyards of the world just to be left alone in a space to call theirs.

Absolute hypocrites.

Jody insisted on washing her hands after touching a doorknob or a curtain, but she had no problem warming up a pitcher, dusting off home plate, and licking her fingers for a tackier grip. Esther sometimes liked hanging out under her bed more than on top of it, and Sage hated spiders with a passion. She reached up and ran her index finger over the dull gray remnants of this web spun from the loins of some disgusting little monster. It wasn't sticky, almost as if morphing with the screen material, and it was clearly a home long abandoned.

It didn't disgust her.

Because the screen was hers, warts, webs, and all.

She took hold of the edge of the frame and slowly slid it across. It made noise, but not that much. From over her shoulder a moth flew in. Not her fault, couldn't be helped. She put her hands on the ledge and stood ready to press herself up to wrangle into the usual sitting position, one foot in and one out.

She hesitated for a moment, on the brink of two worlds, both potentially lethal. Once she broke that plane she'd find out, and probably quickly, whether or not the thin, double insulation she had going on with the bots in her belly let The Sculptor suddenly discover her, scare her, manipulate her, kill her. All would be lost, like being exposed to the Eye of Mordor in *The Lord of the Rings*.

She hauled herself up and got one leg over. As always, the rail she was straddled across was uncomfortable on the tailbone, almost painful. She hadn't committed her shoulders and head yet, she just couldn't. What if the maniac suddenly "saw" her and somehow made the screen frame start coming closed, trapping her crotch to forehead like something out of the *Final Destination* movies? What if he made the roof gutter come swinging down to bash her in the face, made a tree fall on her, sent a meteor from outer space to demolish the house and turn her to jelly and bone splinters?

She just couldn't do it. The risk was too high. There had to be another way.

A car was coming down the street, she could hear it, coming from her blind side. Maybe whoever it was would not notice her in passing. No such luck. It wasn't passing anything. It was slowing, and Sage recognized the chock 'n' gravel sound of tires pulling in and coming to rest in the family driveway.

Now or never. It was the cop car. She'd beaten them here, barely.

Sage pushed in through the opening.

CHAPTER 21

We All Become God's Madmen

E sther was laughing out loud at herself like a mental patient, sweat running down the sides of her neck from under her ears, fingers working the needle and thread the way Sage had taught her to take her mind off her mother's death months ago, clumsy and bumbling, bumbling and stumbling. She'd snapped the thread twice, the black one, and rethreading the needle had been torture. It was all so...tiny, as if made for people half a foot tall with fingers twice as long and as strong. She was climbing and rhyming, trying and crying.

Her eyes kept tearing, her nose running.

And she was laughing a lot. At herself. At her "creation." Sage had told her long ago that quick writing was lazy writing, that fast drawing was sloppy drawing, that every stage of the artistic process was to be treated with love.

Esther wasn't feeling the love here. She was working fast and haphazardly with a procedure that certainly required tenderness and care, but it was the lack of care that made the creation better than she had imagined. Far better.

Footsteps. Up the stairs, quick and hectic.

Esther's heart knocked in her chest.

The door burst open and banged the adjoining wall with a *clap!* Esther dropped the needle and held tight her "art project" up under her throat. Her eyes were wide like saucers.

Jody's were wider.

"You little shit," she said. Her eye black had run, making her look like a weeping circus psycho, and there was a mark on her left cheek like a wide swath of rouge. "Now, you listen," she said, "and you listen to me good. When this is all over, I am going to pay you back like you've never been. You'll lay in bed curled up for a week."

"No!" Esther spouted. "I told him I hurt my own self. You've got to believe me!"

Jody came closer and leaned over, hands on her knees, face darkened in shadow.

"No dice, midget. You're going to own this one. And don't waste your crocodile tears. There will be enough of those to go around when I give you what's coming."

She stopped and seemed to really look at Esther for the first time.

"What the heck is that thing?"

"What thing?" said Esther, pouting.

Jody pointed. "That," she said. "What is it, a teddy bear?"

"It's a stress doll."

"A what?"

"A stress doll!" Esther's eyes were slits, her smile clownish. "I made it myself and it's mine!"

Her sister straightened, and Esther looked at the floor.

"That," Jody said, "is the ugliest, sorriest teddy I have ever seen."

"It's mine!"

"You can have it," she said. "Maybe if Poppy ever takes me and Sage somewhere, you can frighten the babysitter with it."

"May. BE!" she said. "I love him!"

"You would," Jody said. "His mouth is a zigzag of scarecrow horror-stitching, his paws have pads cut in crazy, uneven star-shapes, and his left side button-eye is loose, making him zombified. Most of the stuffing is crammed up into his top half too. Look at his legs dangling."

"I like'um dangling."

Jody laughed dryly. "Well, you're going to need it for comfort, sweet Peanut, stuffing or not, that's for damned sure."

She clearly wasn't bluffing.

When she turned back for the door and came out of the shadows, Esther saw it again, branded there on her cheek. The angry red hand print. Esther knew it all too well. She'd offered her hand up into that bigger hand thousands of times, millions. Her father had always had such a tender warm touch, taking her hand in his, feeling to Esther as if she was being escorted by a gentle king into a cloud to eat marshmallows.

It seemed that those long, loving Poppy-fingers were capable of other flavors now.

It seemed that Esther had done a good job making the pieces she'd cut from the batting gloves look as if they didn't come from old batting gloves too, so there.

She bent back over her teddy doll and kept working. He was coming along, but he wasn't done yet. And it seemed time was of the essence.

Getting shorter by the minute.

CHAPTER 22

They're Here

S age pushed herself into the sun room. There wasn't all too much distance from ledge to floor, so her landing was relatively soft, especially since she was barefoot. She turned to slide closed the screen window, and there was a voice in her ear, sudden and close, the way your own voice sounded to you when you spoke. Sage almost screamed.

It wasn't Hamlet. Nor, was it Norman.

It was him.

Michael Leonard Robinson. The Sculptor. Talking, and not to her, obviously. Oh, it was him, no doubt about it. Though it sounded far different from his Vinny Gatto impersonation, and not quite like the poisonous teasing that had followed it, there was no mistaking the tone of true evil. The thing that terrified her was how intelligent and striking were the word choices, the rhythms, the diction. It was darkly poetic, but a far cry from poetry. It was not emotionless, but it seemed controlled with a mechanistic precision, not angry, but filled with contempt and cruel glee.

"We re-establish convective symmetry soon with clarity," the voice said. "Note: connectivity that was broadband will now be location-specific, and Subject B must secure the on-campus workstation and hold position. Subject A is lost, and so are his treasures. While his hoard was platinum, we adopt Murphy's disfigured stepchild and settle for copper. There will be a delay of approximately fifteen minutes before illusory projections can return, and those that do will be limited to the campus workstation itself. No one leaves the property."

Sage actually understood much of this. It was less dark rhapsody than it was elevated trickster's code, fancy Trumpian speech that would find loopholes in court. Truth was, Robinson had been in the dark since Chief Canfield pulled the trigger. Sage had double-layered his bots, and that had shut down the circus. But Canfield wasn't the only one infected with parasitic A.I. This "Subject B" was Robinson's second-best soldier. With inferior equipment. Chief Canfield had had the ability to be mobile, but the "new guy" had to be on campus at the "work station" to allow for The Sculptor to craft his illusions again.

And in a kind of cold dread, Sage didn't think Robinson had been just notating-to-self. He'd been speaking directly to Subject B, who was approaching the "campus work station" presently. Sage bit her bottom lip. The Sculptor's new transmitter was almost to their doorstep. The only question was whether it was Hamlet or Norman Bates.

Sage tried not to hyperventilate. Easy, blue lakes, clear skies, rose petals, breathe. At least The Sculptor didn't know she was listening; in fact, for now she had the upper hand. She was malware in the circuitry, a spy lurking in the nearest black shadow.

Was the cop with the B-level bots the reason she'd been able to hear both of them in the police car, like signals bouncing between receptors? Or was it as she first thought, a bonus from her precious unborn? Would The Sculptor hear her if she spoke now? Would he hear noises around her? How about when "Subject B" came in off the stoop and she and he shared the same building? Would she trigger all the alarms, sirens, and sensors?

She closed the window as quietly as she could, padded over to the loveseat, and went down to her haunches in front of it. The doorbell rang, terror feathered her spine. Only an archway separated the sun room from the living room, and only the cushy sectional and round nesting coffee tables stood between that and the door. The acoustics would be good, A.I. or not.

The bell rang again.

There was an ominous silence followed by steps running from the kitchen across the hardwood floor of the living room. Bad news. Poppy had said not to answer the door, so either things had changed drastically or this was rebellion. The door opened. In her head, The Sculptor said,

"Assess. Gain trust. Use gentle humor."

Ha. Now Sage would know which cop was the puppet, but hey, then again, did it matter? It was six of one, half a dozen whatever. To one of them she was a copycat villain and to the other, a victim, a target, a tool.

"Hello. Yes?" Jody said.

There was the ghost of a laugh from Hamlet. "You having a costume party? You look like—"

"Alice Cooper," Norman finished.

Typical, Sage thought. So much for being able to peg my two evils.

"Who?" Jody said.

"Alice Cooper," Hamlet replied. "The old metal music rocker who did magic horror stuff with a top hat and cane." Jody didn't respond.

"The school's out song," Norman said.

"Oh, that guy," Jody said. "Sure. Yes. I was playing dress-up."

"Where's your father?" said Hamlet.

"Out."

"Where?"

"The hardware store."

"Why?"

"Broken closet door. In my big sister's bedroom. You'll have to come back later."

"What's your name?" Norman said.

"Jody."

"What's that mark on your face? Did someone slap you? Hit you?"

"It's makeup. Like I said. Playing dress-up."

"Can we come in?"

"No."

"Is your sister Sage here?"

"No."

"Young lady, it is in your best interests to let us come in," Hamlet said. "Now. Old faded rock stars aside, this isn't a game. We just have a few questions. Your sister might be in trouble, and we want to help find her, that's all."

There was a shuffling of feet on the floor of the foyer and then the door closed.

"Scour the premises," said The Sculptor. "If she's there, you go find her."

"First," Hamlet said, "we'd like to have a look around. You can come with us. We won't touch anything. We could start at the busted closet. We're both good at home repairs, and we might have some good advice for your father."

Sage pushed up to a standing position. This just could not happen. She could not let them get to her shoes, not this easily.

But what could she do?

She had no fucking clue. But she couldn't just hide here while her world fell apart. She walked toward the archway, praying she could avoid any groans or a creaks from the floorboards. She got to the edge of the jamb, and as she'd been doing all afternoon it seemed, she crept her head forward and gave a "one-eye" just past it.

The cops were both big men: the probable Hamlet, the one front-running the conversation and towering over Jody, and the probable Norman, half abreast and half behind him on the far side. He was taking notes in a black book. Hamlet had the brim of his hat so low it almost covered his eyes, and his hands were resting on his belt like a sheriff in a spaghetti western.

"So lead the way," he said. "Show us the closet."

"I don't want to," Jody said. "And you need a warrant, don't you?"

The cops looked at each other briefly.

"No, miss," Norman said. "Actually, we don't. This isn't *Cold Case* or *NCIS*. Technically, we are in pursuit of someone who might have committed a felony, so you can accompany us or stand aside. Either way, we are going upstairs."

The back door banged open, and Sage heard her father mutter something that sounded like "Something flickered..." His voice died off. Hamlet's right hand went to his hip holster and he cocked his head, looking through to the rear of the house.

"Professor Winslow?" he said. "Come in out of the kitchen, please. We have some questions...Hey, is that blood on your shirt?"

"Kill him," The Sculptor said. Sage almost screamed. Norman dropped his black book and there was the sound of ripping Velcro. He slid all the way behind Hamlet, put his left hand on the bigger man's shoulder, and made a jerking motion as if he'd just gone up on his toes.

Hamlet snapped his head up, seeming to look for an airplane, and his hat tumbled off his head. He was smiling, ear to ear, so animated that it looked as if he was being sarcastic. His knees gave, and he fell to the floor, exposing Norman behind him, hunched slightly, holding in his fist the long thin blade he'd underhanded into the back of his partner; Sage could see red streaked on silver. Norman slipped the weapon back into its long pouch along the right outer thigh. Jody had backed off and fallen on her bum. Norman ignored her for the moment and looked through to the kitchen.

"I'm the home team, Professor," he said. "Go back to the toolshed. You still have work that needs to be done."

Poppy was out of Sage's sightline, but it wasn't lost on her how defeated he sounded.

"I found it suddenly difficult to…continue," he said. "Then, well, it was like the power coming on again."

"Right," Norman said. "The technical difficulties are solved now, as long as I remain on the premises. Go."

"What took you so long?"

Norman remained expressionless. "Appearances," he said. "They must be upheld. And I was not in the original plan."

"So you're the emergency crew."

"More like a backup generator. Now return to your station and finish what you started. Jody will stay with me in here, and then when you're ready we will bring you your second customer. Workload just doubled, Professor. Go on now, move."

"Good," The Sculptor said. "Radio the station and turn the search for Sage Winslow over to Reynolds and Hanrahan."

Norman probably acknowledged this, but Sage didn't hear him. She was already halfway through the opened screen window frame, on the ledge with one leg in and one out. There was a mystery that needed to be solved. Pronto.

Out back.

In the toolshed.

CHAPTER 23

No More Dead Bodies for Daddy Tonight

S age thought she would hit the ground running. She thought she would hurry into the back yard, approach the toolshed, and rip open the door, simple.

Not so.

There was something going on back here that would be difficult to look at, something hard to take: of that she was sure. What exactly *had* Norman meant when he'd spoken of second customers and the workload doubling? The second customer was one very dead police officer. Was there another? And why was the "backup generator" talking to her father as if a partner in crime? What team was Poppy playing for? And what of the blood on his shirt they'd spoken of? Did he have a bloody nose? Had he cut himself? Had he been fighting? Was he OK?

She passed the back corner of the house and realized she was walking on her toes, as if barefoot in the grass wasn't quiet to begin with. She moved past the birdbath in the small rock garden with the hostas around it, and made her way over to the walkway with the pavers that had all settled unevenly, leaving gaps that weeds had grown through. Poppy still mowed the lawn every other week in the warmer seasons, but he hadn't broken out the weed-whacker since Mom died. He hadn't fixed the toolshed either. Or bulldozed it. He'd left the ugly thing to rot with its missing roof shingles and the hole in the gray panel, down low to the right of the barn doors. There was a bag of mulch stuffed through it, and the whole structure leaned as if ready to fall like a house of cards. The slower she crept, the more frightened she became, and the more frightened she became, the more she wanted to turn and run away as fast as she could.

But where to? The police? They were looking for her already, for all the wrong reasons, following narratives connecting eaten eyes, copycat murderers, and size seven sneakers, no thank you, I'll pass. She stood a few feet from the toolshed and made to take a step forward. Her father's voice from inside made her stop.

"I can't do it," he said. "It's physiologically impossible."

"Well, you must try," said The Sculptor. "It's your house and your mess, so keep cleaning."

Sage heard the psycho's voice as her father heard it, not inside her head as when she'd been enclosed in the sun room, but it didn't matter. His tone was soft and it was awful, like stepping in dogshit without shoes or socks.

"I'm telling you," Poppy said, "this is a two-man job, three maybe, especially considering the…product. It was a stretch before your good-cop-bad-cop scenario, and now it just doesn't make sense. Be reasonable."

Sage let her hand drift down to hang at her side, mouth slightly ajar. As it had seemed during his short conversation with Norman, it didn't sound as if her father was bargaining with an enemy here. It sounded as if he was hacking out an agreement with a coconspirator.

Didn't Canfield say that he could not recall setting up cameras in their house? If not the chief, then who had the access?

Sage put her hands on her hips and shook her head "no" good and hard.

Her father just *could not* be working with The Sculptor...knowing and approving of the fact that a cop had been killed in his living room. Could he? Did she have this right? Of course she did, just stop the denial. Copycat, hell! What if Poppy was somehow the protégé, meant to learn the trade from the inside and carry on the tradition?

"Reasonable has left the building," The Sculptor said. "You helped cause it too. We reap what we sow, Professor. You don't get to slap on a failing grade and then hide all holiday behind your email auto responses."

"I need more manpower," Poppy said. "Reap what I sow, sure. How about letting me use my resources?"

"What resources?"

"My daughters."

Sage gasped. She hoped it hadn't been all that loud. She didn't know the whole story, surely, but Poppy was selling them all up the river. Would he? Could he?

"They're good girls," he continued. "They'll do what their Poppy tells them to do."

"They don't have the belly for it."

"You've got pills," Poppy said. "Manufacture three more. Let me make this a family affair, stronger together, you know the drill."

Sage's hands had floated up to her mouth like a scream-queen, and she started backing up, sickened, scared shitless, confused. She had to have this wrong. The answers were inside the shed. Clear answers. Truth.

She just couldn't do it. She had to run. She just had no idea where to go.

She turned and almost screamed, almost bumping into Esther, who'd somehow sneaked up behind her. The kid had her thumb in her mouth and was holding a demented teddy bear by the dangling back leg. Wide-eyed, Sage took her younger sister by the shoulder, turned her, and marched her back to the side of the house. There was no basement window well cover, and she protectively guided Esther past the void to the nook made by the front corner walls and the overgrown butterfly bush. She leaned down, took her by both shoulders, and forced her to face her.

"You scared the hell out of me," she whispered. "And what's with the bear? It looks like something out of one of the *Annabelle* movies."

Esther took her thumb out of her mouth. "It's not a bear," she whispered back. "It's a stress doll."

Sage straightened. "Well, whatever it is, it's creepy as hell."

"It's beautiful!"

"Stop sucking your thumb."

"But I want to."

"What are you doing out here?"

Esther's face had that caved-in look as if she was about to burst into tears, but her expression hardened. "That cop is a fake."

"What cop?"

"The cop in the living room."

Sage folded her arms. "Did he hurt you? Did he make that bump on your forehead?"

Esther shook her head no. "Negatority," she said. "I bumped it myself. And it wasn't Jody either!"

Sage frowned. "Where is she, anyway?"

"Up in her room," Esther said. "And in the living room there's a police guy on the floor sleeping and the fake cop is there, standing there over him with his eyes closed, his mouth open, and his hands hanging at his sides."

"And he didn't see you come out here?"

"He's not seeing anything right now. But out of his open mouth I could hear Poppy talking to The Royal Silk Man. It sounded soft and far away, like a TV in another room down the hall where you hear it but can't understand the words."

"Who is The Royal Silk Man?"

Esther's expression turned in like a screw. "He's a liar," she said. "He's the man who promised me things. And he had no idea I was looking at the fake cop because he can't do two things at once. He doesn't hear background noise either."

"How do you know that?"

"He told me."

"Told you where?"

"In the church, in my closet. And yours."

"What did he say?"

Tears filled Esther's eyes. "You don't believe me."

Sage sighed. "Of course, I believe you," she said. "I just don't believe it, that's all. There's a difference."

"Well, believe what you want. Bye."

She turned and ran, catching the edge of the butterfly bush and making it weep yellow petals. Sage made to go after her, but from around the corner of the house there came a figure blocking the path.

It was Jody.

With that metal bat in her hands.

CHAPTER 24

You Just Have to Pick
the Sin You Can Live With

"Jo-Jo, we have to talk," Sage said as softly as she could, hands up, palms out to ward off a blow. But with a closer look she saw that her sister was in shock, dull and glassy-eyed. Jody lowered the baseball bat like an afterthought, and Sage took this grand opportunity to take her by the shoulder as she had done with Esther, guiding her into the front yard, farther outside hearing distance of the shed, as she thought there was a good chance this could get louder than a whisper or two. They had important things to discuss. Personal things. They got to the corner of the front yard under the big elm that had branches drooping over the fence and into their neighbor's property, the Dunkirks. It seemed Jody was about to vomit or keel over, but instead she said dully,

"You've been in the shed, have you?"

Sage hung her head for a moment. "No," she said. "I didn't have the courage."

"Best that way. Trust me."

"What's Poppy doing back there?"

Jody shrugged and puckered up as if she was going to bawl. "Nothing," she managed.

"What's that mark on your face? It's a handprint. Who hit you?"

Jody did the quickie-shrug again, and Sage bent her knees and cocked her head to try to make Jody look at her.

"All this doesn't sound like nothing," Sage said. She straightened and folded her arms. "Jo-Jo, this situation is more than fucked up, and we need to work together, all the girls, the three of us."

Jody looked up at her sister. "What can we do?" she said.

Sage sighed. The handprint looked like her father's, but it was hard to believe he'd strike one of his three precious daughters. It was also hard to believe he'd be in league with The Sculptor or one of his subordinates, so yes, maybe she couldn't trust her instincts, positive or negative. She didn't have any evidence either way, that was the issue, but that was also the game here, wasn't it? You worked off of guesses and tried not to fall prey to your emotional conjecture or whatever you'd call it.

"We'll talk about the mark later," Sage said. "For now, we have to get rid of that cop in the living room, even if it seems he's Poppy's...friend."

Jody's eyes went steely. "I'm in," she said.

"It means going against Poppy for now."

Jody rubbed her cheek. "I said I'm game."

"Have you been inside the shed?"

Jody paused. Her face twitched, the right eyebrow. "No," she said.

It seemed like the truth. It also seemed that Jody knew damn well what was happening in there, but Sage didn't push. She felt lucky as hell that the conversation had worked out the way it had.

"Well, I have a plan," Sage said. "And we had better hurry with it, because Norman—I mean, the fake cop might only be immobilized when The Sculptor is occupied, like involved in a conversation. When The Sculptor and Poppy quit talking, he might notice you and Esther are missing."

Jody tucked her hair behind her ear. "He just stands there anyway," she said. "Like one of those British palace guards."

"That said, we shouldn't risk that he might call for you."

"OK."

Sage put her hands in the pockets of her overalls. "Jo-Jo, there is something we do have to talk about. Some…one. A boy. The one I have feelings for. Deep feelings, more than—"

The back kitchen door opened.

"Jody…" It was the voice of Norman. Then in an off key "ding-dong" he crooned, "Oh, Jo—dy…I've got Esther here…in a headlock…don't want to hurt her…"

Esther's voice came out muffled. "Get *off* me!"

"Shit," Sage whispered. "Go back inside, to the living room. Stay there if he'll let you."

"What's the plan?"

Sage blinked. "No time for long explanations. I am going to cause a diversion and lure The Sculptor into a conversation. I'm going to make the fake cop go into his radio-trance."

"And then?"

"Then you bonk him on the head with your Voodoo DeMarini bat."

"You want me to kill him?"

"Jody," called Norman. "Where are you?"

"No," Sage said. "Of course not. It's the difference between a home run and a bunt. You want to bunt. Hard enough to knock him out and soft enough so his skull doesn't do the eggshell business. Can you do that?"

"Yes."

"Good. Then get going. After I'm done coaxing The Sculptor into talking, I'll come back and help you drag the fake cop out of the house. Even knocked out, he can't be left indoors, for good reason, trust me."

Jody made to leave and didn't ask for more info. Good thing. Long explanations ate up valuable moments, and Sage was glad her sister trusted her again. Jody halted.

"Sage," she said.

"Yes?"

"Sage. Don't go into the shed."

"I won't. Don't worry about me, just go!"

Jody went. Sage slipped around the wide trunk of the tree and stood behind it trying to make herself as small and thin as possible. Norman was coming, she could hear his footsteps and her youngest sister's as she was being half dragged. The front door opened and closed and he stopped.

"Back to the house," he said to Esther. "Back through the kitchen. Move, or I'll fry your fingers with the hot curling iron and hold your face to one of the stove burners. Not playing, now go."

Sage heard Esther running off and the back door banging shut. Norman was five feet away, maybe six or seven. Sage could hear him breathing. It sounded watery somehow, and monstrous.

"Hmm," he said reflectively. Then there were footsteps again, retreating back the way he had come, and in that moment Sage considered of a couple of things. First, one could hear the conversations The Sculptor was having with someone else inside the opened mouth of his transmitter Norman; yet if Esther was correct in her assessment, they would not be able to use it, to discern the words, to get information and play the advantage. And second?

Second was that Sage was no more than a coward. After all, she had Chief Canfield's Sig Sauer in her back pocket. What stopped her from simply coming out from behind this very tree and shooting the fucker right in the forehead?

The fact was, she was scared. She was scared that she'd miss, that she would get a misfire, that she wouldn't unlock the safety properly if there was one, that she would mess up the transaction like the clumsy oaf she always had been and wind up taking a bullet herself.

More so; however, she was afraid of success. Though she had every reason in the world to carry this through as an act of self-defense, she just didn't think she could bring herself to pull the damned trigger. She didn't know if she could actually kill a man, or even shoot him in the leg or the arm. It just wasn't in her DNA to do such a thing.

She was a coward, putting Jody in harm's way with lesser hardware. The only excuse Sage had for this at all was the idea that The Sculptor couldn't see her or hear her indoors or out. Using Jody or Esther as the "diversion" could very well allow The Sculptor to keep his silence, just observing, but it was clear that Sage would be a different and more special kind of a prize to him. Especially if he couldn't hear her side of the discussion. It would tempt him. Frustrate him. Maybe make him start talking.

And that brought up another big issue, as Sage had just sworn to her sister that she wouldn't go into the shed. For it officially made Sage a coward and also a liar.

She was going to find out the truth back there.

She was going to make one hell of a diversion.

Meat's Meat, and a Man's Gotta Eat

age waved away a lightning-bug dancing in front of her face and started to make her way to the back yard. It was getting dark, the time of day when the sun had fallen just below the horizon and everything was soft-toned, like watercolors. The shadows stretched long off the roof and the trees in a way that made your heart swell, and if someone had been burning leaves it would have completed the soft emotional portrait.

Sage however, felt itchy, tired, filthy from the day's events. No, fuck-tired, she was exhausted. Disgusted. Frightened. And of all the weird and grotesque scenarios of the day that added up to this moment developing in the back yard, the thing that bothered Sage the most was the angry mark on Jody's cheek. If her father had actually hit her, and that hard, there was going to be a problem. Suspicions of him had been flapping through Sage's mind today like black birds in a bell tower...odd, since when it came to Poppy, she had always been automatically forgiving. An ineffective parent she could take. A traitor—well, we all had our treasons. Sage was never quick to judge until she got the whole story, and she had a feeling that even then, there was more to things.

But violence on one of the girls? In their home? On this very property, their safe zone?

No.

Brutality was something she wasn't going to stand for. Brutality didn't have two sides or multiple facets. Brutality was dumb meanness, and whether it was psychological bullying or physical intimidation, Sage felt it was her mission to call out those who inflicted pain on others, those who typically learned the buzzwords and loopholes so they would avoid consequences, the slick fuckers.

Victims deserved better. Even the word "victim" sounded like someone tight-lipped and cringing, disappearing, becoming a non-entity. Soon they were convinced that they themselves were the ugliness, the stench left on the air, and that was the biggest sin of all.

Sage moved past the birdbath and the two yellow Adirondack chairs they never used and the giant Dutch crocuses and sunny-side-up daffodils Mother had planted alongside the detached garage a year ago so it wouldn't look so "cold and industrial."

She stood in front of the shed doors.

They were gray and weather-shadowed and they didn't sit quite flush with each other. There was hardened sediment in the creases between wallboards, and along the bottom edge there was a growth of something like algae.

There was a sound.

From inside the shed. A sound like retching. Vomiting, and it wasn't hitting the bottom of a pail. It sounded as if it splashed, like throwing up in the toilet.

Sage grabbed the handle, yanked it down, pulled open the door, and crossed over the threshold.

The smell hit her before the visual. One summer when her parents had sent her to Girl Scout Camp, there were outhouses... basically large wooden vats with holes cut in the top boards, and the absolute *funk* of them, the potent density of the rankest and foulest liquids and solids on the face of the earth, had driven Sage from the Girl Scouts, from camping in general, and any kind of outdoor festival event with community piss troughs for the guys and Porta Potties for the balance.

This was worse.

First off, the space was so close it was stifling, and the smell of blood, shit, and vomit was overpowering.

Sage pulled her shirt by the neckline up over her mouth.

On the far-right edge of a dropcloth was their utility flashlight propped on its base facing upward, tossing everything into this Halloween noir effect. Sage's first thought was that Poppy had killed a large pig, like a boar or something, and he was eating it raw. Like the frame of a barrel, the racking of ribs seemed the centerpiece, mostly gutted straight to the backbone, with strings of flesh and fiber hanging off, dripping. Her second thought was that it was a kangaroo, for the separated leg bones lay with other skeletal pieces more undeterminable at the front of the cloth, all in the rough shape of a circus clown's grin, and the femurs and splint bones were spotted with gristle and gore mostly in the joints, and they were too long for a pig, and there were no feet connected, but the hands were skinned down like claws both facing palm-up next to the jug of Clorox Germicidal Bleach holding down the front left corner of the ground cloth, and the disconnected arms had been tossed to the side like grit-riddled boomerangs, and in a crude puddle beneath it all was the saturated terrain of the entrails, marbled like an old-fashioned relief map, mostly blue and fluid white and battleship gray, and there were dark intestines and fat bubbles and parts of organs with bite marks taken out of them.

Off the mat to the far left on the floor, under the steel-tined rake and the spade shovel on the wall, was a pair of work boots, one lying on its side, the other sole-down as if ready for the shoehorn, a skinned foot bone next to it, splintered and broken off half-up the shin.

It did not compute.

To the near-right next to a discarded blood-streaked wood ripping saw was a disfigured head staring up at her, a pig's head surely, a boar's head missing the snout, with teeth stretching up the side in a rictus grin, and the eyes bloody craters, and the skin ripped off the right cheek in uneven layers and the hair, flattened and matted and blood-spattered blond.

It did not compute.

Then it did.

She'd run her fingers through that hair. She'd gripped it in both hands when he'd broken her hymen.

Sage jerked her glance to her father, huddled in the back right corner under the shelving units that had Mom's old gardening stuff, the mop bucket from the basement between his legs. There was blood crusted into his beard and down the front of his shirt, some dried, some gleaming between in dull streaks.

"Sage," he said. "Sage, honey."

"Who?" said The Sculptor. "Where? Is she in front of you?"

Sage let go of the neck of her shirt, reached behind into the pocket of her overalls, and pulled out Chief Canfield's SigSauer. She palmed it. Aimed it. Put her finger inside the trigger guard.

"Don't you say one word to me," she said, eyes wide.

"Professor!" The Sculptor said. "It is as I thought. I can't track her indoors. Grab her and subdue her. Now, or you're going to jail for the murder of Vincent Gatto, I'll see to it."

Sage lowered the gun. Tears filled her eyes like blood in a wound.

"You've hurt me, Poppy," she said. "You've hurt me forever."

She was supposed to be the distraction, tying up The Sculptor long enough for Norman to go "radio-head" in the living room and for Jody to bonk him. But Sage wasn't sticking around. She hoped that Jody was a fast bunter.

She turned and ran. Back through the yard. To the curb, to the street, and across for the woods. It was almost dark. Her feet hurt. She had a headache and heartburn. And the last thing she'd heard The Sculptor say to her father was,

"Chase her. Catch her. Subdue her. Bring the hatchet."

CHAPTER 26

What Psychiatrists Call Alpha Male

"Sage!" Poppy called. "You get back here right now!"

He'd sort of half shouted it like a poorly executed stage-whisper, and Sage hadn't slowed. Now she was already halfway up the street, and in a nightmarish sort of déjà vu she took the hard left that took her through the yard of the abandoned renter's house with the roof stains and the ivy on the chimney. It was harder to see in the growing darkness, and the low-hanging branch back by the tire swing grazed the top of her head. It hurt. Slowed her. Then she had trouble with the gate bolt. Stuck, as if someone had glued it.

This morning it slid across as if it was oiled...

Could The Sculptor have somehow gummed up the works here? Was he that good?

"Sage!" Poppy called hoarsely. "Stop, in heaven's name, please!"

She looked back over her shoulder. He was on the sidewalk at the edge of the grass out front, bent over, catching his breath. He saw her looking, and he straightened slowly. He was a silhouette, a tall black man-shape holding a hatchet.

She turned back to the mechanics at hand and tried again to struggle the bolt across. No dice. She popped another quick look behind, and Poppy was coming, walking, as if he could measure her better by taking his time. She moaned frightened nothings, pulling, pushing, using her palm to no avail, and made herself stop and think and reason that even though she was no techie, a gate bolt had a slot and a groove, and which was which didn't matter, but to get to the latter you had to account for the former, and instead of trying to force it laterally, she pushed upward, and it moved. She slid it across and shoved the wooden slats with her hip as hard as she could.

She stumbled onto the path in the woods, lost her feet, and fell on her side. Rock against hip; she'd bumped her head and there was dirt in her hair. There were shooting stars, pain stabbing up her side, and in the fireworks at the bottom of her field of vision she saw the form of black shadow rising before her on a slant, blocking the outline of the foliage behind him. For a moment he stood there, suspended in time.

He stepped through the gateway.

She kicked the gate door closed. She felt it drive into him, heard him exhale hard, as if he'd been subject to the Heimlich maneuver, and in dark outline she saw that it folded him near double.

Take a bow, Sage thought wildly, crab-walking backward, pushing up, finding her feet, moving. Not uphill toward the dead garden. She went down the path the other way where the trees and overgrowth thickened. She'd be able to see even less, but then again so would he.

"Sage!" he called. "Sage, please hold still. I'm losing you in the gloom and we need to stop this silliness."

She stopped. The volume of his voice implied the distance she'd put between them, and she knew he couldn't surprise-jump her, not in a quick step, not in this moment. Her pant leg was ripped at the knee, she was bleeding. She'd also gouged the knuckle of her left big toe somehow, and she spun around.

About twenty yards back up the path was her father's delineation, a tall opaque rough sketch of framework barely discernible in the failing light trickling through the roof of the forest. The hatchet was part of the shape, as if a blunt extension of his chopping hand.

"Sage," he said. "Be reasonable. I can explain. It was a horrible mistake, and when we have more time to sit as a family I'll lay out the details in a rational manner."

"No," Sage said quietly.

"Pardon?"

"No therapy sessions. What is it called? Oh, right. Rhetoric. Your expertise."

"Not fair."

"Not giving a shit, *Poppy*." She'd spit that last word as if it tasted like feces.

"But Sage," he said, "there are things more important than laws and even our precious morals. Things like family, our future, dance recitals, ensemble performances, baseball games, and youth beauty pageants. We've got to keep our eyes on the prize here."

"No," she said.

He took a step forward and she stepped backward. It was impossible to tell if he saw her do it, but it did seem to give him pause.

"Sage, darling," he said, "he can't hear us out here. I'm not going to hurt you. It is dark and getting darker, but if you can see this, take it as a gesture of faith."

She saw his form move, like a blur of shadow on shadow, and he threw something into the trees, those flanking the path leading off up to the garden. She heard it tunnel through the foliage and land somewhere deep into the forest floor.

Sage breathed no sigh of relief.

"You brought that chopper in the first place," she said. "No backsies."

"Appearances," he replied. "And you know it."

Sage turned. She didn't want to put her back to him, but it was time to make a decision. There were three options. Of course, she could surrender and turn right around and walk back to him.

Uh… no.

She could continue straight on the path she was on, even though she'd never gone that far that way before.

A definite maybe. She knew the horse-path dirt-road-effect thinned down to a groove here, yet she hadn't a clue what came next. Did it lead to a creek? The far edge of the neighborhood? It was dark enough that she could easily take the point of a low-hanging branch straight in the eye. It was also dark enough that she could go thirty feet, cut off of the dirt-line, and hide in the brush. Chances were that her father would pass right on by.

Or.

She could take the sharp right, on the more familiar path that cut through the woods down the slope of the ravine leading to the concrete culvert kids sometimes used as a party space. She hadn't been there for more than a year, and she had only gone down the sharp slope a few times at night with a flashlight, so she could only see the path right in front of her and avoid what filmmakers called "the wide shot" showing the environment and the relative height that would drown her in a crushing state of vertigo. *Don't think about it.* She recalled sitting on the cement shelf jutting out of the earth at the bottom of the ravine. She recalled that if you were there first, you had to straddle the front edge of the big ribbed drainage pipe that stuck out. It was only about six feet off the ground, man-ageable in terms of the relative height, and it was as coveted as riding shotgun. They all called it "bucking the bronco." You just had to be careful not to fall forward into the ditch furrowed into the earth and the narrow trench down the middle where the dirty water oozed through. It would wreck your sneakers for sure.

Footsteps. He was coming.

Sage took the sharp right, remembering the poem by Robert Frost that talked about a guy at a fork in the road, reminiscing that he once took the "road less traveled by." Yeah. And even though it "made all the difference," he'd remembered it with a sigh. He wasn't being happy, he was wistful, and Sage started sidestepping down the ravine as quick as she able.

Poppy wasn't walking anymore. He was running, and she heard him approaching the sharp right up there far too soon. Halfway to the bottom when the path doglegged left, she was also dismayed to discover that everything was slowly brightening, almost as if the darkness was a pair of black veils on top of each other, the first being slid off with meticulous care. She took a moment to glance upward, and there, coming in on an angle, was a set of utility wires running through, and someone had cut huge L-shapes in the trees to clear the way. The other trees did a fair job of maintaining the "canopy effect," but there were divots and weak spots, dull moonlight push-ing through in splinters and pinpoints, and now her father would be able see her. It also brought on a wave of nausea, as it was revealed how high up she still was. And worse, once she got to the bottom there'd be nowhere to run. She could try and fight her way up the far side, as pawing upward was far better than coming down in terms of her phobia, but shit, she didn't even know if the path continued over there. She could crawl inside the big drainage pipe, but then she'd be trapped.

She made for the concrete shelf at the bottom of the ravine, looking at the ground, avoiding the overall perspective that would make her dizzy enough to fall on her face. He'd be able to mark her down there on the cement "stage" like a bug under a light, yes, but she'd be able to see his approach just as easily. She could pull out the gun again. She could aim it and shout out a warning with all the passion left in her. She just didn't know if she could actually bring herself to pull the trigger. Would he know this? Would he call her bluff, walk toward her, put his hand over hers, and simply disarm her?

His hand.

Yes, his big strong hand with the long fingers that left a mark on her sister's cheek. The rotten long-fingered hand that gripped a ripping saw to cut her boyfriend to pieces, next bringing the pieces of the pieces to his mouth like a savage.

She struggled down the lower part of path, her feet landing heavily on roots, briars, rocks, dirt, and tinder. She wondered if there was broken glass underfoot from tossed beer bottles and such, and she almost laughed, since her generation was supposed to be so conscious about the environment, and her feet were numb anyway, and there was so much more here to worry about than surface wounds. Her father's hands were huge and he was more than six feet tall. And though he'd thrown away the hatchet, there was a good chance he was planning to do more than disarm her. I mean, get real, he wasn't seeing her as his daughter anymore no matter how "sincerely" he begged. She was the obstruction, already written off in his mind, already dead, the artsy pink-haired corpse blocking his illusion of the perfect family ideal.

She gangled down to the end of the path and limped onto the concrete apron. Her lungs were on fire. Her legs felt like lead. She reached for her back pocket and stole a glance back up the incline.

Her father was lumbering down the pathway, leaning back with it, coming down hard on his heels, with his arms and hands flailing like some insane orchestra conductor having a fit. She drew out the pistol and aimed it up at him. She wondered if he would slow his advance when he got to the bottom as she had just envisioned he would, doing the creepy soft-sell, all smooth, placid, and rational, trusting that she would finally and fatally trust him. But hell, maybe he wouldn't after all. Maybe he'd just keep coming on like a freight train, plow into her, and launch them both off the concrete.

But soft subtlety, freight trains, and plows weren't in the tea leaves. His feet kicked out from under him, his hands flew skyward, and for a moment in mid-air he looked as if he was on a roller coaster showing off that he didn't feel the need to take hold of the bar.

He landed flat on his tailbone and bumped down the bluff the way you rub down a playground slide in your short-shorts, and his shirt was coming up, and instead of being propelled onto the flat cement of the culvert, he came in a few feet in front of it where there was just a maw where the dirt gave way to the cavernous ditch in front of the drainage pipe.

There was the hint of a lip at the edge acting like a ramp of sorts, and he was pitched forward hard into the furrow. His arms made huge circles in the air, his feet pumping to catch up with the runway, and in the center of the ditch his left foot splashed into the trench. He jerked down three inches, and simultaneously there was a *snap*, making Sage think, *That was what it sounded like when you hit my sister,* and he hurtled in for the crash landing, forearms crossed in front of his face.

He bashed into the far side of the ditch and lay there face down.

Sage looked at it, assessed it.

His right foot was toe-down to the dirt at six o'clock as it was supposed to be, but the left heel was wrenched to seven-forty or so, the toe twisted up on the opposite side at two o'clock and some change.

"Sage," he said, voice muffled in the soil.

"What?" she said flatly. She imagined he was going to beg for assistance, for her to offer her shoulder to lean on, helping him out of the ditch.

"Sage," he said, "come down here and shoot me. Please. Back of the head, I won't even feel it."

"What makes you think I'd care if you'd feel it?"

"Please, Sage."

"Goodbye."

She emotionally severed him for good, the thing in the ditch.

She forgave herself.

She walked off of the concrete platform and started up the steep path to find her way back out through the forest.

CHAPTER 27

Every Town Has an Elm Street

S age limped back into the neighborhood. There wasn't a streetlight until Trent crossed Hempstead down ten or eleven houses, and Sage was thankful for the cover of darkness. She was walking with her arms folded across her chest, each hand rubbing the forearm of the other; it had gotten chilly. She felt as if every part of her body had either a scrape or a bruise, and though she longed for clean socks and a good pair of sneakers, she wasn't thrilled about putting her battered feet under the tub spigot and rubbing soap into the wounds.

Her mind felt numb, calloused, and scarred. She had no idea what she was going to walk into back at the house, but more than likely it was going to end then and there. It was all moot, all for naught, as honestly, she didn't think she'd carried on a conversation with her father in the shed long enough for Jody to carry out her part of the plan. How many sentences had Robinson uttered? Two maybe? That made for an awfully short radio-trance, and in all probability Jody didn't even have enough time to approach Norman in stealth, let alone take a position and execute the mechanics to knock him out cold. Most likely, Sage would creep across the lawn to the side of the house, climb into the sun room, slink to the archway, and peer around the corner to the living room just to see the bodies of her sisters rumpled in a heap on the floor with Norman sitting in Poppy's spot on the sofa eating microwave popcorn and watching Netflix.

There were the occasional garden lamps and walkway lights that looked bleak and gloomy, with dull reflective haloes like illumination in damp caverns, and everyone had their shades down and the curtains closed.

She had to help her sisters any way she still could, even if it meant surrendering to Michael Leonard Robinson. The problem was that it didn't seem he wanted a white flag. It seemed he wanted to keep the nightmare going as long as Sage and her sisters could walk and still breathe.

A leaf blew into her hair, and she rubbed it away absently. She also had to send help for her father, though she sure as hell didn't want to. The "right thing to do" wasn't always the right thing to do, right? What a blurred line between good and evil, poetic justice and justice, truth and rationalization…and Poppy, so good at puzzles. Well, he never figured out how to piece together his own family, now did he?

She was here. Home. Where the heart is. No, nix that. "Poppy" already ate the heart out of it literally and metaphorically, so no more clichés. No more paradoxes pitting morals and practicalities against each other like mongrels in a dogfight. She started across the grass, but she didn't cut a diagonal to the side of the house. She went straight ahead. For the front door. She was just too disgusted and angry to sneak.

She reached around to her back pocket and drew out the pistol. She couldn't believe it was going down this way, couldn't believe it of herself, of the "Sage" she thought she had known, but she was doing this and doing it now, it was happening.

She was on the front doorstep.

She got out her key, put it in, and turned the lock. Game on.

Sage pushed into the living room.

CHAPTER 28

I See Dead People

The house was seemingly deserted, except for the body of Hamlet, stretched out face down on the living room floor by the corner of the sectional like a chalk-line sketch. The flatscreen was on, and it was paused. It wasn't a Netflix special, but rather some YouTube video showing a paramedic with his two fingers on the throat of a crash-test dummy. It was titled "How to Check a Pulse."

Sage stepped carefully past the body of the dead policeman, and that's when she heard it. The breathing. Michael Leonard Robinson was trying to listen in, sitting patiently somewhere while his lab rats scurried in and out of the frequency. He must have heard the door open just now, and if he couldn't perceive who it was, he would guess by an easy process of elimination that it was, in fact, Sage entering the premises. Or maybe Jody had bonked Norman, checked YouTube to see how to determine if he was still alive, and she and Esther had dragged him outside. Maybe The Sculptor was hearing a whole lot of nothing from anyone right now.

Sage sniffed hard; she was about to burst into tears. More probably, Jody had tried to strike Norman, she had failed, and he had reacted instinctively, striking her with such force he crushed her skull, or worse, he'd held her down by the throat, slipped out the long blade from his thigh-sheaf, and slit her down center like a prime cut of beef. And so then, it would have been Jody's body that was dragged outside after all.

To be brought to the shed.

To triple Poppy's workload.

Sage's eyes filled up, they overflowed, and she rubbed her cheek hard. It was probably the latter and worst-case scenario. Norman acted instinctively, killing Jody before reasoning it through, and The Sculptor hadn't been happy. The girls were more fun for him kept alive, and that was why the video was called up in the first place. Norman was seeing if he could put toothpaste back into the tube. It was paused, because he had not been successful.

It was dark in the kitchen, but Sage could see through the dull gloom that the back door was open. Through the storm door's half-screen with the slide-up glass she thought she could see forms moving. She thought she could hear something too, but it was faint, indistinguishable.

She walked through the archway, stepped in something wet, and almost slipped in it. She turned on the light.

On the linoleum was a streak of blood like the paint-stroke of some giant's finishing brush, glazed in a line straight to the door, which now had a glare on the glass. It mirrored Sage's approach. She tried to avoid the swath of gore. She thought vaguely about incriminating red footprints, and she got to the door, pushed it open, and pointed the SigSauer.

"Holy shit!" Jody whispered savagely. "Put that away!"

The secondary light from the kitchen threw everything into a soft and shadowy hue, but this little masterpiece was anything but gentle. Jody had both Norman's feet rooked under her arms, and she'd almost gotten him off the high concrete step, his hands up and back as if he was signaling "touchdown," his head and shoulders still at the front edge, eyes closed, chin to chest. Jody leaned back with it and his head came off the step, bumping to the cement patio. The momentum made her lose her balance, and she let go and fell to her butt.

Esther was off to the right a few feet, holding her demented teddy bear by one leg and sucking her thumb. She pulled it out when she saw both her sisters were looking.

"His head is split open in the back, and you can see his brains," she said, far too matter-of-factly for Sage's taste. "If you grab him by the hair and lift and peek underneath, you'll see. It looks like cottage cheese and ketchup."

"Yeah, thanks for the update," Jody said. "It would have been better to help me with the body."

"It's too heavy," said Esther. "And there's no good place to grab anything. And he smells like poop. And I'm not doing anything I don't want to do anymore, ever, ever, ever." The thumb went promptly back into her mouth.

"All right, Peanut," Jody said, pushing up slowly, looking for a horrifying moment like a battered old woman. Or maybe it was just the smeared eye-black, the red handprint, and the secondary lighting. She walked around the body and stood before Sage.

"Pink hair and all," she said, "you look like shit."

"You look lovely," Sage answered. Jody smiled slightly, since they had both really said the same thing. There was no hug. Her expression darkened.

"Where's Poppy?" she said. "I heard him calling your name."

"The woods. In the culvert. He broke his foot."

"We should send help."

"I know."

Neither did anything about this, and it seemed neither meant to, at least not right away. It was there in their eyes.

"I didn't mean to kill this guy," Jody said finally.

"How did it happen?"

"I was never much good at bunting." She shrugged and looked at her feet. Then the boo-boo lip. Her shoulders started to shake like a tenor's vibrato, and Sage reached for her. Jody moved back a step, putting her palms up. It wasn't a gesture of anger, but more an indication that she was trying to master this on her own. Sage backed off a step.

"What are we going to do with the body?" she said evenly. "And what do we do with the one in the living room?"

"I don't know," Jody said. "I only dragged this one out because you said he couldn't be left indoors. Didn't really make sense, but then again, nothing does. Not anymore."

"I'm hungry," Esther said. "I want McDonald's."

"Not now," said Sage.

"Wendy's? Taco Bell?" Her face soured even more, and she stamped her foot. "Leave the poopers right where they are! No one can see them from their own houses, and they wouldn't even if they walked past our driveway out front!"

Sage and Jody shared a look. She was right. And the shed wasn't an option, thank God, because Norman couldn't be put inside an enclosed space. Sage put the tip of her tongue between her teeth. There were just so many holes in this, so many unknowns. What was their next move? She lowered her glance absently in order to make some sort of quick assessment of the condition of her feet, and that is why she saw it coming.

The hand.

Norman's hand closing around her ankle.

Sage cried out and tried to pull away, but he'd squeezed a split second before she'd been ready. His grip was pure iron, and he was groaning, spouting nonsense sounds like speaking in tongues, and Sage looked back across her shoulder at his face. There was spittle coming out of his mouth, looking very much like the froth bubbling over the rim of a boiling pot of spaghetti. His lips were blue, his eyes entirely rolled back, showing only their whites. He lifted his head off the cement with his effort and started yanking Sage's ankle back and forth, trying to take her down. His position slid a bit with it, and Sage could see the marbled bloody stain he'd left on the cement beneath his head, thick, almost black in this lighting, and she was trying to keep her balance one-legged as he pulled and yanked as if tightening and loosening the same nut with a pipe wrench, and she thought wildly about cottage cheese and ketchup, and she thought of Poppy eating chunks of Vinny in the shed and she started to hyperventilate.

A shadow fell over Norman's face, and there was a snort and a grunt, and Jody brought down the DeMarini Voodoo bat as if she was chopping wood. There was a sickening crunch, and the policeman's face split nearly in two; simultaneously, Sage was hurled out of his grip, literally *shoved* from his clenched fingers as if electrocuted.

She landed five feet away, on her feet amazingly, and instead of pulling a ragdoll, she managed to work the momentum, to bounce off her feet like old rusted springs and throw herself off the patio and onto the grass. She rolled twice and came to rest on her side, facing back toward the kitchen, and Jody was still whipping down the weapon, her shadow up against the wall of the house, gigantic, etched into the gradations of the surface like an old-school monster movie, rapid and vicious, and it didn't sound like a carnival mallet to a watermelon anymore, but more like bringing hammer to anvil through a wet smear of Jell-O.

"Enough," Sage said, pushing up to a sitting position, strength retuning. "Jody, stop. Enough, please, he's dead."

Jody hit him one more time for good measure, dropped the bat on the ground, and put her hands on her knees.

"OK," she said breathlessly. She spit. Hawked up and did it again. Esther was staring at the ground in front of her feet, thumb buried in her mouth, swaying gently like a mental patient out of her holding cell for her hour on the lawn. Jody turned her head and looked at Sage sideways.

"When I hit him, you jumped," she said. "Like you were thrown. What happened?"

Sage knew, but didn't have a brief way to say it. For a moment she'd been confused as to why Chief Canfield hadn't affected her similarly. She made physical contact with him when he was freshly dead also, so why no jolt that time?

She got a sudden chill up the spine.

Because Canfield had passed from this world to the next on his own. The magic was in the transfer, and the jolt had given Sage an insight, a vision. This also had confused her because the image was alien yet at the same time familiar, like a thought you were on the brink of but just couldn't snag.

"Esther's right," she said, pushing up to her feet, a bit shakily. "Morbid as it is, we should leave both policemen where they are and get inside ourselves. Robinson can't tune in now, so we'll have privacy. We make sure the shades are closed, the doors locked, the lights dimmed. We hunker down and hope the police don't miss these two and send backup. And we don't send help for...*Poppy* yet either."

Jody's eyes flashed in immediate agreement, as she'd obviously heard the distaste in her sister's voice when she'd mentioned their father.

"But Sage, we can't hunker down forever," she said. "What are we finally going to do?"

Sage sighed. "We wait."

"For what?" Esther said. Sage folded her arms and shivered.

"For me to figure out exactly what I just saw when Norman—I mean the cop here—died and I got jolted. I was given an image, like a still shot in a movie. It was a room, or rather a 'space' that was big and dark and industrial, like a warehouse or a basement storage area where you could see the pipes and wires coming out of the ceiling. Plus, it was even more creepy because in the background I could have sworn I saw abandoned paintings, like jumbo-sized works of abstract art, but I couldn't make out what was being depicted as they were lying on their sides. At least, I think they were." She made a fist and bumped it on her leg. "Oh, I don't know. It's frustrating, familiar, but I can't place it. I mean, I know what it is in a general sense, but I just don't know where."

Esther pounded her own leg in sarcastic imitation.

"Well, tell us what it is at least—the suspense is a killer!"

"Easy, Peanut," Jody said.

"It's OK," Sage said. "The 'what' is easy. It's the key to this horrible mystery. It's the lair of the spider."

She looked at Esther, then Jody. "It's Robinson's hideout."

239

CHAPTER 29

Tasty, Tasty, Beautiful Fear

They shuffled back into the house, Jody first, Sage second, and Esther in tow. She had offered her hand and Sage had taken it. Such a simple gesture, but so important all the same. There was still comfort and warmth in this family. You just had to cherry-pick, that was all. Jody stopped in her tracks under the kitchen archway leading to the living room, and like bad slapstick, Sage almost bunked into her.

"Whoa..." she said.

"Shit," Jody answered.

"What?"

"Look."

She stepped through and to the left out of the sightline. There was no longer a body on the floor at the corner of the sectional. There was a smear of dark blood on the hardwood the size of a dinner plate, but no droplets leading away from the area, no trail of breadcrumbs.

"He could be upstairs," Esther said hollowly.

"Or the basement," Jody said. "We could—"

"We're not splitting up," said Sage. "Wait a sec." She looked off to the side, front teeth gnawing at her bottom lip.

"What?" Jody said.

"The cop car," she said. "Out front."

She burst for the front door and put her hand on the knob. Jody stepped in beside her, color high, body taut, fingers wrapped white around the grip of the bat cocked behind her shoulder.

"Easy," said Sage. "I'll take the lead on this. No more head bashing."

Jody slowly brought down her back elbow. "You gonna draw that gun of yours then?" she said.

"Of course."

"You gonna use it?"

"Not unless I absolutely have to. Now, lower the bat and take Esther's hand. Please. We don't rush this. Slow, cautious, and smart, not impulsive and foolish."

Jody gave a look to let her sister know that this plan was rather uninspiring, then stepped back and reached down. Esther gave her hand willingly, but stared at the wall emptily. She brought her teddy bear to her chest and rocked it ever so gently.

Sage took the Sig Sauer out of her back pocket, drew a deep breath, and reached with her left hand. She pulled open the door. Night breeze, darkness crisp, darkness cold, and the three girls trusted themselves out to the front step. The lighting from the living room offered a dim spill into the front yard, and Sage was damn glad there were no street lamps nearby.

To the left in the driveway, Hamlet was a grainy sketch at the edge of the secondary glow, and he had the door of the police cruiser open. The girls held still for a moment, watching. He was trying to get his right foot in over the lip and under the steering wheel, yet it was obvious what was giving him trouble. He tried to lift his foot past the rim and almost fell against the side of the car, reaching up for the roof to secure the transaction, and yelping in pain when his hand got past the level of his hip.

The girls started toward him. Sage was scared nearly blind, pointing the gun forward, trying not to shake. Jody let go of Esther's hand and stepped in beside her elder sister.

Hamlet had seen them, of course, and had gone for his gun. But it brought his shoulder and elbow just past the "pain-plane" and he shrieked, going for broke now, hopping on one foot, trying to shimmy into the vehicle no-hands. He got a foot in and couldn't finish the transaction, losing his balance and falling back along the side of the car. He dropped to the ground flat on his rump, bit back a scream, and tried again to reach for his firearm.

Jody got to him first, just as he was unsnapping the holster. She had tossed her bat to the grass, a promise was a promise after all it seemed, and she dropped to her knees, grabbing for his wrist. There was a short tug of war as the weakened officer fought for control of his own limb and Jody strained with everything she had.

Sage got mind-freeze something awful. She wanted to go in and put the gun to his head, but she didn't want to be close enough that he could just take it from her with the good hand opposite the side-wound. She wanted to assume a position and aim, saying, *"Hold it! Don't move!"* yet was terrified the thing would go off accidentally and blast her sister in the back of the head. Jody got to her feet and started lifting and then bringing his arm down like the lever on a pump trolley. Hamlet yelped with each extension upward like a tortured animal, and finally he fell back to the asphalt, thumping his head, eyes tearing down the sides, nose running, chest heaving.

"Mother?" he gasped. "Mother, I'm frightened."

Jody straightened and backed off a step, both hands up as if to say, *"Whoa, this fluff ain't my flow."*

Sage stared for a moment, mouth ajar. Was this a fake-me-out? Was this somehow the work of the fiend, banking on her sympathy and basic affection for others so she could be grabbed, stabbed, or choked somehow? Was there another "Sculptor-robot" in the car that they hadn't accounted for, maybe in the back seat or the trunk or even on the other side of the vehicle crouched down, waiting for a moment of vulnerability?

She shook off a shiver and wondered just what The Sculptor had turned her into. Was she someone so cold and callous that she ignored a dying man's last plea? For his mother, for God's sake?

Fuck the fiend.

No, YOU fuck the fiend, she thought crazily, pocketing the weapon.

She knelt beside Hamlet and rested her palms on her thighs, head cocked a bit. In the background, Jody was saying something about boobytraps and basic stupidity, and the policeman's chest hitched and stuttered. She leaned down and in, and was met with a waft of gentle cologne and the hard kind of sweat Gillette or Axe wouldn't even begin to cover over, and she scooped under his head, his neck hot and damp. She took the back of his skull in the crook of her arm and strained back to pull him to a sitting position. And they were cheek to cheek, razor stubble, his breath hot on the back of her shoulder, and she brought her other arm around to complete the embrace. It was like holding a tree trunk, a sweltering redwood, his hands dangling down by his sides like loose kite streamers.

"I'm here," she whispered into his ear. "You don't need to be scared anymore."

"Mother?" he murmured hoarsely. Then he died in her arms, she felt the shudder. She held onto him tightly and wept. So much pain and death, I mean, why, fucking why?

"Sage, c'mon," Jody said. No response. She put her hand on her sister's back and rubbed. It was clumsy and tender and it did the trick. Sage eased Hamlet down, released him, and got to her feet slowly. Jody turned her to face her and studied her a moment.

"What?" said Sage.

"Your mascara."

"What about it?"

"You made it run down your face all jagged and shit. Worse than it was before."

"Well, it isn't a beauty contest."

"No," said Esther emptily. "But it sure is lucky-ducky."

Both girls looked back, and their baby sister was a broken doll standing in the grass, shoulders slumped, clothes disheveled, expression all dull and listless. She dangled the deranged stuffed animal by its paw next to her right leg and she pulled her left thumb from her mouth again.

"Lucky-ducky!" she said again.

"What's lucky, Peanut?" Jody said. "Two dead cops?"

"No, stupid," Esther said. "It means two more guns. It means that now there's a pistol for each of us."

CHAPTER 30

This Is No Dream. This Is Really Happening

They took Hamlet's firearm. Jody claimed it. She even promised that she would get the other cop's pistol for Esther, since no one seemed too excited to rush out back and step around the wet meat splattered across the patio.

They took other things too—the spoils of war. Hamlet's police-duty belt was loaded: holster, handcuffs, chemical spray, taser, utility flashlight, baton holder (no baton), and a radio. Sage helped Jody roll him up to his side to get it out of the sheath-holder-thing and straightened to look at it as Jody let him fall to his original position. On the back it said, "Motorola, APX NEXT," and the front was a darkened touch-screen. Sage was wary of checking this for fear of someone on the other end being aware of it, but it bothered her that Hamlet hadn't radioed for backup that would have been here by now.

She tapped the screen. Nothing. She turned the two knobs on top and pressed in the touch-bars on the back of it.

Nothing.

Jody had put on Hamlet's belt and was adjusting it.

247

"Hey," she said, "it isn't that deep. It needed a charge. Maybe the unit is on the dashboard and it runs off the engine battery or something."

"You should push him under the car," Esther said. She then turned and pointed back in the general direction of the dead community garden that Sage felt she had visited years ago. "People coming from that way will see. That wouldn't be very nice."

Sage almost burst into tears again. A first grader reasoning about the way to hide a body was a sin on so many levels that it felt pornographic. She handed the dead radio to Jody, reached over the body to shut the car door, then squatted. Hamlet's left hand was turned palm-up inches from her toes. The fingers were curled in like dead spider legs.

"I suppose I'll push at the hip," she said.

"Yes," said Jody. "I'll take the shoulder."

They gave each other a look, then bent to it. He was still warm. They pushed. The progress was sluggish, like a sled hitting a dry patch of grass, and they got him half in. Stuck. Something was catching on the undercarriage, and it didn't take a genius nor better lighting to figure that it was his head—more specifically, his face.

Sage and her sister didn't need to communicate on this one. It had already gone so far that it didn't even seem abnormal to desecrate a body like this. They got into crab-walk position, sat, and planted the soles of their feet on him. They didn't even count to three.

Sage strained with it, but Jody was the one doing the heavy lifting. After a few seconds of continued resistance she altered her angle and used her right foot on the side of his head, knee up, then pistoning her heel into his ear as if she was stamping out a fire. Her neck cords were up, and there was a moist ripping sound, and she got an inch of give. She moaned, Sage whimpered softly almost in harmony, and finally they scraped him under far enough that there was no body part creeping out from under the edge.

Jody pulled her legs in and sat where she was, tucking her hair behind both ears. She folded arms and stared at the asphalt. Sage was sitting cross-legged, and she put her face in her hands.

"Someone's coming," Esther said.

"Where?" Jody said, twisting back.

"There."

Esther was facing away, pointing, and Sage turned slowly to follow Jody's gaze, which followed Esther's indication.

For a moment there was nothing, but then, yes, it appeared that the shadows were moving along the sidewalk up the street in front of the abandoned house with the tire swing. It was coming toward them.

It was a man-figure, tall with three legs, one bent at the knee with an odd shape dangling from the end of it, one clumping forward, and the third—knobby and unyielding like a fence post.

It was Poppy, and he was limping toward them in bumps and scrapes, using a thick forest branch as a crutch. But of course there was no handle nor an underarm crutch pad, and taking a bold step forward, Poppy's grip suddenly slid down the shank, jamming the top of the branch hard up into his armpit.

He cried out, twisted in, took a tumble, hit the sidewalk. To Sage it sounded wet somehow, like bloody meat and old bones in a bag. She got out her gun, Jody held hers at ready, and they took a few steps forward so they were shoulder to shoulder with Esther. They moved together across the lawn in diagonal. Up the street, Poppy was a shadow etched in scratches of moonlight, and he had turned himself face down and was trying to push his chest from the pavement into what looked like the "Baby Cobra" yoga pose. He went for broke then, yanking in, trying to plant on the point of his elbow so he could work to the hip, but it scraped past the perpendicular and dropped him to a shoulder. He screamed, then went guttural trying to contain it, and on their side of the street two houses up, the Dickersons' porch light went on.

Sage quickly pocketed her weapon.

"Hide yours," she said, and Jody dropped her pistol to the grass. She also unclasped the police belt and let it fall into the darkness at her feet a split second before Mrs. Dickerson pulled open her door and slipped out to the edge of her front step. She was wearing a long, off-white terrycloth bathrobe with roses and vines on it.

"You girls OK?" she said. "I thought I heard something out here." She looked back up the street to Poppy trying to push to his feet in the shadows, and she gripped together the collar of her bathrobe up at her neck.

"Is that you, Brad?" she called. "Do you need help? Should I call someone?"

"Mrs. Dickerson!" said Sage, trying her best to mask the urgency. "We already did that. Look." She swept her arm back toward the house.

Mrs. Dickerson looked over them and squinted at the police cruiser sitting idly in the driveway. Sage prayed they had pushed Hamlet in far enough underneath it.

"Oh," Mrs. Dickerson said. Sage didn't wait for the woman to consider and then reconsider her possible liabilities.

"Poppy sleepwalks!" she blurted out, faking a laugh. "He usually just goes downstairs and cooks something. Thank God he didn't ever put napkins in the toaster or anything! This is the first time he's ever left the house. We didn't know where he was, so we called the police. They're waiting for us inside. We told them that Poppy would only listen to us in this state, so when we heard him out here just like you, we came running." She turned to her sisters. "Well, c'mon! Let's go get Poppy!"

They raced across the street. Mrs. Dickerson slowly went back inside, still hesitant, and Sage would have bet the farm she would be watching their every move from behind the living room curtains.

The three girls approached Poppy together.

From his stomach, he watched. He was smiling.

It wasn't the happy type.

CHAPTER 31

Hell Is Only a Word.
The Reality Is Much, Much Worse

od, did he stink! To get him up and onto his good foot, both Sage and Jody had to dig their fingers under each elbow, drag him up to his knees, and then go under with his arms across their shoulders. Both girls strained up from their squatter's positioning to legs straight and lock-kneed, and since there was such a difference in height, he had to push himself up off their collarbones. Finally he leaned back down and in, flat on his forearms in the crooks of their necks, and they teetered with him there for an awful moment that felt as if they were all going to take a tumble. Somehow they kept the ship upright.

He felt damp and crusted, spoiled and rancid and greasy.

"Thank you, girls," he was saying, whispering harshly. "We're a family again, and it'll be all right. Just get us back to the house and we can talk...you know, reason our way into—"

"Quiet now," Sage whispered.

He *so* disgusted her. He was heavy and clumsy, and just when they found a rhythm, having him hopscotch his working leg between them, grunting and thumping, he'd come close to slipping off one of their shoulders, or he'd bang the lame foot against Jody's knee and cry out like a tortured hyena.

"I know you don't want to hear this," he gasped, "but it is in this family's best interest to get back on Robinson's wavelength. I wish I could take everything back, but like a lot of things in this life you have to play the hand that you're dealt."

"Quiet, Poppy, please!" Sage hissed.

From behind them the lighting had just brightened, elongating their shadows before them and pointing past Esther leading the way like a dented hood ornament. Then there was another spread of brightness from behind, and another, and it seemed the whole street was turning on its floods. The Winslows were almost home, five steps or so until they would be directly across the street, and Sage thanked holy God for that cop car. While there was a chance it would draw out nosy neighbors to gather in little gossip circles, it was doubtful they would actually approach the Winslows' front door. They'd figure the situation was being handled. Hell, no one called the cops when the cops were already there, right?

"You'll thank me for this when you're older," Poppy murmured.

His breath was putrid. Sage could smell it when he leaned down right before every leg-drag, and she wanted to vomit. The idea that both *"Poppy"* and the girls could share the same agenda out here was absolutely ridiculous, biblically ironic, and faking her toleration of his stench and his poison was far more than difficult. They made the quarter-turn counter-clockwise, bunny-hopping it, making the opened front door across from them bounce in the sightline.

"There is nothing stronger than our bond," he said, nearly breathless, and Sage could feel him shifting to look at her, then Jody, and Esther. "We are a family," he continued, laughing hoarsely. "I'm telling you, lying there in the woods I wanted to end it all, just ask Sage, just ask her. But I realized then and there that I would keep us all together as a unit, a team, one for all and all that, right? The future is ours, and we just have to be together on this thing, this one little thing."

Enough of the fucking clichés, Sage thought. *And keep my name out of your mouth.*

They maneuvered the curb, almost tipping over left, but they didn't. Together, they stumbled and bumbled across the street to the driveway and then to the grass.

They had almost reached the front door. A bunch of tiny gnats circled in a honeycomb shape a few feet from the archway, and to the left a couple of floodlights went dark. Show over.

"We should have sold tickets," Poppy muttered, totally grossing Sage out as they had been thinking similarly. They strained up the step, taking a second to rebalance before going in, and Poppy gave them what seemed his best final plea.

"We can't abandon things," he said. "Your mother would have wanted us to fight through this. Together. We're not quitters. Dammit, Esther stopped the dancing lessons only because the room above the music store smelled like cobwebs and books, and she still regrets it, don't you, dear, don't you? And Jody. You gave up playing the drums, and now you realize how cool it would have been to have earned a spot in the school marching band during baseball's off-season. You still talk about giving it another try, yessir, I'm right, aren't I right, sweetie-pie?"

They were about to start moving together across the threshold, and he leaned down, almost touching Sage's crown with his lips.

"And you, Sage. How about the school theater? You would have been a wonderful techie, helping paint the flats and construct the scenery, but you were shy and it felt awkward and uncomfortable and it was only because it was new. Think of it! With your artistic gifts you would have been student-stage manager by now!"

Sage stopped dead in her tracks, and it wasn't because her father was panting so close that it felt as if centipedes were crawling in and out of her ear. There was something in what he'd just said, something related, something significant.

She couldn't quite make the connection. Then suddenly she could. A chill went down her spine and the blood felt as if it rushed straight out of her face.

"Bathroom!" she commanded, "No time to get him upstairs, so we'll use the half-bath down here. Esther, go make sure the door is wide open and turn on the light. Then we'll have to find the Neosporin and alcohol and cotton balls, lots of them!"

"What?" Poppy said.

Jody picked up on it immediately and joined Sage in straining him forward. He hopped to keep up.

"Wait," he said, the word bouncing out of him. "What—how—when?"

Ahead of them, Esther ran through the kitchen, darting left. Sage prayed her father kept on coming, sort of on autopilot the same way you fell into single file or marched in tempo when others established the pattern. If he decided simply to sit down where he was, she didn't think they could haul him, not all the way.

He didn't sit.

They trudged through the kitchen and Poppy started trying to resist and in response Jody said something about getting gangrene and solving the "skin infection" before worrying about the bone splint and that they had to get him ready for the hospital, and he was protesting rather loudly that there was no time for the hospital, and they had gotten him to the bathroom doorway. Esther moved back farther to the shadows of the pantry.

As if a sleeping giant suddenly awakened, Poppy slipped his forearms off sideways and made to grab Sage and Jody hard by the shoulders. But both did instinctive duck-unders, backing a quarter-step behind him, and by his own flawed instinct he stood for a moment propped on one foot trying to maintain his balance.

They pushed him in, hard.

He pitched forward and banged face-first into the cold-water spigot at the back of the sink. It kicked the water on in a rush and left a bloody smudge on the steel; he tumbled back, thumped down to the floor, and turned on his side toward the toilet. He bitterly spit out a tooth, the saliva sticking to it, still connected to his mouth like a laundry line. He spit again and it made a bloody spray on the linoleum.

He started writhing then, gargling like a monster, trying to push up, and his foot was poking out through the archway. His bad foot. Sage chanced a look at it for a quick moment and almost barfed. It should have been lying on its side, on the ankle, but it was facing upward off the stump, toes high, heel down and mostly disconnected, like the boot you'd half kicked off after shoveling the driveway.

Both Sage and Jody simultaneously grabbed for the edge of the door and yanked it across, shoving it home. Dull percussion, flush on Winslow's shin just above the break, and he hollered and tucked into himself to a fetal position. His foot dragged in with it, and Sage and Jody slammed the door shut on him. Both put their hands flat on it, both leaning in with all their weight.

"Esther!" Sage whispered harshly. "Go shut the front door we left open, then hurry down to the basement to the red toolbox and find the claw hammer. It's in the tray on top, I think. And go to the low shelf by the water heater and grab the Chock Full o'Nuts coffee can with all the screws, nails, and junk in it. Bring the hammer and the can up here to us quick as you can, before he figures out a way to get vertical and try to shove his way out of this, go!"

Esther darted off, shut the front door, pitter-patted back, flung open the basement door, and clumped down the steps. Sage prayed the poor thing didn't trip and fall, and from inside the bathroom there were thumping sounds, muttering, cursing. Sage's and Jody's knuckles were bent in and wrinkled-white, they were shoving so hard, and suddenly the water in the sink shut off.

Silence.

Both girls saw the knob turn.

Then he threw a shoulder into it, or at least that is what Sage pictured, as the dull thud sent shivers back through her elbows and shoulders, bucking the door open an inch. Both girls screamed, dug in, and shoved it back closed. Sage was smiling hard, all teeth, and it made her face hurt. She was pretty sure that if her father had had the use of both feet, he could have splintered the door by now, demolished it, busted it right off the hinges.

"Tough titties," she murmured to no one. Beside her, Jody snickered, and the door thumped again, harder, squeezing open at least two inches, and Sage and Jody shoved back with everything they had. The door banged shut a second time.

There was jostling on the other side, a rubbing that seemed to bump down the wood, and then a *wump* sound down low. Groaning. Then weeping, as if his mouth was pressed right up to the gap between the wood and the linoleum.

"Sage," he managed to say through the slit. "Sage honey, I didn't mean to kill your boyfriend. I really didn't. You have to believe me. Robinson couldn't have wanted this, hell, he can't even spy on us now. I don't quite know why he lost his edge here, but I think that you do. Tell me, Sage, tell me all you've discovered. We're better as a unit and you very well know this."

Sage grimaced. "How do I know you're not the new Sculptor?" she said. "How do I know you're not a copycat or even the original freak-a-zoid? How do I know that Robinson isn't actually *your* copycat? I mean, we were filmed in our bedrooms. Maybe you couldn't find the cameras in the ceiling fans after you ripped them down because you set them there in the first place, just *acting* like you were looking for them."

"Let me out right now then, and I'll look at them with you, prove my innocence."

"Yeah, right," said Sage. "Innocent of one thing, innocent of them all. Good logic, Professor. I feel like I'm watching Fox or CNN garbage. Do you think I'm that much of a dumbass?"

He laughed. It sounded like the squawk of a rooster being slaughtered.

"Never," he said. "I love you, Sage, like I love your sisters, so deeply it hurts."

"Yeah," Jody snorted. "Like the way you slapped me so hard I flew halfway across the kitchen and banged into the pot rack, huh?"

"I'm sorry," he said. "OK?"

"It's not OK," Sage answered. "You're a killer and a cannibal and a shitty fucking father."

"It was an accident no one could have predicted."

"Really?"

"Yes, really," he tried. "Go on, Sage. Go up to my bedroom and look at my computer. Look at the messages from Robinson, look at them all. He planned for me killing Chief Timothy Canfield, trust me, it's on there. I didn't have a chance to go look at it, but Canfield told me he got a similar message. It was never anyone's intention to kill Vinny Gatto."

Sage laughed bitterly, forced it. He did have a point in that Canfield had told her the same thing, but fuck it, there was no reason to go parsing things, giving him an inch to stretch.

"Yeah, good try," she said. "One of us pressing the door shut out here is better for you than the two of us. Sorry, I'm not that lame and I'm not that stupid."

Esther rushed up to them, breathless. She had the claw hammer under one arm and the coffee can hugged to her chest. Her stress doll teddy bear was sitting in it, feet spilling out over the edge, head lolling to the side like a broken child half sunk in a toilet.

Sage thought for a second and chanced that her father was still sprawled out on the floor, as the direction of his voice had just indicated. She let her pressure off the wood as gently as possible, took the hammer from her sister, and waited a moment for the kid to remove her new toy. Esther did, and kissed the ugly thing up by the dangling eye-button. Sage picked as quietly as she could through the contents in the can Esther still held at chest level, and she yanked out a nail. Slightly bent. A couple of inches or so, it would do.

She aimed it at an angle in the middle of the decorative door casing, or molding, or whatever you called it. She hoped the sound wouldn't drive her father into such a panic that he'd gain some kind of inhuman strength, or such a rage he'd somehow find a way to push his way out on one leg. She hoped she didn't bash in her fingers.

She hoped.

She backed the hammer off a few inches, counted to three, and then tapped it. To get a starting nook and bury the tip. Success! It was embedded. Down through the slit in the bottom of the door Poppy shrieked. Thumping, banging, chaos, and thankfully Poppy didn't have any leverage. Sage pounded the nail through the beveled wood casing. It took three strokes. Wasn't perfect, but it was in, and she was pretty sure it was sunk into at least three-quarters of an inch of door.

Esther had put the can on the floor and sat by it, digging in, getting another nail ready and reaching it up to her big sister. This one was three inches at least, and Sage didn't bother with a starting nook, she just reached up and pounded, and on the other side of the door Poppy went nuclear. He thwacked and thrashed and hollered and punched, but the nails held, as did Jody, and Sage banged in four more big ones.

After about three minutes, she'd nailed in at least twenty-five all up and down the left side, some at knee level.

At four minutes or so, Poppy stopped screeching.

He wept, though, and ever so softly. It sounded blubbery and snot-filled, and Sage was as unmoved as were her sisters. She went down the right side, amazed at how calm and methodical she'd become, and she got a kitchen chair to stand on to nail in the top. By the time she finished the job, the door looked as if it was wearing some strange metallic lizard-skin, jagged but uniform.

Sage stared at it, Jody next to her, and Esther next to Jody. Sage jerked her head as if to say, *"Follow me,"* and she led them back into the living room. She checked the front door. Unlocked and relocked it. Turned to her sisters.

"It's cool out," she said in a low voice. "I am going upstairs to put on socks and sneaks, a sweater and a jacket. You both should do the same."

"Where are we going?" Esther whispered.

"Yeah," Jody echoed.

"To see him, to face him."

"Who?" Jody said.

Sage shivered visibly. "The beast," she said. "Michael Leonard Robinson. It's the only way to end this, and I know where he's hiding now."

CHAPTER 32

Congratulations. You Are Still Alive

They looked like the most pathetic threesome in history, shuffling their way up the darkened street as if on some doomed religious pilgrimage. It wasn't so far from accurate either, as it was entirely possible that the girls were going to die tonight, like actually crucified. But what was the alternative? Sage was no detective, yet it was difficult to ignore the fact that there were three dead bodies on the Winslow property, a crime scene drenched with the blood-evidence and forensic whatever, which tied the whole family to murder. In fact, if Sage were on the outside looking in, she could easily come to the conclusion that "The Sculptor," or at least the latest incarnation of "The Sculptor Killer," was a sick middle-aged widower and his three oddball daughters: all cannibals, vampires, cop killers.

Oh, and it didn't stop there. How about the original "Sculptor," or rather, "The Scarecrow Killer"? For real, maybe it had never been Michael Leonard Robinson in the first place! Maybe he was the fall-guy somehow. Of course! Sage had seen the pics on Google this morning: those grotesque photos of the college coeds, impaled on poles with their faces disfigured. Maybe the "Evil Winslow Quartet" had been the doer all along, now moving on from the original obsession to something more timely, more gender-sensitive. And the smoothest transition? Well, who was the first to show up at the original highway kill-sites? Cops. Most probably male.

Fact. Hamlet was dead in their driveway with his mutilated face scraped into the undercarriage of his own cruiser, and Norman's face was splattered across the back patio in glorious technicolor.

Looked like a pattern of disfigurement, now didn't it?

And Poppy being nailed into the bathroom? New fall-guy. Gosh, those notorious killer-girls were clever!

"Hey," Sage said aloud, "even though it hurts like anything, between us we have to consider that Poppy could have been the bad guy all along, even back two years ago. The victims were all college coeds, right? He would know his way around a campus…"

"Yeah," Esther grumbled. "And before he bonked them, he probably told them to shut up like he told me today, and no one gives me shut-ups anymore, no one, not ever."

"Easy, Peanut," Jody said gently. She stopped, took her hands out of the kangaroo pocket of her hoodie, and put her arm around Esther protectively. The three made a semicircle. They were five blocks away from the house now, across from the Rutherford Apartments and the gas station that had gone out of business. Both properties were flanked by dark woodland. The wind made all the shadowy leaves flutter at the tree line, and above there was a low moon, black clouds, and black sky.

"I don't know if *I* believe that one," Jody said. "It would make it so that he was killing people back when Mom was alive. I mean, I'm mad at him and all, mad as ever, but I don't know. I just don't know what to believe."

Sage nodded. Good point. She had brought it up because she didn't know whether *she* really believed it. She sighed. She must have at least thought it *plausible,* or else she wouldn't have thought of it to begin with. So the finger-pointing was addictive, of course. The Sculptor offered you a truckload of dirt, rich with manure, fertile with your own bullshit, and you couldn't help but grow your own horror story from it. Hell, false manifesto? It was originally thought to have been written by a college professor. Like Poppy. The Sculptor was into puzzles. Like Poppy. The Sculptor was from Lower Merion. Like Poppy. The Sculptor was a man big enough to tote around his "Scarecrow Statues" and Poppy was six foot four inches tall.

"No," she said. "Jody, you're right. We keep our eyes on the prize. We find and expose Michael Leonard Robinson and end this. It's the only way. Without him—dead or alive—we look like we're guilty, all four of us."

"And you're sure about this?" Jody said. "You're sure he's hiding at the high school?"

"Positive."

"In the basement?"

"Yes," Sage said, voice shaking a bit. "I saw it when Norman, I mean, *the cop* had a hold of my ankle right before he died. At first I couldn't place anything in the vision, but it was the weird artwork that was vaguely familiar, the big pieces of artwork lying on their sides in the background. Then it clicked when Poppy mentioned the school theater. What I saw was a bunch of flats, big stage-scenery flats that the techies made for the street scenes in *Oliver Twist.* It was supposed to be the mid-year musical but it got delayed because of the construction renovations."

"In the auditorium?"

"Yes," Sage said. "Closed off, and they moved all the theater stuff down to the basement along with the piano, the music stands for the orchestra, the bleachers, the footlights, the stepladders, everything. Both spaces are off-limits now. It's perfect for him."

"But wouldn't the janitors find him down there?"

Sage shook her head. "I don't think so. The basement is humongous, a cluttered storage area, spanning the length of the whole school. And now he has all this theatrical equipment, like lights and scrims and curtains, things that would come in handy for him as he hides in the shadows like a poison black snake. He's also got cameras and old computers, power tools and heavy-duty cables. Fuckin'-A, it's not just a hideout. It's a crowded lab space, a horror-theater with a lot of industrial gizmos."

"And kids one floor up," Esther said.

"Yes," Sage answered hollowly. "He has had all the kids that he needed. To observe. To study. To choose from."

"And he picked you," Jody said.

"Yes, he picked me. And we are going to go force him out into the light." She absently felt for the handles of the eight-inch bolt cutters sticking awkwardly out of her left jacket pocket, and then she dipped into the right and touched the cold grip of Chief Canfield's pistol. "One way or the other," she concluded bleakly. Jody nodded and patted the shape of the service revolver she had on her hip underneath her sweatshirt.

"Don't worry Sage. Besides this, I also have—"

"No," said Sage. "Don't. Whatever you're hiding, keep it to yourself the way we talked about. It's better that way. This jerk is an expert at making people backstab each other, so let's not give him an advantage we don't have to."

"OK," Jody said. "OK."

Sage nodded and bent into the wind, leading the way. They were a quarter-mile from Lower Merion High School, a hop, skip, and a jump, and Sage's feet hurt. She had a dull headache. She needed a shower and the wind felt sharp on her forehead. She'd pulled her hair back and fastened it with her two-piece Celtic slide and hairpin, "the sticker," three inches long and made of electroplated zinc alloy, perfect for punching if you buried the butt-end in your palm and brought the shank up between your middle and ring fingers. She made sure at home to practice sliding it free and making a fist with it. Still, the exchange was always awkward, and she didn't think it would do her much good in the end. She had Norman's mace zipped in the inner pocket of her jacket, but reaching in and withdrawing it was a clumsy business. She had a steak knife hidden in her left sock, but the only way she could think of toting it without cutting herself was to wrap up the serrated blade with duct tape. Then she'd circled the tape all around her shin two times to strap the blade in place. She hadn't a clue how long it would take for her to yank the thing free, and when and if she did, she hadn't a clue as to its effectiveness. I mean, sure, it would hurt to be on the receiving end of a stabbing motion, but Sage knew it wouldn't pierce, sink, and bury.

This was a fool's mission.

And she wondered exactly what method Robinson would use to murder all three of them once he stopped grinning and laughing.

CHAPTER 33

Sometimes Dead Is Better

The school was a darkened hull, its security lights making dull pools on the concrete apron in front of the main entrance doors. Weak secondary light was spilling into the closest tier of the parking lot, and there were only three vehicles there: a pickup truck that maintenance used, the minibus with the special wheelchair lift for students with handicaps, and a row deeper in, a battered brown van with a busted side mirror on the passenger side.

Sage led her sisters east along the lot's back perimeter. Suddenly she was positive that Robinson knew they were coming; in fact, he was probably watching somehow. She hadn't thought of alarms, but was convinced that the freak had nullified them. She wasn't sure exactly how they were going to get to the roof, to the trapdoor above the theater, but she had a feeling they could save themselves the trouble and walk right in through the front lobby. He'd have unlocked the doors for sure.

And he was waiting for them in the basement, the bowels, his lair, fucking creep.

Hell no. The last thing Sage was going to do was make it any easier for him.

"This way," she murmured. They'd made their way around to the far side of the front building where, across the grassy slope, there was a loading dock, two huge dumpsters, and a fenced-off area where they kept racks of backup generators and other industrial things that looked as if they belonged in an electrical power station. The next part back between buildings was a dark alley, deep and thin, with a nook at the rear that had a cluster of exposed piping going straight up the outer wall of the auditorium. Sage and her sisters were going to have to climb the pipes somehow, and she'd had the vague idea that they might do it one by one, feet flat on the wall, holding tight the ends of the belt she was currently wearing, which would be slipped around the back of the pipe to shuck-up foot by foot.

But what if the pipes were fastened to the wall every seven feet or so with some sort of mounting bracket that would block them?

Well, some things you had to do on the fly. Some things you had to dive your way into, and like the Freddie character said in the Queen movie, *"Oh, we'll find a way..."*

"C'mon," she said, starting down the slope. They were officially on school property now. Trespassers. Villains about to become murderers. If they were lucky. Her sisters had fallen in step behind her, and the three slowly approached the dark set of buildings. The closer they got; however, the more dreadful the place seemed, and crossing the access road, Sage saw that the lighting was somehow worse this close up, the mouth of the alleyway blackened like midnight in a cave. She stopped. They had not brought a flashlight.

"Wrong alley," Esther said. Sage turned, stared for a moment, and almost burst into tears. Every time she looked closely at her baby sister the poor thing seemed to be worse, frayed, as if she'd lived in the basement for seven years. Her hair was tangled and clotted, her face gaunt and skull-like.

"What do you mean, 'wrong alley'?" Sage said.

"I mean, we have to go in over there." Esther pointed back to the left, to the fenced-off area with the turbines, reactors, and converters or whatever the electrical engineers would have called them. There was a gate at the front of the cage chained with a padlock and a sign fastened to the cyclone fencing above it that said "DANGER HIGH VOLTAGE."

"Through there?" Sage said.

"Yes, to the back, where there's a ladder."

"A ladder," Jody said. "Where? I don't see a ladder."

"It's covered."

"With what?"

"Cloth, stupid."

"Hey!" Jody said.

"Quiet, both of you," said Sage. She went down to a knee before Esther and tried to take her hands. Esther put the right one holding the demented teddy bear behind her back and sacrificed her left. Sage had a strange feeling that she looked as if she was about to kiss her little sister's ring.

"How do you know about a ladder inside a restricted area on the property of a school you don't even go to?" she said.

Esther frowned. "I know lots of things. I've climbed that fence hundreds of times, millions, and I've climbed the ladder to the roof too. Billions of times. Bazillions."

"Why?"

"I like to think from high places. Just don't be stupid enough to go touching anything inside the hazard-cage."

Sage stood and peered back over her shoulder at the restricted area.

271

"No 'stupids,' Cupcake," she said absently. The fence surrounding the danger-zone made a perimeter of about twenty feet across and thirty or so back, and though there was no razor twine looped along the top rail, there were those nasty twists that looked like sharp two-pronged forks. Maybe Esther was light as a feather and nimble as Peter Pan and all that, but Sage didn't relish the idea of getting one foot over, then slipping somehow and landing crotch-first on the forks.

She got out the small bolt cutters and walked to the gate. "You're sure there's a ladder in there?"

"Yes," said Esther. "It's next to the locked door at the back, in its own little alleyway to the right of it."

"I don't see it," said Jody. The three of them stood before the gate.

"Of course you don't," said Esther. "You're not supposed to. If you could, all the kids would try climbing it."

Sage stared at her sister a second longer, then back through the fence. She squinted. The machinery and electrical apparatuses blocked the ground-level view, and the wall behind looked grainy and black. About fifty feet up there was a huge piece of ductwork cutting across horizontally, blocking the sightline at roof level. Sage looked down at the padlock. It was old and rusted, clasped through two links of the thick chain tucked around and between the steel gate rails. She'd never cut anything with a bolt cutter tool, and she'd never broken the law like this, not really. She'd smoked weed three times. She drank peach schnapps once, over at Mollie Tanenbaum's house when her parents were out at an art show. It made her dizzy and spazzy. She took hold of the padlock and put the opened jaws of the bolt cutter on either side of the shackle.

There was no way she was strong enough to squeeze the handles together, no way.

She squeezed and was amazed at how steadily and easily the blades worked their way through the steel, like fabric scissors cutting through leather. It was like an illusion, a magic trick. No wonder the diesel types and techies liked tools. She cut through completely with a *snap* and a *plink,* and Jody reached to grab out the lock. After feeding the chain back through once or twice, the gate was clear. Sage pulled it open and walked in with her sisters in tow. She was careful not to touch anything, and there was a low hum that she felt more than heard, almost indiscernible, like those background movie sounds that made everything ominous before the jump-scare.

On the building-wall there was a door that looked as if it was made of dark maroon steel with a peep-window that had those diamond wire shapes in it. To the right, at first glance, it seemed as if the façade was uniform, but when Sage stepped in closer she saw that there were a couple of seams about three feet apart going straight up the wall.

"Masking cloth," she muttered.

"Told you," Esther said.

Sage reached for it, pinched the fabric, and it felt gauzy, like a black veil. It was fastened above her a few yards up on both sides with black string looped over subtle black concrete screws, and when she looked down she saw the cloth attached similarly on both sides at ground level. She squatted and detached both. The breeze made it look as if part of the wall was rippling, and Sage rose and stepped inside past the cloth.

The inner "alley" was a three-foot-wide niche cut into the concrete, going a mere four feet inward, and high above on the right there was one of those eternal cemetery lights shaded dark blue and offering a dull glow along the length of the steel ladder bolted to the back wall.

Sage approached and started to climb, and behind her she heard Jody offer to put the teddy bear in her sweatshirt pocket. Esther refused to do so.

"No one takes my bear, nobody," she said. There was a pause, and then a muffled, "See?"

Esther had put the scruff of its neck or one of the arms or legs in her mouth. Sage heard her climb on below her, coming up quickly. Time to get a move-on, and Sage went rung to rung as fast as she could without slipping. And fast was good, as Sage was determined that her fear of heights wouldn't go holding them back.

It got noticeably cooler at the top behind the ductwork as it was open-air, and Sage got to the top, sliding her knee up over the lip and pushing onto the roof before she had a chance to think about the exchange as a flashpoint for falling. Soon enough, she was standing up there in the dark wind, joined by her sisters, with the shadowed forms of the roof vents and draft hoods making shapes around them like sleeping monsters. Sage shivered.

"The alley with the pipes looks bigger across now," she said.

"Yeah," Jody said. "But we can jump it." She walked off right and approached the edge.

"Not that close!" Sage said. "Be careful, please."

Jody leaned over it, glanced to the other side, and turned back.

"Looks worse than it is," she said, returning to them. "All in your head. We go twice as far in the long jump in gym class."

"Well, I don't," Sage muttered.

Jody had just re-entered the "the huddle."

"No choice," she said.

She turned on her heel then and ran back for the brink. Sage wanted to scream but clamped shut her mouth, both terrified and equally amazed at her sister's "burst-speed." The baseball coaches had always called it something more technical, but to Sage it was simply the idea that a batter, after hitting an infield grounder, had to go from being stationary and slightly off-center to all-out full speed, especially a righty having to cross over home plate and beat the throw to first base. And Jody was *flying*, and she clapped her takeoff foot extra hard at the launch-point and jumped out across the abyss. It was tough to tell from this angle, but it looked as if she made it by two feet at least, her sneakers scraping and braking on the rough terrain of the neighboring roof.

"See?" she called over. "Piece of cake."

Without warning, Esther then burst away and sprang across the roof, propelling herself at the break point and making the other side easily with four or five nimble landing steps. She turned back toward Sage.

"C'mon then!"

Sage put her thumbnail between her teeth. She didn't want to do this, didn't think she *could* do it. If she fell short, she'd die, and she wasn't athletic. What if she punked out? How many feet across was the gap? Three? Four and a half? Five or six?

"I'm going to go in deeper over here and see if the rooves connect," she said weakly.

"They don't," Esther said. "I've been up here, remember?"

Sage didn't know what to say. She felt as if frozen, muscles sluggish, ready to fail her at the critical moment, and it was going to end here, before the fight, before she had a chance to pay back this rat bastard for ruining her life.

Ruined my fucking life.

Suddenly something overcame her, head to toe, as if she could feel the blood pumping in her chest, in her temples, back behind her eyes, and it was hot blood, angry blood, the venom of rage.

Ruined.

Someone was screaming.

By the time Sage had connected the fact that the scream was coming from her, she'd bolted halfway to the launch point. She was screaming and the wind felt sharp and her sisters were screaming back at her, pumping their fists for her, screaming themselves raw, and Sage tore the rest of the way across the roof knowing she might die and not giving a shit.

She hit the launch point.

The timing and the length of stride had been off by a half-step, however, and she sprang up and out into the air off her right foot about a yard back from the drop as opposed to something more ideal, like three inches or so.

The wind tastes like adrenaline up here, she thought. It didn't make sense, but it made perfect sense, and her sisters were still screaming when they were all supposed to be coming on in stealth, and Sage didn't care, and this was a one hell of a rude-rush, soaring across the edge of the sky, and the roof on the other side for a bare moment fishbowled as if she was seeing it through the curved windshield of a copter miles above the helipad, and then it came up to meet her in one hell of a hurry.

She came in hard with a yard or so to spare, but she landed poorly, flat-footed and awkward.

Pain burst like rage in both soles, and she could swear she'd just broken every blister she'd garnered walking outside all day barefooted. She rolled forward in a heap, coming to a stop on her side, breathing hoarsely, feeling ugly and broken.

Jody came from behind and grabbed her under her arms. She grunted, lifting her to a standing position, and Sage didn't say anything about the blisters. Her sisters might have asked to see them, and her strap-on weapon would have been exposed. Their plans were haphazard and juvenile, but at least they could stick to their own rules.

"This way," she said, moving forward, trying not to hobble. Jody was quick to fall in step behind her, and she put her hand on Sage's shoulder, making her halt and turn.

"Hmm?"

"You forgot these." She handed Sage the bolt cutters. They were all standing between two waist-high industrial vents, one capped off with what looked like a Middle Eastern turban, the other like an Asian conical rice hat. They were "going international," Sage thought crazily.

"They fell out of your pocket on your smooth landing," Jody concluded.

"Hardy-har."

"It's over there," Esther said, pointing back left about ten paces. The surface outline of the trapdoor was indiscernible, but the padlock was picking up glint from the moon. That wasn't good. The first lock had been rusted, dull and weakened. Maybe the bolt cutters wouldn't be so magical this time around.

They all approached and knelt on three sides of the trapdoor built into the flat surface of the roof. It was steel, painted dark gray, and the hasp looked heavy duty. Its loop, or what Sage thought was called the "staple," looked to be as thick as the shackle on the padlock. She brought around the bolt cutters, set the opened jaws on the steel of the lock, and pressed in, one-handed.

Nothing, and she used both hands, and it went nowhere, as if the shackle was plated with titanium or something. Hands were on top of hers then, Jody's hands, and together they squeezed, and it hurt playing "middle man" between the cutter handles and her sister's powerful grip, which had been strengthened tenfold from holding a bat firmly in her hands and hitting three hundred a night for years off the tee in the basement. Sage clenched her teeth and felt some give.

There was a flat *snap* as they severed the shackle, making it *toink* and pitch in place for a moment as if struck by a bullet. Jody reached, fingered it out, and tossed it aside. She folded the hasp open and took hold of the door handle. She strained up with it and Sage got her fingers under the edge. The door was heavy with suction at first, almost as if the space below housed some massive beast sucking its breath inward for spite, but the beast's magic power was short-lived, and Jody and Sage hauled the door up and over, making it fall back and *clunk* to the roof.

"Knock-knock," Esther said listlessly. Jody came over and tucked her little sister's dirty hair behind her ear.

"Don't worry, Peanut," she said. "A second ago, we were yelling so loud it hurt my throat. If you're worried about cops, it's obvious that they aren't anywhere nearby. If you're worried about Robinson—"

"He probably knows we're here already," Sage finished, her own voice listless and numb. "I was thinking about that back when we first arrived at the edge of the parking lot, but I thought we had to do everything possible to—I don't know...I mean, what if he guessed we'd know he knew and loaded the front doors with dynamite or... ?" Her voice trailed off into the wind and she leaned over the edge of the opening, her hands in fists up under her chin. There was the dim glow of a safety light or something from somewhere within, and the space smelled faintly like burnt wires and sawdust. "Uh, that's going to be a problem," she said, pointing downward.

"What?" Jody said, looking in herself. "It's the catwalk above the back of the stage. C'mon, Sage, you can do this. Looks like it's got safety rails." She glanced at her sister. "You've been up on it, right?"

"No," she said quietly.

"For real?"

Sage nodded. She looked at the dark sky, then to her sisters.

"I told you guys that I quit the theater tech group because it was too much like a clique, but I lied. I quit because there were so many names of things and so many technical safety measures and protocols that my mind always froze up, as if I'd just breathed in gas, making my head loopy. It was anxiety, big time, but I'm not comfortable talking about it the way other people are, and I didn't know anybody. I was scared to climb the ladder up to that catwalk. There's also a spiral staircase, but that was totally 'haunted house,' and I was supposed to know the difference between the stationary lights hanging off the rail up there and the 'warmth' of the follow-spots, and what a pinrail was, and the way to get to the fly loft as well as how to adjust the proscenium curtains, but in the end I was too chicken to even climb a damned ladder."

She looked back down into the opening.

"And now I have to jump again, but this isn't in the dark between rooves." She pointed. "You guys see a catwalk bridge, right? I only see how high up it is through the grating."

"It'll hold," Jody said. "We're only about ten feet above it. The drop only looks farther because of the distance to the stage underneath. Look, I'll jump first."

Sage stopped her. "No," she said. "I'll go first. If I'm going to face a serial killer, I have to be able to get over the dumb stuff."

She lowered herself to sit on the edge with her feet dangling. It felt as if she was going to throw up and she forced herself to lean out across for the edge opposite, stretching her torso over the drop and clamping down her fingers on the far lip. It would be better this way than simply sitting and pushing off; if she could hang for a moment, she'd erase a few feet.

She shimmied up until the near edge was under her butt, and then she came off, cutting an arc down through the air, coming fast. She hadn't accounted for the fact that the momentum would make her swing out on the back end like a pendulum, and on the rise, of course, she couldn't see through her own body. It felt as if she'd swung out past the safety rail. And her hands were slipping.

She held on with everything she had and felt herself coming back.

She let go. The fall took forever, far worse than the slow-mo of the helicopter jump. She didn't land when she thought she would, and a split second later the grid of the catwalk rushed up to meet her, thumping her roughly, and she felt the breath whoosh out of her and she ragdolled, bunking her head on one of the low safety rails. For a moment she felt as if she'd passed out and drifted through a flicker of dark dreams, because she was looking down at her sisters from above, and they were peering up at her from behind the edges of the square portal, and she wondered how they could do this without falling back into the sky, and down was up, and then things settled, reversed.

Sage shook her head hard. On the back of her skull there would be a lump she hoped her hair would hide. She pushed to all fours. She stared down between her hands and froze.

Now, with a much wider viewing angle, the auditorium was a disturbing alien dreamscape, the stage directly beneath her bald and unchanged from the back end they called "upstage" to the mid-point of the "playing area," yet from there to where the "apron" was supposed to be it was utterly demolished, splintered, cratered and scarred like the moon, with planet buggies in the orchestra pit that looked like push-dumpsters for scrap, and lunar roving vehicles that appeared to be mini-bulldozers that said "BOBCAT" on them, and all the other space-age equipment cluttered around the robot cranes, doubling as concrete breaking hammers, pry bars, shovels, power drills, and circular saws, all scattered about the seating area that had been ripped up, the chairs removed, the mild grade littered with piles of crushed stone, plywood, and what looked like work-stations and pallet racking, all circled by humongous scissor-lifts rising up into dark recesses.

"You all right, kid?" called Jody.

"Yeah," Esther echoed. "You OK, baby-doll?"

It broke the spell, and Sage checked her pockets. The gun was still there. The bolt cutters weren't, but she knew they didn't need them anymore. Once they got off the catwalk and down to the cluttered floor space, they'd have access to more tools than they'd know what to do with. She smiled ruefully.

"I am like a baby," she said. "And I am going to crawl to the side to give you guys room. I'm not guaranteeing that I can stand up, though, because I don't trust my balance."

"Don't look down," Jody said. "In fact, look up at the underside here. Is there a ladder there, maybe folded underneath?"

Sage gazed upward, and in the shadows it did seem as if there was something hooked on the north side of the opening, fastened to the ceiling. She made herself grab the footrail and push up off her knees. Then came the waist rail, and the top one at chest level. She got her feet under her and held tightly, feeling woozy. Next to her right hand was what looked like a steel clip, and it was directly under the ladder up there that looked like a long rack of alien ribs, half-reptilian, half-machine, nesting up there in the shadows.

"There is a ladder," she said. "But I don't know how on earth you get up to it so you can detach it. There's a clasp here, like a buckle or something to fasten this end, but again, I don't see how to get up to it." She looked at her hands. "Seems that to grab the ladder we need a ladder."

Jody laughed dryly. "I'll bet there's a crank somewhere, like the basketball hoops in gym class and the one at Latchkey. But you don't know where it is because you didn't pass theater-nerd 101."

"Exactly," Sage admitted.

"So dumb!" said Esther.

"Who, me?"

"No, silly. If there's a ladder, why was the trapdoor it leads to locked on the outside? It doesn't make sense. So dumb."

"Lots of things don't make sense anymore," Sage said. What she didn't voice was the nagging suspicion that it was The Sculptor who had put a lock on the trapdoor outside, so he could fire-bomb the auditorium or some such cruel shit. Cage in the techies stuck up on the catwalk. She shuffled a few careful steps, still clutching the rail like an old woman in a handicapped stall, and she paused for a moment, taking a careful glance to the side, stage left and away. Just before the far wall there was the spiral staircase twisting its way beneath the platform down to the floor like the ladder next to it. And in terms of the rail that she was clutching onto for dear life, it was over yonder, where it extended to the right-angled corner-point, that there was a big crank handle fastened to it with gears underneath, like a supersized gadget in a Sherlock Holmes movie. It was connected to a cable that went taught on a slant overhead and then was lost in the dark maze of girder work, piping, and what looked like scaffolding connected by elbow joints.

"Don't jump," Sage said. "I found your crankshaft."

She was proud of herself when she finally reached the mechanism without puking or falling down or freezing in place as if she was playing "Red Light/Green Light," and she was even prouder for figuring out how to work the darned thing without help from her sisters. There was a lock-clip with a tab in a groove you had to thumb out, and before she knew it she'd cranked down the ladder. Now to fasten it. Slowly but surely she made her way back to where she'd just jumped and almost killed her damned self, and she soon discovered that the locking device on the railing had a similar clasp as the crank, and by the time Sage clipped the foot of the ladder in place she felt fairly confident about her equilibrium and all that. As long as she didn't let her gaze fall lower than her waist.

Her sisters came down the ladder. Then it was the same old-lady-walk for Sage to make it back over to the spiral staircase.

Climbing down was an ordeal that took what seemed like forever, but it was better than it would have been if Sage didn't have a supportive sister in front and behind her.

When the three finally had their feet firm on the stage's rear floor area, Sage felt a swell of pure joy. They'd made it! Then the feeling curled in and puckered. They were close now. Too close. To possible death. To the devil himself.

Jody had wandered out to the splintered edge where the stage was torn away, and she seemed to be scouting a path among all the construction paraphernalia.

"Don't bother," Sage said. "The entrance to the basement is back here. The first thing they demolished was a part of the adjoining wall to the choir room, and they built a concrete ramp going down a level. Claire Finnigan told me. She'd borrowed my biology notebook, left it in her music class, and then over the weekend the construction started. The whole space went off-limits all of a sudden, and I was pissed actually. I had some doodles in the margins that were pure fire."

Jody returned and pointed at the back wall. "I don't see a ramp. I just see the big garage door behind all those dangling wires."

"That's the door. It leads to the ramp."

Jody made her way closer to it. "There's no lock," she said over her shoulder.

"Of course not," Sage said. "Why bother locking it when all the doors to get in the auditorium are locked to students and staff to begin with? Common sense, right?"

Jody turned. She used her pinkie to pick at something between her teeth.

"There's no handle either," she said finally.

Sage didn't have an answer for that. The steel corrugated door curtain had no lift handle or T-grip as their garage did at home. Maybe there was another crankshaft somewhere. Esther was looking at her, staring actually, and she was simultaneously occupied with chewing on her teddy bear's eye, creepy as hell, but it was better than sucking her thumb...

"Button," Esther said, sort of slurred. Sage was tempted to tell her not to speak with her mouth full.

"Yeah, Cupcake," Jody said. "It's a button your teddy has for an eye and you're going to pull it straight out of its head. It's literally dangling by a thread, and you don't want a blind bear, do you?"

Esther popped it out of her mouth. "It's not a bear," she said. "It's just cloth and stuffing, and I'm not a baby. It's a stress doll. I'm stressed." She bit it back into her mouth, then spit it out promptly. "It's cold and gross now." She cradled the bear. "And I meant that you have to hit the button."

"What button?"

"The one hanging like a banana on a vine over there."

Sage turned, and there was a thick piece of electrical cable with a rectangular housing on the end of it hanging to the left of the door. In the middle of the housing there was a red button protruding. It looked cartoonish, like Poppy's old favorite with the roadrunner and coyote, but it wasn't funny, ha-ha. It was more funny, ironic, like not funny at all, in one of those opposites where the innocence of the kiddie thing made it twice as scary.

Sage walked in toward it, moving the hanging cables aside like jungle foliage. She reached up and grabbed the housing. She hit the red button.

A motor kicked on, rumbling and echoing throughout the space, and the door started coming up, vibrating, screeching its wheels in the side-channels. A dull glow spread out of the opening and slowly filled everything with dull murky ocean colors, making the sisters look pale and washed out like corpses. They approached the edge of the entranceway. Inside, the lighting seemed to come from some sort of emergency system similar to the lusterless illumination in the ladder-niche outside behind the "high voltage" area. The wide ramp here had a downward grade for about thirty feet, then seemed to do a 180 to come back and go farther down a level beneath them. Like the ball park.

To the basement.

Suddenly the space brightened in perfect syncopation with a stinging synthesizer sound, very much akin to the trick John Carpenter used in the first *Halloween* whenever there was a surprise Michael Meyers sighting. All three of them jerked with it like puppets on wires.

"Fuck!" Jody growled.

"Jesus Lord!" Sage said.

Esther had shrieked something inarticulate.

Before them, the walls started bleeding in three-dimensional anime, overbright crimson dripping and seeping, advancing along the floor in streaks as if subject to bursts of high wind.

Then illusion shut off, back to dim lighting, and an amplified voice filled with richness and reverb said,

"Greetings."

CHAPTER 34

Welcome to My Nightmare

S age had assumed there would be some level of organization
to the basement storage hoard, but it was literally just clutter
and heaps, hodgepodge medleys and disarrayed mishmash,
sometimes impeding the pathway so much that the girls had
to go single file. Every hundred feet or so there was a construction
string lamp hanging up near the ceiling, tossing shadows across
everything in a littered sort of dark patchwork, and after weaving
through all the theater stuff they had to climb over a pile of boxes
filled with invoices and paper waste, some of the cardboard stove
in on top and others burst at the side seams. There were bleacher
sections and boxes of pool noodles and kickboards, bookshelves,
and stacks of steel folding chairs. They passed carefully through an
area crammed with racks of science glassware and gas canisters, and
then made their way through a dark chamber that housed music
stands, instrument cases, flags and wooden twirling rifles, old computer monitors and boxes of basketballs, footballs, soccer balls, and
lacrosse sticks. About two hundred yards in, they came to a fork.

In the middle, splitting the pathways at the front of a cluster of office furniture, portable whiteboards, and old AV equipment, there was a piano, a Steinway, and the only reason Sage recognized it was the association with the John Shirley character in one of their favorite family movies, *Greenbook*. Sadness filled her. What a family they had been, even after Mom died.

The piano started playing.

The three girls jumped, the puppet thing again, and Sage stared in horror at the keys depressing themselves, plinking and doinking to the Aretha Franklin song "Won't Be Long," featured in the film she'd been just thinking about. It was a happy song, a road song, a pump-me-up song, but without the drums, the bass line, and the vocals, it accented the offbeat, making it ghostly and wicked, more like a swansong in a haunted old western saloon.

Worse, it proved that Robinson had studied them all too well, that he'd manufactured this moment, predicted them down to a T. And worse than worse, he could see them now, or at least he could hear them, as he must have done at the top of the ramp when he kicked off the synthesizer note and the three-dimensional blood show. Sage had been so shocked back there that it hadn't clicked, but now it was abundantly clear that here, in this place, Robinson didn't need a human transmitter.

The piano stopped.

"To the right," his voice said, still heavy on the reverb. Like dutiful soldiers, they complied.

More like lambs, Sage thought.

They walked shoulder to shoulder down a rough alleyway made up mostly of old cafeteria equipment on either side of them: baker's sheet pan racks, rolling tray towers, microwave ovens, ice cream display cases, big steam table units, stacks of plastic milk crates, toaster ovens, and even a couple of dingy refrigerators that looked as if they came from the 1950s.

At the end of the makeshift hallway, now crammed on both sides of them, were throngs of theater costume mannequins, all in states of disrepair, chipped, some eyeless, some missing limbs, some patched with duct tape. The two groupings had been positioned to form a wide aisle leading up to a set of old theater curtains blocking the way, floor to ceiling, dull green, closed in their familiar design like some humongous street clown's accordion. There was a whirring noise and the curtains slowly opened, the hooks scraping along the drape rods.

There was a pathway now about twenty feet across between the drawn curtains, and the opening led to an inner sanctum that was pitch-dark. Suddenly a spotlight kicked on, casting down a bright cone shape on an angle from upper stage right. It revealed a bare floor that was painted jet-black.

"Come forward," said Robinson, his voice all feathers and honey. "You didn't come all this way to merely be spectators."

The three approached cautiously to a step or two before the curtain-line, and as they did, another set of lights came up in the wide theater space before them, museum lighting, glowing down in soft arcs from behind a strip of masking curtain spanning the back upper edge of the scenery. It was all backdrop, the long rear wall constructed of the *Oliver Twist* stage flats, lying lengthwise with two gaps at the far right and left edges, like two missing molars, both embedded as part of the strange mural cutting its corner-points on diagonals with scrim material covering them. The "gauzy drapes" were colored dove-white, and each was about ten feet across. The scenery paintings continued down the sides toward the proscenium curtains, establishing a "playing space" about the size of the audi-torium stage, and dead center before them at the back—the "hood ornament," so to speak—was a set of flats depicting Jacob's Island by featuring rotten bridges crossing tidal ditches at the foot of a row of slum houses. Sideways it was disorienting, as if the drainage was suspended in mid-air before flooding the stage.

The spotlight and the overheads went suddenly dark, and footlights blazed from inside the two corner gap areas. Now visible behind the gauzy façades were silhouettes, man-shaped, and behind them were buttons and dials and gauges, blazing and blinking. Promptly the overheads came back on, the footlights clicked off, and the material covering the twin "corner control booths" flicked back to dove-white.

"My lovelies," Robinson said.

Sage wanted to vomit. "What?" she said. "What do you want from us?"

He made a humming noise in the back of his throat for a moment.

"First things first, my darling," he said. "We have to establish the rules and conditions. Before you, in the two work-stations behind the scrim theater drops, you just observed two men in front of their instrument panels. One of the silhouettes is fake and the other one is yours truly. If you take a run at me at any time, it will be pure fifty-fifty, like a coin toss. If you guess right and make it to my control chamber, we will have the final tussle you undoubtedly crave. If you guess wrong, however, the moment you touch the drape you will be electrocuted, two thousand two hundred volts, the same as would run through a modern-day electric chair. If you are thinking of splitting up, you must deal with the fact that one or two of you will certainly die, while the balance fights for life in a deathly dance with the friendly old cripple."

"Friendly?" Jody said. "You're a pig."

"And you're a wicked witch," he returned, in a tone of casual boredom. "Not that I don't appreciate your...industry when it comes to using that baseball bat of yours, but enough of the ironic imagery alluding to *The Wizard of Oz.* You are no more wicked than I would try to convince you not to pay attention to the man behind the curtain. This is no movie and it is no drill. I have studied all of you for months now, and I am five steps ahead of you at every turn. Please know that all three of you could possibly die tonight."

"Fucker," said Esther.

"Names, names. What fun, Cupcake, but I must insist that we discuss more of the conditions, not only for my benefit, but for yours. Please observe what is above you, ceiling-high in a glorious panorama, not quite a 360, but close enough to keep this thing interesting."

Perimeter lighting blazed on, up where the creases in the ceiling would be, above the *Oliver Twist* flats and extending out past the stage space into the hallway. It was a huge horseshoe shape, and just below the peep-lights was a double roll track with dolly-cars attached by running and side wheels. There was a unit every foot or so, flatcars about two feet square, and atop each was a mechanical contraption on a swivel base, child-sized and robotic, all steel slides, piston-rods, knuckle gears, and clamp units. Each had affixed to it an archery bow, and they all had arrows nocked in place and drawn back.

"You are all in my sights," Robinson said, "and you will remain so until the end of this tableau. Since commands in English would be too slow in response to an attack, I have formed my own verbal codes. Here is an example of the consequence for disobedience. Let's just say that Sage disappointed me. Instead of saying something like, *'Units thirteen, fourteen, and fifteen, give a warning shot half an inch from her nose,'* I would simply say, 'Ulrachh!'"

There was a *twang* sound, and from due right came three arrows whistling through the air. Sage felt the breeze as they whipped past her face and *thwacked* into the mannequin just to the side of her, one in the eye and the other two through the top of the cheek. Sage had bitten back a scream, and noticed now that the three attacking bots had already nocked brand-new arrows. She also noted that the mannequin that took the punishment here just happened to have a Styrofoam head as opposed to hard plastic. So the arrows would sink in more dramatically, of course. If Jody had been standing here, she would have been the one exemplified.

"Now that the unpleasantness is out of the way," Robinson said, "let's exercise a lesson in courtesy. If you would be so kind, I would insist that you step forward into the stage-space one at a time, remove your personals, and then disarm yourselves."

There was a sound from stage left, a rolling sound, and Sage recognized it as that of a "truck" or a piece of flooring on wheels. Usually a techie pushed it, but here the movement was automated, and when it came into view bearing its cargo Sage felt what was left of her spirit sink. It halted before them, about fifteen feet in from the makeshift proscenium curtain line, and clearly, from the very beginning, this had been a fool's errand.

It was a metal detector, the walk-through type shaped like a big tuning fork. Sage recognized it immediately. They'd had it at the front entrance of the school for the first three weeks into September. Parents complained. Channel 3 did a feature on it, and it had been removed. Stored down here in the basement. Perfect.

There was no cable; he'd even figured a way to go cordless. On both sides of the device on the roller cart were sawed-off podium bases and on top of each was a gray plastic bin, of the sort they used the airport.

"You first, Sage my darling," he said. "You see the storage trays. The one to your right is for personal items. You approach that one first. The tray on the left is for weapons, and it's like confession now, isn't it? Ah, but in the end you'll be appreciative when you walk through without setting off the alarm. It buzzes in a manner that is just so displeasing. Oh, and take note, my dear, that if you simply choose not to come forward, I'll kill one of your sisters. I won't tell you which because showing is so much more potent than telling, but rest assured that my 'arrow-bots' will turn her into a pincushion. And so please, pretty please, my sweet, please make your entrance."

She stepped past the curtain line, praying with everything she had that the metal detector was defective somehow. Maybe it had gotten damaged in transport from the front lobby to this God-awful place. Standing before the back right corner-point of the platform, she fished out her keys.

"Oh, no, no, darling," he interrupted. "Those go to the left in the 'bad girl' bin."

"Really? For real…"

"There are times for risk and times to play it safe, dear. This is the latter. Better for you in the end, I think."

She walked across and tossed the keys in the weapon bin. She walked back to the right and took out her wallet. She would have put in her cell phone as well, but she hadn't brought it. None of them had.

"Do you want my sneakers in the bin too?" she said.

"Why?" he said. "You catching a plane?"

She didn't even bother answering. If she was going to make a move, it would have to be now. She currently had an unobstructed shot at the two control stations on either side of the roll cart at the back corners of the stage. No problem, she would simply have to draw the gun from her jacket pocket faster than a cowboy and shoot into both. And she'd have to be quick. She'd have to get it done before he could belt out one of his code words, turning her into a pincushion.

"And I'll have that gun now," he said softly. "I can see the butt of it protruding from your right jacket pocket. And don't even think about firing into the scrims. This isn't Hollywood, and the draw would be awkward. You might even catch an edge on the pocket lining, and before you'd have a chance to set your finger in the trigger guard, I'd have put ten arrows into you: two for your eyes, five in the throat, and three of them straight through your heart."

She walked slowly back to the left and reached into her coat pocket, slowly sliding out the pistol. She held it by the grip with the tips of her forefinger and thumb like making an "OK" sign, and she heard Jody moan in despair behind her. She put the pistol in the gray bin.

"Now the knife strapped to your shin, please."

She felt herself jolt, couldn't help it. "How—?"

"You've bled a bit, dear. It's soaked through your sock—not much, mind you, just a dot on the white-collar lining of your sneaker, but it would be best to get rid of the implement causing the irritation, don't you agree?"

"I thought you were blind."

"Better than sight, I have implanted impulse conductors affixed to conduits that have meta-contact with the cerebral cortex. But Sage, do you really want to waste time with the science lesson?"

She twisted to the floor. This was hopeless. She shucked up her pant leg, pushed off her sneaker, removed her blood-spotted sock, and started digging at the tape holding the knife in place. She could see where the tip of the buffered blade had bluntly scraped her down toward the ankle. It had bled a bit, yet it had already clotted. She must have done it to herself on the roof-jump or the swing out onto the catwalk.

She worked the edge of the tape until she'd scratched up a pulling-tab, and she yanked it. Of course it split, only yielding a strip, and suddenly enraged, she used both hands to twist the knife as if turning an industrial gate valve. With a grunt she snapped the adhesive, wrenched the knife free, and dropped it to the floor.

And she still had to get the rest of the tape off her leg.

"Fast is best, darling," Robinson said, doing that psycho mind-reading bullshit again. Sage cupped her hands around the limb and molded the tape back where the knife had been.

"I've bled enough for you tonight, motherfucker. No more."

"Well, that remains to be seen. Now put the knife up in the weapons bin."

"Put the lotion in the basket?" she said. "You remember what happened to that guy?"

"He was merely a foil for Hannibal Lecter, his better. And I am more the latter, my dear."

"That remains to be seen."

"Enough," he said. "Place the weapon in the bin and walk through the metal detector. If you tire me further, I'll do a lot worse to you than ripping off duct tape."

Sullen, she pushed to her knees.

"You didn't put your sock or your sneaker back on, Sage."

She grabbed the knife and she stood. "Don't need them," she said. "Maybe the unevenness will bug you, mess up the symmetry of your psycho theater. Hope it does, too."

She put the knife in the gray bin.

"Now walk through," he said.

"My coat has a zipper. So do my jeans, let alone the fastening button."

He sighed. "I preset the detection threshold high enough not to register those things, dear. Now walk."

She stepped up on the platform. There was no movement, no rocking motion, and in the back of her mind she marveled at the way he had something on wheels so well anchored. She walked through the metal detector.

The alarm blared. Somehow he had it hooked into the sound system too, and it hurt Sage's ears. She put her hands over them. The stage went momentarily dark, and red and blue police lights swept their beams across the theater space.

The sound cut off like a blade in syncopation with the lights coming back full. Sage slowly brought down her hands, humbly came back, and reached into her coat's inner lining-pocket to get out the small spray can of mace. When she went to put it in the gray bin; however, she stopped short. The bin was empty, no gun and no knife.

"Shitty magician's trick!" Jody spat from her position at the curtain-line. "The tray has a false bottom and the podium base is hollow. He hit a button or something and flushed the toilet when the lights were flashing. Bravo, asshole."

"Ummschdadt," he said quietly.

There was the *twang* sound and an arrow zipped across from top right. Jody's arm jerked as if someone had bumped her hard on the shoulder in passing, and she screeched and brought up her hand. It looked like a strange geometrical shape, and it was the arrow buried to the halfway point through the webbing between her thumb and index finger.

"Oh my God!" she cried. "I'm going to *kill* you."

"Doubtful," he answered. "And stop whining. It isn't your throwing hand."

"Bastard!"

"No, dear. My mother and father were married, thank you. No worries, though. I wasn't depending on you for vocabulary. Oh, and by the way, I wouldn't pull out that arrow. That's when it really starts bleeding."

"Bastard!"

"Redundant!" he said. "You're all so predictable. Not that I mind, as it makes you good lab rats, but this portion of the show is taking too long. I'm getting restless, and we don't want that, do we? Jody, get ready to move your ass to the metal detector. Sage will complete her part of this by placing the can of mace in the gray bin along with that ridiculous hairpin she's wearing. She'll do one more walk-through for safety's sake, and following that, I am warning you both not to make any sort of exchange when you pass each other to switch places. Jody, you will put your trinkets in the right-side bin, and of course your keys and all your weapons in the left. Do it promptly, no games."

"*Bastard!*" Jody whispered.

Utterly deflated, Sage placed the mace in the bin and pulled out her hairpin. She put it in with the mace and made haste, walking along the edge, coming back around and walking back through the metal detector. No sirens this time, no fanfare, and her hair was in her face. She stepped off the platform, pivoted, and shuffled back to her place at the proscenium curtain line, not even having the courage to acknowledge her sister with a look in passing. This was a miserable failure, all of it. She turned. Jody stood at the back left edge of the platform.

"I don't have keys," she said, "and I don't do trinkets."

"Give me the gun then, Jody," he said. "I can't see it, but I know you have it." He laughed. "And you shouldn't need it anyway. You know from baseball that the gear has nothing to do with talent. The gun's almost like cheating. Same as on the field: you should still be able to hit it flat and hard to left center even without your best cleats and a composite bat with spring action barrel flex."

Sage almost barfed. Jody had said those exact words a month ago, complaining about a teammate who bitched about the lack of traction he got with sneakers, practicing with the indoor pitching machine. This wasn't just clever psychology. Robinson had been listening to them, learning them, wearing them like skins so he could turn them inside-out here on show-night.

Jody used her good hand to go under her sweatshirt to her waist-band and pull out the service revolver, either Norman's or Hamlet's, didn't matter. Clearly, Esther had the other one, and too soon Robinson would confiscate it as well, flush their hopes down the makeshift podium-toilet.

"My hand hurts," Jody said.

"It's supposed to hurt. Drop the gun in the bin and give me everything else. If my calculations are correct and my psychological profile is accurate, you have your own can of mace in your pocket, a short-handled barbecue fork in your sweatshirt pouch along with a police taser, and a cigarette lighter you taped to the back of your neck."

Sage couldn't see Jody's face, but her jaw must have dropped as her shoulders wilted. She put it all in the bin, yelping pathetically when she pulled the lighter off the nape of her neck. Sage thought Robinson was going to make some wry comment, connecting it with the duct tape still wrapped around her own shin, but he didn't. Instead he said,

"I'll have that meat hammer now."

Jody made a sound Sage had never heard before from her. A pitiful wail.

"We'll have none of that," Robinson said. "There's no crying in baseball and no weeping in the theater, not this one."

"I can't feel my hand, mister."

"Not my problem. You brought it on yourself. Now give me that hammer."

Jody reached down, careful not to touch the arrow to the floor, and pulled up the left cuff of her sweat pants. The tool Poppy used to tenderize meat was stuck in her calf-high sports compression sock, tied around with a bandana under the head. She unfastened it, straightened, and put the weapon in the bin.

"Now walk through," he said.

"What about this?" she said, holding up her pierced hand.

"If you hadn't noticed, the arrows are plastic-tipped, painted silver. It's the only way the school district could arrange the contract so that the implements weren't considered lethal weapons, go figure, go archery team." He chuckled. "And if you do somehow unveil me, well, there you have it. I'll leave you to your instincts and industry to try to use that embedded arrow against me. It's only fair, no?"

"Bastard," she said. But it was hollow, no fire, no grit.

"Walk through the detector," he said.

She did. No alarms, no police-lights. She slinked back to her place at the curtain line to the sound of the gray bin opening and clattering her weapons down into the podium.

"And now..." said Robinson.

"No!" Esther said. "You can't make me, I'm seven!"

"Old enough," he returned.

"Fine!"

Sulking, she flounced up to the platform, climbed on, and moved to the bin on the left. All business as if to spite herself, she unzipped the right side of the jumbo kangaroo pocket of her bulky winter Danskin Now sweatshirt. She pawed in and yanked out the service pistol. Into the bin it went. Next, she dug out Sage's stone carving hammer, same pocket, and she reached to drop it next to the firearm. She took a moment to look in at both sullenly, hugging her teddy with both arms, rocking gently. Then she pivoted and made to walk through the metal detector, head down, determined, no non-sense. Still, with a half-step to go before going through, Robinson's voice stopped her cold.

"Oh, no, no, no," he said. "First things first, darling, put the teddy in the bin to the right. That's where the personal items go."

She turned a 360, looking all around, eyes wide, and she gripped the bear even tighter to her chest.

"No!" she cried. "I won't be without my stress doll, not for a minute, not for a second!"

"But that's the rule."

"I don't care!"

"And you are a spoiled brat who needs to learn a lesson or two."

"No!" she shouted, crumpling to the platform, clutching her teddy bear. Then she was whining, next screeching, then kicking and thrashing and shaking. This was no hissy-fissy. This was an all-out, no-holds-barred tantrum. It went on for what seemed like hours, and after curling in, she leveled off, whimpering, moaning.

"There," Robinson said. "Now that you've cried it out, you can put the teddy in the bin."

"Are you fucking insane?" Jody said, a bit of the fire sparked back in her eye. "She's a small child! Let her go through holding the bear, for shit's sake."

"I know you don't have a heart," Sage added. "But have some mercy. Besides, this is messy. Of all things, I don't think you wanted it messy, not this way."

There was a moment of silence, for all but Esther groaning and quivering, and Robinson's voice was even and steely.

"Esther. Winslow. Stand up and put that bear in the personal items bin."

Amazingly, she struggled back to her feet, worn out, pouting the whole way. She gave her precious teddy a last tender cradle-rock, then gently, oh so gently, she placed it in the gray tray on the right.

Stone-faced then, she walked toward the archway of the metal detector. Then she walked through it. No alarm sounded. She turned back, retrieved her teddy bear, and jumped off the platform. She walked back toward her sisters and at the curtain line sat at their feet, cross-legged, her precious teddy bear crooked in her left arm coming across her stomach. Promptly, she stuck her right thumb in her mouth. It almost made Sage burst into tears.

But there was no time for that.

The lights went dark, and she could hear the platform rolling away. Before the sound had fully receded, however, three spotlights came on, all in a row about three feet apart, dead stage center.

"Positions, please, for scene two," Robinson said. "Esther, you are to take the one to your left. Yes, get up to your feet, that's right, well done, now walk into your light-space and own it. Yes, perfecto, oh, no, no, no, don't sit down, you must stand, yes, well done. Now, Jody, you are to take the one in the middle, and Sage must enter the beam on the far right, chop-chop, get a move-on, let's go."

"I still can't feel my hand," Jody said. "And my arm is tingling."

"Better then to make haste," he replied. "Positions."

As if in a trance, they obeyed. Everything seemed surreal and nightmarish, and Sage felt only as if she was going through the motions, as if already dead. She moved under the beam of light she'd been assigned and happened a glance at the arrow pierced through her sister's hand, protruding in such an odd perpendicular. In sick fascination, Sage realized she'd never quite seen a wound like this, not even during her Emo phase when she listened to Billie Eilish and watched horror movies each night on Netflix. She blinked hard. Jody hadn't bled much, oh miracle of miracles, but the skin around the puncture was purple and swelling.

"Now, my darlings," Robinson said, "it's time to role play. Funny, the way you are facing the flats, with both engineer's control booths within your sight, when an actual performance would be delivered back out through the proscenium arch. Toward your audience of crash-test dummies and mannequins. Your world outside of this place."

"Oh, you're so deep," Jody muttered.

"Yes," he responded. "And I hope the reverse angle won't impede your performance."

"What performance?"

"Ah," he said, "the improvisation of course. I am going to ask you a question, and the one with the best answer lives."

Sage felt herself bristle. "That's what this is about? Answering riddles? So you can act like you've outsmarted us and then go and kill us?"

"It's not about riddles, Sage."

"Well, what then?"

"You haven't guessed?"

"Clearly, no."

There was a pause, and the microphone on Robinson was so sensitive that Sage heard his breathing change, a faint *click* as he swallowed.

"Um, yes," he said, all silk and velvet, voice breaking a tad in the back of his throat, and Sage realized in amazement and disgust that he was getting emotional.

"Yes then, right to it," he managed. "I recovered from the murder attempt at the forge two years ago and rebuilt myself. But there wasn't much left, at least physically, that was as proficient as it had once been. Nothing was easy, and my industry, my...artistry had new limitations. It made me reflect, think about my life, my talents and deficits, my personal worth. And the equation kept coming up empty. Until I realized that I wanted a daughter."

"What?"

He gave a nervous laugh that seemed horrifically vulnerable.

"Yes, a daughter, Sage, dear. Someone to share things with, someone to nurture. I searched long and hard, far and wide, and decided on you three as the final...contestants."

"Like a game show," Jody said.

"Like a game, yes. I had to put you all in situations that would expose your weaknesses and virtues, your metacognitive abilities and your respective lexicon of strategies unveiled under pressure. I essentially had to get rid of your father and make you all turn against him, so I could become the surrogate parent. I had to make it seem to the outside world that one of you, or more importantly all of you, were The Sculptor killer all along. That way I'd have your devotion, your... love if you will, though forced at first by circumstantial blackmail."

"I would never love you," Sage said, "and neither could my sisters."

"I disagree," he said smoothly. "Of all the children I observed, you three were and are the most loving and forgiving, and at the same time brave and resourceful. I am so...*proud* of you. That is why this part of the show is so aesthetically pristine, so glorious and so heartbreakingly tragic."

"So you're going to choose," Esther said. "One of us."

"Precisely, my child."

"Well, it's not going to me. I hate you."

"Well, then I'll have to kill you, now, won't I?"

Esther put her thumb back in her mouth and with her left arm hugged her teddy bear tightly. His voice returned to its usual tone of condescension and bombast.

"In this scene we are going to borrow a plotline from William Shakespeare's *King Lear,* and focus on the foolish game he plays with *his* three daughters, announcing his 'retirement' and his desire to split his kingdom into three portions between them. He asks them who loves him the most, quite transparently digging for vows of devotion that would determine the relative size of each daughter's coming inheritance. There is almost a fairy tale quality to it, until the evil sisters, Regan and Goneril, compete with each other for the bigger lie, both claiming they love Lear more than the earth, the sea, the mountains and heavens. Then Cordelia, his youngest, makes the grave mistake of telling him the truth, claiming half her love goes to her husband and half back to him."

Sage shook off a shiver. "So you're telling us to make vows of devotion to you?"

"No, Sage dear, that would be stupid. Easy lies interest few and make little difference in the vast scheme of things. Here tonight, each of you will get a chance to speak, and my question is quite different from that of King Lear. The question I pose to you is what do you see as my biggest flaw? Please consider the political nature of the question and all the implications and possibilities. In the end, I might kill all three of you. I might kill one, maybe two, it depends on your answers. Unlike the foolish King, I know when I am being lied to, but the more truth you give, the deeper down might be your grave. Do you pamper and coddle me, or am I more in the mood for Cordelia tonight? Do you give me something close to the whole truth, or do you parse and hedge? What gives you the advantage? What is your goal, and to what lengths will you go or what depths will you stoop to attain it?"

"Right," Sage said. "Straight to it. Your weakness is that you are an insecure misogynist who was defeated two years ago by a tenth-grade Goth-girl."

Yeah," Jody continued. "And you're no good without your bots and your gadgets."

"And," said Esther, "you can't hear background noise. You told me so, yes you did."

There was silence, and for a moment Sage thought he'd lost his ability to amplify his voice. Then he spoke, softer than before, yet brilliant on the edges with rage.

"That's what you decide to show me, here in this arena?" he said. "Blunt truth, no level of artistry, no technique, no ambience? Do you realize that your lives are in danger? Do you think that I'm bluffing?"

"Who cares?" Jody said. "Let us go. You're boring."

"Yeah," Esther said. "You talk like a teacher."

"And, so you have three Cordelias," Sage said. "You're not worthy of a comparison to *any* human being, not even a character as weak as the foolish King Lear. At least he had his fake-o moment with two of his daughters. You're so pathetic you can't even get one of us to lie to you."

Another hesitation, but a short one this time.

"Affirmative," he said. "Scene three. The Theater of Death."

Everything darkened except for the spotlights, and when he began it was evident that his voice had gained an artificial sort or clarity, an extra spread of richness, and though it was trivial and totally irrelevant, Sage wondered if he was using "Autotune."

"Bitches," he said. "I mentioned before that these last two years I had to measure my new advantages and deficits, and as a result of the latter, my ability to recreate the nanobot technology you've heard about and read about online was affected negatively. That doesn't mean I could no longer utilize the science, but the product came out to be inferior to its predecessor. No nuance, no partial free will in the subject making the perfect hybrid. My current nanobots make people obey, that is all. Dumb servants that I cannot even track when outside. Still, they did help me infiltrate your house, for example, for camera and audio installation."

"Who was it?" Sage said.

"Jeff Needleman first. Remember, you had him over to work on a group project for social studies last May. He set things in place. Then Cindy Lucas visited to cram for the geometry final. She completed the positioning of the micro-surveillance equipment that would self-destruct and disappear when I needed it to."

"Why not just make and transport the creepy spy stuff in a burst of your super-duper pixels then?"

"Good question, Sage dear, I'm impressed. To be brief, the pixel technology creates illusions. In terms of the short run, they have real bite, real physicality, but more long-term paraphernalia needs to be constructed in actuality."

"Then why not just make Jeff Needleman's and Cindy Lucas's replicas?" said Sage. "They were only over for a 'visit.' Wouldn't they have made more dependable 'dumb servants?'"

"No, dear. The pixel technology works well in terms of inanimate objects, all liquids and gases, some solids. Manufacturing people, however—well, that part of my research and development is still in its infancy. My human configurations have a current shelf life of seven minutes maximum. I don't know why at this juncture, but please understand that I will. In fact, I must. As you just guessed, Needleman, Lucas, and the five other high school students I infected make for weak soldiers. I have only been able to use them about once a month because of their tender age and the inferior bots. If they were to be 'activated' even twice during the given thirty-day period, their brains would shut down temporarily like fried batteries. They all assisted with making the parts for the arrow-bots positioned above you in metal shop as well as the preparation here last week, literally moving things for me, and the latter therefore has rendered them useless to me today. As for the other idiot with a badge whom I recently 'bot-liberated,' he would know no such time constraints, his quote-unquote 'brain' fully matured, so called. But either way, I am still burdened with the disadvantage of not being able to monitor any of my 'soldiers' outside. Still, as you probably guessed, when here in my building I don't need a human transmitter at all."

Sage folded her arms coldly. "He told me different."

"Who?"

"Chief Canfield. He said he got 'infected' two years ago in your truck."

"Alas, no. That was in his programming. He was indeed recently anointed with an only slightly higher grade of the inferior bots, my only recent advance in that part of the science, thank you, that made it so he didn't have to be 'on site' for me to boomerang my illusions off of him. Still, I had to make him think that his 'parasites' came from the old days, since the original devices could be 'read' by the operator, me, outside of four walls. Thinking that his supposed 'old-school bots' possessed the aforementioned flaw would lay the groundwork for his nagging suspicion, false of course, that it was something in him, some internal weakness, that made it so the bots had this 'new' limitation. My weakness became a strength. Context is everything. In the end, however, I consider the destruction of the old, more powerful bots a great loss, all blown to smithereens at the forge: those implanted in Canfield's receptionist Erika Shoemaker, your 'Goth-girl,' Meagan Mullin, and myself, after they overloaded my eyes and exploded."

He laughed softly through his nose. "But now that you mention Chief Canfield..."

Sage tensed. Any hope of tact and fair play was out the window, if there had been any of that in this to begin with.

"Tell us, Sage," he said. "Is Poppy the only cannibal in the family?"

Esther squirmed. "I'm too young for this conversation."

Robinson laughed again. "Time to grow up, dear. This is serious business, discovering who and what your father is, and who your sisters really are. Isn't that right, Sage? Three Cordelias? What if they were to turn on one another like rabid hyenas? Would that be blunt enough for you? What if one of you was pregnant with Vinny Gatto's baby and what if she got information from Chief Canfield before his unfortunate demise, that my nanobots, untethered otherwise, would travel through the esophagus and straight to the human eye? What if she guessed that once nestled in one set of eyes, the bots would be sluggish to detach and re-travel. What if she literally ripped out Canfield's eyes and swallowed them, guessing that the bots would

307

finally loosen from their original, now-dead receptacles and find a new pair of live ones close by through the uterine wall? Yes, that would be quite interesting. It also makes one wonder if even inferior bots can learn and develop, especially if the new host has no biases, no false presumptions, and most importantly, no tangible optic receptacles. Maybe the bots join in the creation of the eyes, the mind, the whole being, eliminating future weaknesses by accounting for them first with this lovely blank slate. What a wonderful experiment, watching them grow up together, and so thank you so much, Sage. I wouldn't have thought of that one all on my own, no way, ain't no how."

Jody was looking. "You're pregnant?" she said. "With Vinny's baby? For real?"

Sage stared at the floor.

"I'm too young for this!" Esther cried.

"I was going to tell you," Sage murmured.

"What else should we tell dear sister Jo-Jo?" said Robinson. "Should we give her the other news? Should we let her know that Vinny impregnated her too?"

"What?" Jody said.

"I'm too young for this!" Esther screeched.

"I was going to tell you," Sage said. "I just couldn't find the right moment, that's all. And then I sort of forgot. I mean, we've been sort of busy, right?"

Jody's eyes were so wide they looked as if they would burst. "You forgot?"

"Enough," Robinson commanded. "There is treachery in this family: lies, murder, abuse, the whole package. I will spare you further pain. My adopted daughter will be Sage. She will make me a grandfather, and together we will raise her child as a superior being with the world as his playpen. As for the two of you, Jody and Esther, a dark fate awaits you. As I before intimated...while it is unfortunate that my ability to advance my nanobot technology has waned, my pixel technology has strengthened and grown. Two years ago I could turn the room to a snow globe so you could taste the flakes. Currently, just as printers can make guns, my pixels have substance with the exact weight and density of that which they depict, at least for the limited time period I require here. In other words, a knife can cut you. One of my pixel knives can cut you the same. Let's have a demonstration! Let's play!"

He cleared his throat.

"Not to be impolite, but Sage, dear, you will have to move fifteen steps to your right. As is, you are in the field of play."

Sage held her ground.

"Have it your way then," he said. "Heat, spotlight three."

She felt it immediately on the sole of her bare foot. By instinct she lifted it, but then was the smell of burning rubber. She squealed and jumped out of the spotlight. She still could feel the heat from it, searing, almost pulsing, and she moved fifteen steps to the right.

"And now you, Esther. Move fifteen steps left."

She complied, walking backward. Jody was alone at stage-center, still glaring at Sage. The Sculptor's rich voice filled the stage space.

"Please take note, Jody Winslow, that either you or your sister Esther Winslow will be executed. You, Jody, will decide who dies, plain and simple. A non-answer or an answer of 'neither' means that I kill the both of you. Clear?"

Jody said nothing.

"I'll take that as a 'yes,'" Robinson said. "And now for some please-touch pixel technology!"

From the stage there was a burst of fire-red glow-dots a few feet in front of Jody. They made a five-foot-high fountain shape, blossoming up in delicate curves and cascading down to the floor surface. They pinged and danced like marbles on stone, then turned to gentle wisps that smelled like freshly cut grass and ballpark franks. As if a magic wand had been waved, a contraption was now left in the wake of the pixie dust. It looked like some weird abstract statue of a person, a partial skeleton made of curved steel plates, slats, pins, and tabs. The feet, legs, hands, and arms were connected to a spine that had its vertebrae padded with small leather cushions. There were no ribs. There was no head either, just what looked like a helmet connected to the neck at the back. Said helmet had steel bands "basket-woven" at the rear of it, yet the front was totally open-faced, save one band going across the top like a roll bar. Hanging off the left chin-side was a leather strap. The apparatus was shaped like a baseball player standing in ready position for batting, and about seven inches to the right of its steel feet was home plate.

"It is custom fitted," Robinson said, "to you, Jody, every crescent and contour. If this is your choice, you will get into position with the spine cushions at your back, the rear side of your legs and feet pressed snug against the backing frame. Then you'll strap in your head and take your batting stance. No need for a bat, though. This pitcher wants to give up a free base!"

There was another "poof" of waterfalling pixels farther in toward the scenery flats, and lo and behold, there was a pitching machine back deep stage-center now facing outward, the type with an arm.

"You've got to be kidding," Jody said.

"Move fifteen steps to your left, back toward the curtain line so you don't block Esther's view please," said The Sculptor.

As Jody began to comply, there was a small puff of glitter-green fairy dust at the top of the skeletal player-frame, and now the chin-strap was fastened, holding in place a large coconut, head-sized, about eight or nine inches.

The pitching machine whirred. The arm started rotating, and The Sculptor said,

"Jody, you should be honored. This spectacle is called 'Batter Killer,' and this is what a hundred and fifty miles an hour looks like."

The arm came around and there was a *shhhooo* sound, and like a bullet the ball shot through the air, straight for the coconut seated in the helmet's open-face frontal area where Jody's forehead would be. There was a sharp *clap* both brittle and wet, and the coconut exploded, the shell rupturing like grenade shrapnel, milk spattering. The ball bounced off stage, and then there was silence. All three girls slowly lowered their arms that they'd instinctively crossed protectively before their faces. All three were speechless and shocked. Amazingly, they hadn't been injured by the storm of shards, though Esther had a few slivers embedded in the forearms of her hoodie and Jody had droplets of coconut milk in her hair.

The baseball stuff vanished, no fairy dust, those days were over it seemed.

Now, back where the pitching machine had just been, there was a chamber, a long rectangular casing. It spun slowly as if on display in a showroom, about six feet high, a yard and a half wide, and at least five feet deep. To Sage it looked like a coffin. When it came around revealing the front panel that had originally been facing away, Esther screamed. There was a black border around it with a depth/height of around twenty inches, framing the long centerpiece like a painting.

It was a door. Esther's closet door from home.

"We met in the closet in the dark, Cupcake, didn't we?" Robinson crooned. "It's where you'd come to share secrets, hear my voice, take my advice and be soothed by it. What a glorious whereabout in which to come to your end, no?"

The door swung open ever so slowly, screaking like a low voice. Inside, the space was bare, painted bright white, and there were grooves, some on weird slants, cut into the floor and the sidewalls.

"The extravaganza before you," said Robinson, "is called 'The Closet of Blood.' It has an invisible tripwire and is triggered to commence its cycle exactly one second after you break the plane of the archway. I have a manual switch in here too, so don't worry, no misfires, and just to let you know…because I only want the very best for you, Esther…I modeled the engine off of the type used in the school's ride mowers, the big John Deere X590's, and since there is normally such a high whine and grind that can only be made by a Briggs & Stratton, I've added a set of twin mufflers to make it purr. I even manufactured an exhaust orifice in the rear so you'd smell the oil, the pistons, the petrol. If your sister chooses this for you, Esther, I envy you. Now for a demonstration! This is what it looks, sounds, and smells like in action."

The motor kicked on, emitting a low thrum, a pulsating whisper. The smell of engine oil began to waft its sleepy odor about the space, and then something popped up through one of the grooves cut into the closet's bare flooring. It was a huge circular saw blade maybe twelve inches in diameter, making that high spinning *zing* noise that sounded like wood shop, and it protruded until its halfway point, then receded back into the floor base just as the next blade emerged on a slant from the side, and as it submerged, another blade surfaced, and another and another. In quick succession, there were seven blades altogether that bristled in from seven different angles, and by the end of the sequence all three girls were screaming.

"Quiet," Robinson said. He'd turned up his volume as if expecting this reaction, and it took a moment, but they all shut their mouths. Jody's face had turned beet-red and Esther clutched her teddy bear to her chest, shaking. For a moment the only sound was the soft whir of the engine, and there was something odd here, something at the periphery of focus that Sage had noticed, something that could possibly make a difference, but she couldn't nail it, she couldn't focus, because all she could think about was spinning saw blades and exploding coconuts.

"Encase," Robinson commanded.

There was a rectangular box now, colored dark gray, where Esther just had been standing. From inside there was a dull pounding.

"She can't hear us," Robinson said. "Now, Jody, decide. Which of you dies? Will you take your last at-bat, or will dear sweet Esther have her final hideaway? Remember, please, that if you answer 'neither' or choose to not speak, I kill you both. I will be perfectly content to comfort my adopted daughter and help raise her son without ever having to deal with either of you again. So what is it? Which of you perishes?"

"Me," Jody said with clenched teeth. "I am the one who will die."

Sage wanted to protest, but there was nothing she could say or do to change this. Still, there was something she'd noticed…if only she could bring it to the forefront! It was like having an itch you couldn't get to, or that moment leading up to a sneeze.

Jody was looking at her, head cocked, eyes trying to relay something. She'd noticed it too! She'd nailed it! If only they could speak freely!

"Uncage," Robinson said, and the black box imprisoning Esther vanished. She was breathing heavily, hair hanging in her face, looking very much like the TV girl in *The Ring*. Robinson's voice sounded regretful.

"Darling Esther," he said. "Your sister has named you as the one who should die."

Sage expected Jody to throw the tantrum this time, but she didn't. She was trying to catch her younger sister's eye. Esther shook her hair out of her face and met her gaze. Jody gave the slightest quiver of the head back toward the "Closet of Blood" and with a measured voice, calm and precise, she said,

"Peanut, it's not true." She kept her sister's eye and called, "Mister, you tricked us. But if my sister's gonna die, I want to wear a blue veil. It's my favorite color, and I want to wear a blue veil, the thick kind, like a curtain." Esther's eyes were still question marks, but after chancing a glance in the direction Jody had indicated, there was something different. She knew. Whatever Jody had been trying to convey, Esther knew!

"It is time," Robinson said gravely, "and please understand, Jody, that I have no desire to grant strange requests for last-minute funeral clothes. You should know better." He cleared his throat. "And Sage, my darling, just in case you had plans in your head of somehow trying to stop this, I must put you now in your own kind of cage."

The floor beneath her in a ten-foot circumference suddenly vanished, and it was some kind of film or recording beneath her feet, but it was three-dimensional and it looked real. It seemed as if she was balancing at the peak of a church spire thousands of feet in the air, almost to the rim of space. Sage moaned, swayed, almost swooned. It was an illusion and she knew this, but that didn't seem to help.

Then she knew. It finally clicked, what Jody had discovered and what she'd communicated to Esther. "Blue veil," hell! She'd been talking about the stage flats, the ones lying sideways deep stage-center, depicting Jacob's Island, with its rotten bridges and crossing tidal ditches at the foot of a row of slum houses.

Tidal.

Dirty blue water. And when the "Closet of Blood" had revved up to run its blade sequence, kicking out a bit of extra exhaust, the "scenery flats" just behind it had rippled slightly. That's what Sage had noticed in the background but not quite registered! They weren't flats made of wood slats and canvas. They were curtains painted to look like flats made of wood slats and canvas. Robinson wasn't in one of the "control rooms." He was deep stage-center behind the fake flats, the curtains he could "see" or "sense" them through.

Jody started breathing deeply. She crouched. She grabbed the arrow shaft with her right hand at the place of puncture in the left. She was psyching herself up to rip free the arrow. She was going to use the pain to "startle" herself into action. Sage understood this on an intellectual level, but her emotions were slow to catch up.

"Wait!" said Robinson. "Jody, don't even think it! Your baby! You can't! You're a conservative!"

Jody sneered. "My body, my choice, asshole."

She pulled hard and screamed as the arrow shaft started ripping back through her tissue.

Sage leapt off the spire, screamed, fell, and pushed to make it back to her knees. The illusion below her felt like infinity, and she was free-falling, off balance, spinning through clouds, fast toward tracts of land and trees with everything revolving around her like a spinning vortex tunnel in a carnival house. She pushed, she clawed, she made it to the edge of the illusion somehow, and then over it, and her choice was to keep crawling or take the time to get back her feet to make a run at her sister. She crawled hard, her knees and palm-heels pounding the stage, and Jody tore the arrow back through, shrieking, and Sage made a dive for her.

But Jody had that burst of speed, and Sage wound up falling on her elbows, grabbing at air. Jody sped for the closet, leapt up and out, and broke the plane of the entranceway. The engine whirred. The blades zinged, and just before the door swung closed Sage got a clear view of Jody's body parts falling like stones, her torso split at the middle, pitching her waist and legs to the left, and her head and one shoulder sliding down to the right.

The engine cut down to its hum, and through the closed door blood seeped out through the bottom crack, dripping down the base to the stage.

To Sage it didn't compute. It couldn't be, not here, not this way.

From behind the curtain painted like Jacob's Island there were sounds, cries of rage. It was Esther. She was screaming with hard exclamations as if voiced in CAPITALS, each followed by a percussive *THWUNK,* like a hatchet sunk hard into a wood stock.

"You are NOT a nice man, and you're a LIAR, and you HURT my Poppy and I'm too YOUNG for all this, and you KILLED my sister!"

Sage hurried toward the curtain. It had been tacked to the stage and the fasteners had been yanked out at the bottom where the muddy blue river spilled sideways. Jody had been the diversion. And Robinson never heard Esther coming. He couldn't hear background noise, as in the foreground had been the *thrum* of his engine and the *zing* of his blades. Sage pulled up the curtain.

Robinson was a huge man, but since he had no legs and only one arm, he looked like a monstrous maggot. He was in a reclining position, lying upon a strange contraption that supported his body with what looked like a complex array of pistons, most probably to move different parts of his torso and his good arm so he could manipulate his machinery. Behind him was what looked like one of those old-fashioned telephone switchboards common in black and white movies from the 1950s, with nests of twisted cords and mini-cables, pull tabs and switches, buttons and blinking lights, all connected to one master wire inserted in his arm intravenously. He was shirtless, wearing nursing scrub pants with the leg parts cut off and sewn back in to cover his stumps. His flesh, from the past burns, looked more like sports mesh than skin, most perforated along his flanks and the near side of his bald skull. His face was big-boned, with a high forehead and a wide cowboy jaw. His eyes were gone, and soldered into the sockets were a number of different colored wires twisted and pigtailed back into the control board at five different contact points. As for his fresh wounds, he had a wide barrel chest that had been stabbed through and stove in three or four times; it was difficult to isolate the puncture wounds through the thick smears of gore. His throat had been absolutely annihilated, scrambled eggs with ketchup, and Esther had also punched distinct holes just above his right eyebrow, at the top of his nose bone, and straight through the mouth, taking three of his teeth.

She was covered in blood, all his evidently, her right arm so drenched it looked as if she was wearing a red industrial factory glove. She had spatters on her chest, slathers gleaming dully on her neck below the ears, and enough on her face to make her eyes look like moons. She didn't say anything. She handed her weapon to Sage.

It was the stress doll teddy bear, but it didn't look like that now. First off, it was turned half inside out; second, it was ripped; and third, it was saturated dark red. Sage inspected it for a moment, pinching and moving the wet fabric with her thumb and index finger similar to the way she'd so delicately sacrificed Chief Canfield's gun ten minutes ago.

Oh my.

They'd all been fooled by the childlike sewing job on the outside of it, as that was *Esther's* clever diversion. Her work inside was smart and sophisticated. Evidently she stitched Sage's rock carving chisel point inside the chest and belly, and it appeared that she crazy-glued strips of one of Jody's old batting gloves around the top of the shank for gripping. She had matching batting glove patches inside both arms, which she could stuff in with her middle finger and thumb to go patch to patch for friction and holding power.

Sage bent at the knees to put the teddy bear dagger on the floor. She rose slowly, and Esther was staring, eyes so white and so wide in contrast to the dark red "war paint" drying around them. Sage reached for her, put her arms around her. She rocked her back and forth warmly and gently.

And both of them wept for their sister.

Two Years Later

The prison door had no window, just a center-mounted port opening with a sliding safety shutter on the outside and a tray rack for food-pass on the inside. There was no window on the far wall of the cell either, just a sink, a steel shelf, and a toilet. The bed frame was a low stainless one-piece single with a bunk pan, no coils, and the mattress was foam sealed with polyurethane-coated nylon. It was a BIP model with a bump and no pillow, and it was fireproof. There were no posters on the walls. The epoxy flooring was a dull gray with no sheen.

Bradford Winslow was sitting on the gray floor with his back against the east wall by the sink. He had his knee up like a pup tent. His other leg was splayed out, the prosthetic limb itching him, just below the big toe, of course. The phantom effect had been worse, but it seemed to have a memory. It liked coming home sporadically to touch base.

The door-shutter slid open.

"Visitor, Winslow. Do not rise off the floor. Do not approach the opening. Do not breech the front half of the cell at any time during the encounter."

Winslow had been mouthing the words, and now he said,

"Yes, Officer Murdock, of course."

The door unlocked and swung outward, revealing two figures, and Winslow blinked as if looking at silhouettes partially blocking the sun. They entered, the door closed behind them, and they stood waiting, hand in hand. It was a mother and her child, and he was a year old and had been able to walk independently at six months. At first she had read to him regularly, baby books like *Good Night Moon* and *The Very Hungry Caterpillar,* until at seven months he was reading them back to her. At nine months he was reading storybooks with plotlines, and at eleven months he had read every science fiction novel and political thriller in the Wynnewood Public Library.

"Hello, Sage," said Winslow. "Hello, Nelson."

"There's no need to address him," she said flatly. "We have an agreement."

He nodded, smiling sadly. Sage had on purple eye shadow with silver tints, accented in cat style with the wings and dramatic black waterlines. Her hair had grown long, past shoulder length, and she'd had it straightened and dyed midnight black with a lavender streak on the left. She kept it tied back tight in a long ponytail just like Paulina Villareal, the drummer in her new favorite band, The Warning. But he wasn't allowed to address any of that either.

"My fake foot is troublesome lately," he said. "There's something wrong with the suspension system. The straps need to be adjusted at their anchor points."

"I'll look into it."

"I get to walk in the yard an hour a day under strict supervision, two armed guards, one at ground level and one in the northwestern tower."

"That's for your protection."

"I want an hour and fifteen minutes."

"I'll look into it."

"I want better food. Lebanon baloney on stale white bread does not a proper lunch make."

"Don't be greedy." She paused. "Do you have it? There's nothing on the edge of the sink."

He took a deep breath that made his shoulders move.

"Yes. They didn't want it in view of the portal. It's over there." He indicated with his head the direction, and Sage turned back to the door. There, under the food rack back in the crease, was a small tab of folded wax paper, stuck there with the chewing gum the ex-professor had been given by Officer Reynolds in the wood shop two days ago. She bent in, plucked it off, put it in a napkin, and stuck it in her purse. She turned back and took Nelson's hand again.

"Who is manning the front visitors' entrance?" she said. "I don't know him."

"His name is Donahue. He's been informed."

She nodded curtly and made to go.

"Sage," Winslow said, "he's advancing faster than they can keep track of, isn't he?"

She paused. Nelson looked up at her questioningly, then back at Brad Winslow. He was big for his age, cute as a button in his OshKosh overalls and Sponge Bob T-shirt. Sandy blond hair, mouth like a cherub. Sage shrugged indifferently.

"I don't understand it on a technical level, but I see the results every day. He has A.I. embedded in him and the two are growing simultaneously. When he hits a plateau, he needs more...

nourishment. The powers that be don't appreciate delays and plateaus. The remedy has to be a certain code of DNA or familial molecular configuration. That's all I know. We agreed you wouldn't test me on this and that you would be rewarded. It's working. Don't be selfish."

"Speaking of rewards, how long this time?"

"Shelf life is fifteen minutes. That's up two minutes since the last one. As I said, don't be greedy."

He pursed his lips and looked straight ahead.

"I...couldn't finish last time. I...felt as if they were watching."

"Not my problem. And they're not. I could sue. They don't want that kind of publicity."

He looked at his daughter. "You shouldn't bring the boy here."

"I won't let him out of my sight."

"And you have no idea how he does it?"

"No. As I told you, I can only prompt him, as I am going to do thirty seconds after I walk out of this room."

"How is Esther?"

The air grew quite thick.

"They are letting her out on the lawn for independent time without a wraparound now. She's been clean of self-harm attempts for three weeks, but she's still drawing the pictures. It's tragic, and I miss her. And I still miss Jody. Every day."

"Ah," he agreed, still smiling weakly, looking ahead at nothing. He knew better than to say he missed her too, that he missed Sage herself, that he felt devastated about Esther, their family name, Vincent Gatto, his poor parents. But these were all triggers, borders he wasn't allowed to cross. Not if he wanted his reward...

She pounded on the door three times with the meat of her fist. The door opened, she exited, and Winslow forgot about the fact that in one day, just one single day two years ago, every living member of his immediate family except Sage became a murderer. He forgot about all the news reports, the social media memes, the rumors, the stories…he forgot all that as if a switch had been pulled, because the slamming home of the cell door was a trigger as well. Suddenly he was just too excited, too filled with emotion to be dragged back down into all those old memories, those realities. What was so soon coming now wasn't just a worthwhile payoff; it was the only reason that he still wanted to live.

He struggled to his feet, using the wall as he'd been taught in rehab, climbing it with his weight on the flats of his palms, slipping once, losing a bit of ground but not failing at the attempt overall. And he was counting, and he was way under thirty seconds this time when he got upright, and now he was standing, and he gave a half-turn leaning hard on his good leg, so anxious he could barely contain himself.

In the middle of the cell there was a sudden eruption of pixels in a fountain shape, lavender and quicksilver, five feet eight inches high, cascading to the floor in waterfalls that danced off the epoxy floor and turned to gray wisps that smelled of her favorite perfume, Tom Ford Black Orchid. In a burst then, the pixels were gone, and standing before Bradford Winslow was a woman. She was wearing the black cocktail dress with the slit, the one she'd had on at the last faculty meeting at David's house in Newark three years ago, the one that showed off her beautiful calves and hourglass midriff.

"Honey," she said, eyes sparkling.

"Georgia," he whispered. "I need you."

"I know."

"I want you so badly."

"Then have me," she said.

He reached for her with incomplete hands, for a moment reminded of what he'd sacrificed in the wood shop for this brief encounter, what had been left in wax paper under the food tray, left for his grandson's "nourishment" in order to skip past a plateau.

No worries. This time it was only the tab of the left pinkie down to the first joint, and though his right hand was fingerless with the exception of the thumb at this point, there was plenty on the other to play this thing lefty.

The love of Winslow's life melted into his arms.

And for a short fifteen minutes, he only knew love.

Movies Referenced in Chapter Titles

Chapter 1 / When a Stranger Calls / 1979

Chapter 2 / The Blair Witch / 1999

Chapter 3 / Saw / 2004

Chapter 4 / Se7en / 1995

Chapter 5 / The Thing / 1982

Chapter 6 / Child's Play / 1988

Chapter 7 / Scream / 1996

Chapter 8 / Candyman / 1992

Chapter 9 / The Amityville Horror / 1979

Chapter 10 / Insidious / 2011

Chapter 11 / The Witch / 2015

Chapter 12 / Feardotcom / 2002

Chapter 13 / Twilight / 2008

Chapter 14 / Misery / 1990

Chapter 15 / Psycho / 1960

Chapter 16 / Freddy vs. Jason / 2003

Chapter 17 / The Shining / 1980

Chapter 18 / A Nightmare on Elm St 3: Dream Warriors / 1987

Chapter 19 / Hellraiser / 1987

Chapter 20 / The Return of the Living Dead / 1985

Chapter 21 / Bram Stoker's Dracula / 1992

Chapter 22 / Poltergeist / 1982

Chapter 23 / Planet Terror / 2007

Chapter 24 / Horns / 2013

Chapter 25 / Motel Hell / 1980

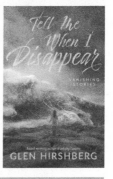